PATRIOTS: VOLUME THREE
THE TURNCOAT

DANIEL REED—The eldest son of a prominent Virginia
family, he has pledged his life to the cause of freedom.
Now there is no turning back from war, and he grimly
thinks there will be a terribly long and bitter rebellion.
But hope burns anew when he meets the n____ appointed commander in chief of the rebel a____ _____
Washington.

ROXANNE DARRAGH—Time ____
patriot risks her life in the ____
alty—and honor—will ____ _____ ____ ___ of
all: she will have to ____

ELLIOT MARKHAM—S____ ____ Boston businessman with Tory symp____ ___secretly supports
the patriots' cause. And it is h____ who will be chosen to
ferret out the traitor suspected of supplying rebel secrets
to British troops.

QUINCY REED—The impetuous sixteen-year-old will
reveal his courage when he joins a rugged frontiersman on an expedition through dangerous Indian territory,
and saves the life of a settler's young daughter. But he
faces certain death when he is captured by a savage
band of Mohawks.

MURDOCH BUCHANAN—The rough and ready Ohio
Valley pioneer guides a group of adventurers across
uncharted lands. But when his party is taken captive, he
challenges a fearsome war chief to battle.

SAGODANEGA—A ruthless and ambitious Mohawk
war chief, he vows to become leader of *all* Indians of the
Iroquois Nation and drive the settlers from the land.
To this end he schemes with British redcoats to kill
the enemy.

PATRIOTS—Volume III

THE TURNCOAT

Adam Rutledge

 Producers of **The First Americans,**
The Holts and **The Frontier Trilogy: Westward!**

Book Creations Inc., Canaan, NY • Lyle Kenyon Engel, Founder

BANTAM BOOKS
NEW YORK • TORONTO • LONDON • SYDNEY • AUCKLAND

THE TURNCOAT

A Bantam Domain Book / published by arrangement with
Book Creations Inc.

Bantam edition / January 1993

Produced by Book Creations Inc.
Lyle Kenyon Engel, Founder

DOMAIN and the portrayal of a boxed "d" are trademarks of
Bantam Books, a division of
Bantam Doubleday Dell Publishing Group, Inc.

ISBN 0-553-29201-3

Published simultaneously in the United States and Canada

Bantam Books are published by Bantam Books, a division of Bantam
Doubleday Dell Publishing Group, Inc. Its trademark, consisting of the
words "Bantam Books" and the portrayal of a rooster, is Registered in
U.S. Patent and Trademark Office and in other countries. Marca
Registrada. Bantam Books, 666 Fifth Avenue, New York, New York 10103.

PRINTED IN THE UNITED STATES OF AMERICA

OPM   0 9 8 7 6 5 4 3 2 1

THE
TURNCOAT

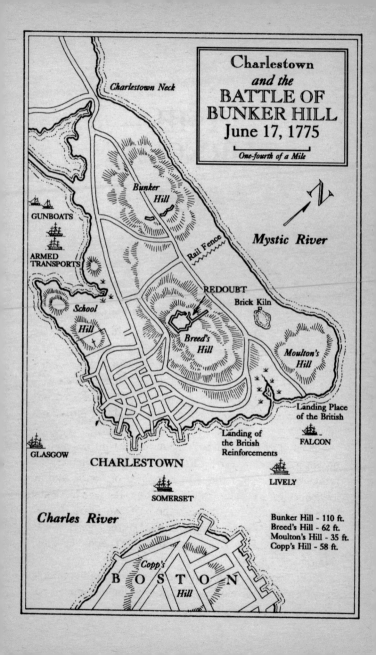

Chapter One

With a fully packed pair of saddlebags slung over his arm, twenty-two-year-old Daniel Reed emerged onto the porch of Gresham Howard's large, comfortable house in Saratoga, New York. A fine-looking black mare that would carry Daniel to Boston—away from his brother and his best friend—was tied just outside the white picket fence that enclosed Howard's front yard.

Daniel was a well-built young man with a thatch of brown hair curling out from under his black tricorn. His brown eyes had lost the soft innocence of youth, and he looked somewhat older than his age, his lean face hardened by what he had gone through the past two years. It was May 24, 1775, a fine spring morning, but for Daniel, it was a day on which he was saying good-bye to people he cared about.

The door behind him opened, and a lad in his middle teens, bearing a strong resemblance to Daniel, stepped out

1

of the house. "Well, I suppose I'm ready to go," Quincy Reed said to his brother. "I wouldn't want to wager on when Cordelia will be, though. You know how women are."

Daniel had to smile at Quincy's comment. The boy's experience with women was limited, but Daniel was sure his little brother would not appreciate it if he pointed out that fact.

"I'm sure it won't be much longer now," Daniel said as he turned to face Quincy. "Eager to get on your way, are you?"

Quincy shrugged. "It should be an exciting trip, and I'll be seeing a lot of new territory. I've gotten used to the idea—but I'd still rather be going back to Boston with you, Daniel."

"You know that's impossible." Daniel hoped Quincy wouldn't start another argument on this subject because they had thrashed it out more than once during the two weeks they had been guests in the home of Gresham Howard, the owner of one of New York Colony's leading wagonyards. As far as Daniel was concerned, it was settled; he would return to Boston to report to the Committee of Safety on the capture by patriot forces of the British forts at Ticonderoga and Crown Point, while Quincy and their friend Murdoch Buchanan would accompany Gresham Howard and his daughter, Cordelia Faulkner, to the Ohio River valley. Gresham and Cordelia wanted to get as far away from the coming war as they could, and had willingly sold his lucrative business in order to undertake the journey west.

"I know, I know," Quincy said. "I told you I'm used to the idea. But that doesn't mean I won't miss you, brother."

"Nor I you, Quincy."

The door opened again, and a tall, brawny, redheaded man in buckskins and a coonskin cap emerged from the house. Murdoch Buchanan was a burly frontiersman who looked perfectly natural with two flintlock pistols tucked into his belt, a long rifle cradled in his arms, and a heavy-bladed hunting knife sheathed at his hip. He was every bit as dangerous as he appeared, but as he grinned at the Reed brothers, it was clear he had a gentle side to his nature as well.

"Mr. Howard will be here any minute with the wagons," said Murdoch, "and I dinna mind telling ye, lads, I be more than ready t' get away from this town."

"Saratoga's not so bad," Quincy protested.

"I'm no' talking just about Saratoga. 'Tis all towns I be tired of. Give me the clean air o' the wilderness, where a man canna smell the stink o' fireplaces night and day."

Daniel thought the air was not as bad as Murdoch made it out to be, but he had to admit the frontiersman's senses were keener than his. Murdoch had lived on the edge of civilization for several years before coming east to visit relatives—the same trip on which he had met and become fast friends with the Reed brothers.

Murdoch looked at Daniel and went on, "I dinna envy ye, going back t' Boston. Ye'd best keep your eyes wide open, Dan'l, and watch out for the redcoats."

"I will," Daniel promised. "I'm hoping I'll be able to slip back across the Charles River. After all, Mr. Revere did it easily without the British catching him, even though they had a ship in the harbor to watch for just such attempts."

"Aye, but with everything that's happened since then, they've probably tightened up their guard."

Daniel inclined his head in acknowledgment of the point Murdoch was making, then turned to look down the street when he heard a loud rumbling. Two large, canvas-covered wagons, each pulled by a team of sturdy mules, rolled toward them. Gresham Howard handled the reins of the leader, and an employee of his wagonyard drove the second vehicle. They came to a stop in front of the house, near the saddle horses that belonged to Daniel, Quincy, and Murdoch.

Howard jumped down from the seat, moving lithely for a man of his age and bulk. He was short and heavyset, with thinning brown hair liberally touched with gray and a neatly trimmed beard of the same shade. His clothes were well made but not ostentatious, and a pipe was ever present in his wide mouth. He lifted a hand in greeting to the three young men who stood on the porch of his house.

"All of you ready to go, are you?" Howard asked.

"I think so," Daniel said. "We're just waiting for Cordelia."

Howard laughed heartily. "Then you may have a long wait, my boy." He waved a pudgy hand at the wagons and went on, "I had them loaded with provisions and any other supplies we might need during the journey. I suppose we'll be relying on hunting to give us some fresh meat along the way, Mr. Buchanan?"

"I've told ye more than once, call me Murdoch. And the answer t' your question is aye. There's more than enough game for fresh meat."

Howard turned to the man who had driven the second wagon. "You can go back to the yard, Earl," he said. "Thanks for giving me a hand."

"Sure, Mr. Howard," replied Earl. "Glad to help. The boys down at the yard are going to miss you, squire. You were a good man to work for."

"You keep doing the same job for the new owner as you always did for me, and I'm sure he'll be a good man to work for, too," Howard assured him. "Thanks again."

As Earl turned and headed to the wagonyard he passed a man walking toward the Howards'. Daniel saw the stranger coming up the road but paid little attention to him until he stopped in front of the house and called, "Howard! Gresham Howard! I want to talk to you!"

From the porch, Howard frowned and said, "I should

think you and I have little to say to each other, Stone. What do you want?"

"Just thought maybe we could patch things up 'fore you leave," said the man. He was tall, thin, and middle-aged, with a lantern jaw and gray hair under his tricorn.

"A former competitor of mine," Howard whispered to Daniel, Quincy, and Murdoch. "We've had a number of arguments in the past, about both business and politics. It shouldn't require much time to take care of this."

Leaving the others on the porch, Howard walked to the gate in the picket fence to talk to Stone. Their voices were pitched low, and though Daniel could not make out what they were saying, the discussion did not appear to be friendly, and he doubted Stone's assertion that he wanted to "patch things up."

Suddenly, Daniel saw Stone step back, pull a pistol from his belt, and level the weapon at Howard.

"You're nothing but a damned Tory, and you always will be!" Stone said harshly. "I'll not let you run away so you can continue to help the king!"

"Wait, Stone!" Howard stood still, not wanting to shock the angry man into firing. "You've got it all wrong. I've changed. I support the patriots now!"

"Liar!" grated Stone. "You're just trying to save your loyalist skin!"

Murdoch and Quincy were ready to move, but Daniel put out a hand to hold them back. If they charged Stone, the man would fire, and Howard would be struck in the chest. They had to talk sense to him.

"Mr. Howard is telling the truth," Daniel said loudly, to get through to Stone. "He doesn't back the Tories anymore. In fact, he's been helping us."

"Who're you?" growled Stone, his eyes darting toward Daniel.

"My name is Daniel Reed. This is my brother, Quincy, and our friend Murdoch Buchanan. Maybe you've heard of them—they were at the battle of Fort Ticonderoga with Ethan Allen and the Green Mountain Boys."

"That doesn't mean anything. Howard's still a stinking Tory."

Daniel shook his head. "You're wrong, Mr. Stone. Now why don't you put down that gun before somebody gets hurt?"

Murdoch's hand was wrapped around the butt of one of his pistols. "I can drop him, Dan'l," he said quietly.

"The man's a patriot, just like us," Daniel said. "He's wrong, but he's doing what he thinks is right."

"Howard'll still be just as dead."

It was a reasonable observation. From the look on Stone's face, the man was possessed with anger. The barrel of his pistol quivered with the rage that gripped him.

Abruptly the sound of hoofbeats in the road made everyone—including Stone—look toward the settlement. A rider galloped toward them, and in the second that Stone's gaze turned away, Howard darted to the side, out of danger from the pistol's muzzle.

Murdoch's fingers shifted from the butt of his gun to the hilt of the knife, and he plucked it from its sheath, aimed carefully, and threw. The blade glittered in the sun as it flew across the space between Stone and him, and it was the weighted butt end that struck Stone in the shoulder.

The man cried out in pain, and the gun slipped from his numbed fingers before he could fire it. His right arm flopped limply at his side, but he staggered forward and bent to pick up the fallen weapon with his left hand.

Quincy, however, bounded across the yard and scooped up the pistol, then backed off hurriedly and covered the now disarmed Stone with the gun.

"Are you all right?" Daniel asked Howard.

Howard's face was pale, but color was seeping back into his cheeks. "I'm fine, Daniel. I'm fine."

His face twisted by rage, Stone asked, "How can you protect this—this traitor?"

"Everyone can make a mistake," Daniel told him forcefully. "Gresham Howard has made his share. But now you're the one who's mistaken, Stone. Howard's a good man, and he's on the side of liberty. You've got to give a man a chance. That's one of the things we're fighting for, isn't it?"

Nursing his still-numb arm, Stone sneered contemptuously and spat in the dirt. He turned and started to walk away.

"Aren't you going to call the constable?" Quincy asked Howard.

"I don't think so," Howard replied, feeling steadier now. "I'll be leaving Saratoga behind soon enough. No need to cause trouble for Stone. He was wrong, and I'm willing to leave it at that."

"Even though he wanted to kill you?" Quincy sounded amazed.

"Your brother said it best, lad. You've got to give a man a chance."

The rider who had caused the distraction had reined up in front of the Howard house. Now he swung down from the saddle. "Hello, Gresham," he said as he and the men came up the walk. "What was that all about?"

"Nothing important, Cyrus," Howard told him. "What brings you here?"

"I've got news."

"I knew it had to be something important to bring you racing up like that," Howard answered as the newcomer climbed the three steps to the porch. Howard introduced his companions, then went on, "This is my friend Cyrus Groener. He owns the best mercantile in Saratoga."

Groener was a middle-aged man who revealed a bald head when he took off his tricorn to wipe sweat from his brow. "I appreciate the compliment," he said in a high-pitched voice, "but I've got something important to tell you. I knew you'd want to know right away, so I came as soon as I heard about it."

"Heard about what?" asked Howard, keeping his growing impatience under control.

"The Second Continental Congress is meeting in Philadelphia. They've been at it for two weeks, in fact."

Howard frowned at the news. "And we're only just now hearing about it?"

"A rider brought word to my store not a half hour past," Groener assured him. "Information travels slowly these days, what with all the problems going on."

No one had to tell Daniel, Quincy, and Murdoch about the turmoil gripping the colonies. They had witnessed it firsthand: the Boston Tea Party, the battles at Lexington and Concord, the capture of Fort Ticonderoga. War fever was sweeping through the land.

Howard took his cold pipe from a coat pocket and put the stem in his mouth. As his teeth clenched down on it, he asked, "What's the Congress doing?"

"Word has it that Ben Franklin and Samuel and John Adams are trying to talk the colonies into forming a single army to fight the British, and when the delegates heard that we'd taken control of Lake Champlain, it changed everything."

Indeed it had, thought Daniel. With the capture of Fort Ticonderoga, the patriots had gone on the offensive, instead of fighting defensive battles as they had at Lexington and Concord.

"If the Continental Congress can forge a workable alliance among the colonies, there'll be no turning back from war," Howard mused.

"There'll be no turning back anyway," Daniel said. "Even if we gave up now and begged for forgiveness, British pride wouldn't allow it. The king and Parliament would insist that the colonies be punished beyond the point of endurance."

"I'm afraid you're correct, young man," Groener agreed. "You're the lad who captured that wagon train filled with British arms, aren't you?"

"Not by myself," Daniel replied. "I had plenty of help from a lot of good men, some of whom gave their lives."

"Yes, of course, I understand that." Groener turned back to Howard. "I knew you'd want to know about this, Gresham, since you've given up those Tory leanings of yours."

"I'm sure there are a great many loyalists who are sincere in their thinking," Howard said. "I just don't happen to agree with them anymore. That's what I was trying to tell Stone when he pulled the gun on me. But I want to thank you, Cyrus. I appreciate the information. There's naught we can do about it at the moment, but all intelligent men owe it to themselves to keep abreast of the news these days. Everything is changing so quickly."

To men like Howard and Groener, it might seem that change was coming rapidly. To Daniel, it was as though a hundred years had passed since the day not quite twenty-four months earlier when he had ridden into Boston, the long journey from his parents' plantation in Virginia behind him, to read for the law at Harvard and prepare for a career as an attorney.

"What about intelligent women?"

The unexpected question brought Daniel's thoughts back to the present. Cordelia Faulkner had stepped out of the door in time to hear her father's last comments, and her question had an acerbic tone to it.

She was beautiful, with blond curls framing a face highlighted by large blue eyes. The traveling outfit she wore enhanced her ripe figure. Despite the fact that she was only in her early twenties, she was already a widow, but she had not mourned her late husband. Perry Faulkner had been a brutal criminal who cared only for money and power, and was willing to sacrifice everything—even his lovely young wife—to get what he wanted. Faulkner had died by Daniel Reed's hand, and although there was no romantic attraction between Cordelia and him, the shared danger of foiling Faulkner's plans had cemented their friendship.

But the relationship did not blind Daniel to Cordelia's stubbornness or her sharp tongue. She was a young woman who was accustomed to getting her own way, and he doubted that would ever change.

"I didn't mean anything, Cordelia," her father said. "I didn't know you were listening."

"Well, I was, and it seems to me that it's just as important for a woman to know what's going on as it is for a man. You men think we're all just helpless females without a brain in our heads and that we have to be protected from any sort of unpleasantness—"

"That's enough, Cordelia," growled her father. "You're right about wanting to know what's happening with the rebellion, but you've no call to browbeat me. Are you ready to leave?"

Cordelia sniffed. "Of course I am. You told me to be ready this morning, so I'm ready."

Daniel, Quincy, and Murdoch exchanged glances but wisely kept their mouths shut. They had traveled with Cordelia and knew her well enough to know when to remain quiet.

"My trunks are all packed," she went on without pausing. "They're ready to load on one of the wagons as soon as you gentlemen are disposed to do so. I hope you left plenty of room for my things, Father."

"There's room," Howard said, "as long as you didn't try to take everything from the house."

"I only packed the things I really need."

Daniel was curious just how much that would turn out

to be. The first time he had met Cordelia, she had been fleeing for her life with little more than the clothes on her back, and they had been men's clothes, at that. Now, he suspected that she would have at least two big trunks stuffed with things she intended to take on the journey west.

"Murdoch and I will load your things on the wagon, Cordelia," Quincy said. "We'd be glad to, wouldn't we, Murdoch?"

"Aye," he said dryly. "And I appreciate ye volunteering me for the task, lad. I was just about t' speak up myself."

The big frontiersman followed Quincy into the house, up to the second floor to fetch the trunks from Cordelia's room.

On the porch, Groener said to Howard, "The town's going to be sorry to see you go, Gresham. You've been one of our leading citizens ever since you came to Saratoga."

"People have to move on," Howard replied with a shrug. "Before this war is over, you may wish you'd gone west yourself, Cyrus."

Groener laughed. "Oh, my dear wife would never move. She thinks you're touched in the head to leave behind a home and a good business. But we all have to do what we think best." He shook Howard's hand. "I'm going to miss you, Gresham. You be careful out there on the frontier. Don't let the savages get you."

"I'm more worried about redcoats than redskins," Howard said.

Cordelia waited until Groener was gone, then looked at her father with raised eyebrows and said, "Savages?"

"You know there are Indians between here and the Ohio Valley, Cordelia," her father said. "We talked about that."

"You told me we didn't have anything to worry about from them," Cordelia shot back.

"Not with Murdoch along. He's a scout, a frontiersman. He knows how to handle Indians."

"Well, I certainly hope you're right. It seems to me you're placing a great deal of faith in one man, though."

"When the man is Murdoch Buchanan, it makes a difference," Daniel said. "He'll get you through safely, I'm sure of it."

But Daniel was not as convinced as he sounded, and while Quincy was worried about the dangers Daniel might face in Boston, the trip upon which the four were about to embark could prove much more perilous. Not only were there Indians to consider, but as Gresham Howard had indicated, there were British troops scattered throughout the area. And with everything that had happened in recent weeks between the colonists and the British, any redcoats who encountered a small group of travelers might not ask where their loyalties lay before opening fire.

With a thumping sound that carried clearly outside the house, Quincy and Murdoch wrestled the first of Cordelia's trunks down the stairs. As they slid it out onto the porch, Howard looked at it in dismay and said, "I hope those mules I bought are as strong as they appear."

"They'll need t' be," Murdoch said. "Dan'l, give your brother a hand with tha' end o' the trunk, if ye dinna mind. Be careful, though. Ye're still on the mend from tha' wound ye got fighting Faulkner."

"I'll be careful," Daniel said, taking hold of the handle with Quincy. Together, they hefted the heavy trunk and carried it out to the first wagon. Howard hurried ahead of them to drop the tailgate so they could load the trunk into the vehicle.

There was room in the second wagon for Cordelia's other trunk, and when it was loaded, along with two much smaller bags containing Howard's personal belongings, the travelers were finally ready to depart. Quincy tied his saddle horse to the rear of the second wagon and scrambled up on the seat. He would take turns handling the reins with Cordelia, who had enough experience at driving wagons to do her share of the work. Quincy held out a hand to her and said, "You can ride up here with me if you like."

Without hesitation, she smiled up at him and took his hand. "I'd love to, Quincy," she said and climbed easily to the seat and settled down beside him.

Smiling, Daniel watched the exchange. Quincy had had a crush on Cordelia from the first moment he saw her, and she had taken advantage of that, relying on him as an ally every time there was an argument. At first Daniel had assumed that Cordelia was using his brother for her own ends, but now he sensed she was genuinely fond of him. Though Daniel knew that her feelings were nothing like what Quincy wished them to be, he hoped that his brother did not get hurt too badly by her.

Howard climbed onto the other wagon and took the reins. Meanwhile, Daniel and Murdoch mounted their horses. Daniel would ride with them for a time, accompanying them down the valley of the Hudson River until the party reached the Mohawk and swung west. From there, Daniel would head east toward Massachusetts.

"Is everyone ready?" called Howard, tightening his grip on the reins.

"We're ready back here," Quincy replied.

"More than ready," Murdoch confirmed, grinning. "Let's start putting some miles behind us."

Howard cracked the whip above the heads of the mules and shouted at them. The animals surged forward against their harness, and the wagons lurched into motion. Daniel and Murdoch took the lead, and when Daniel glanced over his shoulder, he saw that Cordelia was leaning out to gaze wistfully at the house. Her father, on the other hand, had his eyes fixed steadily on the road ahead.

That was the wisest course, Daniel knew. These days, it did not pay a man to look back. What was important was what lay ahead.

Chapter Two

The travelers reached the Mohawk River the next afternoon, and so far, Quincy had thoroughly enjoyed the trip. Riding on the wagon with Cordelia allowed him to sit beside a gorgeous woman who liked him and was interested in what he had to say.

Of course, he knew that she didn't have any romantic feelings for him. She was just a friend; after all, she was seven or eight years older than he. She was a woman, he told himself, and had even been married. He supposed she thought of him as a child, even though he was nearly seventeen years old, and in most places that was considered old enough to marry. One of these days he would work up the courage to ask Cordelia how she felt about him. But not today, he decided. Today there were other things to do.

Gresham Howard hauled in his mule team and brought the wagon to a halt atop a hill that overlooked the small village of Half Moon. Through the trees, the travelers could see the Mohawk River curving off to the west, winding its

way through thickly wooded hills toward the settlement of
Schenectady. Before leaving Saratoga, Murdoch had drawn
a map and explained that they would follow the Mohawk
across New York, then turn southwest toward Pennsylvania
and the Allegheny River, which would in turn take them to
the mighty Ohio. It was a roundabout route, but the terrain
would be easier for the wagons to negotiate than going farther south along the Hudson and then turning west. That
would have placed the Appalachian Mountains in their
path, and Murdoch wanted to avoid those rugged heights.

"Well, here we are," Howard called to the others.
"That's the Mohawk River below us."

"I want to get down, Quincy," Cordelia said. The
young man wasted no time hopping down from the wagon
seat, then turning to assist her.

Daniel and Murdoch dismounted and, holding their
horses' reins, stood at the crest of the hill. At the bottom of
the gentle slope the road divided, and one path headed almost due east; the other followed the Mohawk.

Quincy and Cordelia walked up beside Daniel and
Murdoch. There was a painful lump in the boy's throat as
he said, "I suppose this is where we say good-bye, Daniel."

"Yes, it is," his brother agreed. He frowned. "I
wouldn't have suggested that you go west if I didn't think it
was the right thing to do, Quincy."

"I know. If you get a chance, you'll let Mother and Father know where I am, won't you?"

"Of course." Daniel shook his head ruefully. "They
must be pretty worried about us, but if they've been in
touch with Uncle Benjamin, they'll know we haven't been
in Boston in quite a while. And he's probably told them all
sorts of stories about the two of us being fugitives, too.
Somehow I'll get word to them and let them know the
truth."

"Thanks, Daniel." Quincy gripped his brother's hand

and made his voice firmer and more confident than he felt. "I know we'll see each other again—soon."

"You have my word on it," Daniel promised. Suddenly he drew Quincy into his arms and hugged him tightly for a long time. Like all brothers, they'd had their disagreements, but the bond between them was strong.

Pulling gently away from Quincy, Daniel turned to Murdoch and shook hands with the frontiersman. "I'll miss you, my friend," he said. "Take good care of Quincy for me."

Murdoch slapped Daniel on the shoulder, and the exuberance of the farewell slightly staggered the younger man. "Aye—though I guess before 'tis all over, the lad may well be taking care o' me."

Gresham Howard strode up and extended his hand. "I may not have known you for long, Daniel," he said, "but I think you are a fine young man, and I wish you the best of luck in your efforts for the patriot cause."

"Thank you, sir. And good luck to you, too."

That left Cordelia. She looked at Daniel and said rather haughtily, "I suppose I should tell you that I'm going to miss you, but to be absolutely truthful, I'm not sure that I will. You were always very bossy to me, Daniel Reed."

"Somebody had to be, or you'd have been in trouble *all* the time, instead of just most of it," Daniel replied, grinning. Becoming more serious, he added, "Good luck, Cordelia. I wish you only the best."

For a moment her control threatened to break. Quincy saw her façade of charming arrogance begin to crumble, but she regained her bearing, gave Daniel a perfunctory hug, and linked arms with Quincy. The move took him by surprise, but he certainly did not object, not when he could feel the warmth of her arm pressed against his.

Daniel swung up into the saddle, waved to them, and put the horse into a brisk trot down the hill.

"We might as well get moving, too," Howard said, but

they stayed where they were and watched Daniel until he reached the fork in the trail and took the eastern path. Within moments he was gone from sight, cut off from their view by the trees that lined the road.

"Now we can go," Quincy said, and wondered if he would ever see his brother again.

The same day, May 25, 1775, that Daniel Reed said good-bye to his brother and headed east, in Boston, General Thomas Gage, commander in chief of the British forces in North America and military governor of Massachusetts Colony, paced impatiently around his office. The window behind him overlooked Boston Harbor, and every time he swung around, he could see *H.M.S. Cerberus* floating at anchor at one of the piers. The ship had arrived earlier in the day, bringing with it the king's response to Gage's request for thirty thousand more troops to deal with the upstart colonists.

"Three men," Gage muttered as his gaze fell once again on the *Cerberus*. "I ask for thirty thousand, and German George sends me three!"

"What was that, sir?" Gage's adjutant asked from the other side of the room.

Gage waved a hand. "Nothing, nothing," he said sharply. He was a loyal soldier of the Crown, and although in private moments he might vent his frustration by referring to King George III by the well-known, unflattering nickname of "German George," he knew he had no business doing so in public.

The general's secretary knocked on the door and stuck his head inside the office. "They're here, sir," he said in a low voice.

"Send them in," snapped Gage. He went behind his desk and stood at attention to greet his visitors.

The secretary opened the door all the way, and three men filed into the room. They wore the red coat, white breeches, and high black boots of the British army, and the insignia on their uniforms indicated that they had attained the rank of major general. The first man into the room was tall, well built, and impressive looking, with a dark complexion and a stern demeanor. He was General William Howe, an officer with a fine reputation, whose standing was further enhanced by being the brother of Admiral Richard "Black Dick" Howe, England's premier naval commander.

Following Howe was General Henry Clinton, a small man whose fine-boned build and wispy fair hair gave him a boyish appearance. He was, however, in his late thirties and had been a soldier and an officer since his teens.

The final visitor was the most handsome, with sleek, dark hair and an elegant air that made his army uniform seem like the height of fashion. "Gentleman Johnny" Burgoyne was how most people referred to him, including the troops under his command, and he was as famous a playwright and man-about-town as he was a soldier.

The king had referred to the men as the "triumvirate of reputation." They were the most able officers England had to offer.

Would they take the place of thirty thousand troops? Gage had serious doubts about that, but he could not afford to offend such distinguished colleagues by voicing that opinion. Instead he cleared his throat and said, "Sit down, gentlemen. I trust you had a pleasant voyage?"

Burgoyne slouched into one of the chairs Gage's adjutant had placed in front of the big desk. "Pleasant enough," he replied as the others took their seats. He went on, "Truth to tell, I'd rather be in London right now, but as soldiers of the Crown, we do as we're told, eh?"

"One's duty is more important than personal considerations," murmured Clinton. It was clear from the sharp sideways glance he directed toward Burgoyne that he held little affection for the dashing officer.

Howe said stolidly to Gage, "Please tell us what you can about the situation, General."

"Of course." Gage sat down, clasped his hands together on the desk in front of him, and asked, "You know about what happened at Lexington and Concord, I take it?"

"A dreadful business," Clinton said. "Absolutely shocking to think that subjects of the Crown would dare fire on His Majesty's troops like that."

"Shocking, yes," agreed Gage, "but not totally unexpected. The trouble over here has been developing for a long time, and Lexington and Concord were simply the sparks that lit the fuse."

"And that fuse is still burning?" asked Burgoyne.

"Even hotter," Gage replied grimly. "Two weeks ago, rebellious colonial militiamen attacked and captured Fort Ticonderoga and Crown Point on Lake Champlain."

The trio of major generals sat up straight, surprised by the news. "Indeed," muttered Howe. "Then they've gone on the offensive."

"Yes. The whole countryside is aroused. Reports from outside Boston indicate that, as we speak, militiamen are swarming toward the city. A sizable force of patriots, as the rebels call themselves, has already assembled in Cambridge, on the other side of the Charles River."

"Have they occupied the Charlestown peninsula?" Clinton asked sharply.

"Not yet," replied Gage. "You're concerned, of course, about Bunker Hill and Breed's Hill?"

"Well, aren't you worried about the same thing, General?" Howe asked. He leaned forward, a scowl on his heavy features. "If the rebels control those hills and place cannon upon them, they control Boston as well. From that position, they can rain down fire upon us."

"They could bombard the city into submission," Burgoyne added, his air of sleepy nonchalance gone.

"I know, I know, gentlemen," Gage said. "That is one

reason why I wrote an urgent letter to the king requesting reinforcements, so that this problem can be cleaned up before it becomes even messier." He could not resist adding, "You three are the king's reply to that request."

Clinton flushed angrily at the tone of Gage's comment; Howe's scowl deepened; Burgoyne merely lifted an eyebrow.

Howe said tightly, "We shall endeavor to do our utmost to see that you are not disappointed, General."

Weary, Gage lifted a hand and massaged his temples for a moment. "I beg your pardon, gentlemen," he said. "I did not mean to disparage the abilities of such fine officers. I honestly wish this situation had never arisen. The colonists see me as some sort of stubborn monster, I suppose, forgetting the fact that my good wife is an American herself. To be forced to order British soldiers into battle against British subjects— It is a burden, gentlemen, and one which I will gladly share with you." He straightened his shoulders and regarded his visitors sternly. "I need not remind you that none of the feelings I just expressed will leave this office."

"Certainly not," Burgoyne said. "If the truth were known, others in the army agree with you, General."

Gage knew quite well that Burgoyne was referring to himself. *Perhaps,* Gage thought, *Howe and Clinton feel the same way. Not Clinton—the twit is so ambitious all he cares about is winning battles and the king's favor.*

"All right," Gage said, pushing all that aside in his mind. "The question is what are we going to do about this rebellion, gentlemen. And I warn you, whatever it is, it must be done soon, before the colonial army grows any stronger."

West of Schenectady, in the colony of New York, fourteen-year-old Mariel Jarrott stood at the top of a low, grassy hill and anxiously scanned the small valley and fields in front of her. She pushed back one of the long blond braids that had fallen forward over her shoulder and murmured, "Dietrich, where in heaven's name have you gotten to?" Worry clouded her pale blue eyes.

He had been with her only minutes earlier, playing contentedly as Mariel gathered dandelions on one of the gentle slopes behind her parents' farm. She had turned her back on him for mere seconds, but when she turned around again, her little brother was gone.

It had taken little time to search the hill, but the toddler was nowhere to be found. Mariel wondered how far he could have gone in such a short period of time, and, still carrying her basket, she walked down the hill into the valley. She knew she was more than a quarter of a mile from the cabin that her father, Conrad Jarrott, had built with his bare hands several years earlier. Occasional Indian raids, usually by the Mohawks of the Iroquois Nation, had prompted Jarrott to issue firm orders to his children not to stray from the farm.

Mariel's worried look did not detract from her beauty. Her skin was fair, her blond hair was thick and lustrous, and her slender body displayed the curves of blossoming womanhood. At the moment, though, she felt very much like a child: afraid for herself, afraid for Dietrich, and afraid of her father's reaction when he found out that she had allowed the two-year-old to wander off.

A sudden flash of movement ahead of her caught Mariel's eye. She stopped and stared and saw it again, and this time she spotted the top of Dietrich's blond head as he made his way through the new, spring grass. She caught her breath, and a mixture of relief and anger flowed through her. "Dietrich!" she called, and when the little boy looked up, she added, "You stay right there!"

She ran through the grass, quickly covering the twenty yards between them, and as she came up to him, out of breath and panting, he looked up at her innocently and said, "Mariel run fast."

Dropping to her knees beside him, she suppressed the urge to pull him into her arms and hug him. Instead she said sternly, "Yes, Mariel run fast. I had to run to find you because you frightened me when you wandered off, Dietrich. Do you understand what I'm saying?"

He smiled, but Mariel knew there was only so much reasoning one could do with a toddler. So she gave up, hugged him tightly, and said, "We'd better get back to the farm before Father notices we're gone. He'll give us both a hiding if he does."

Dietrich caught hold of her hand, then pointed with a pudgy finger at a nearby field. "Dandelions," he said.

Mariel looked and saw a meadow covered with fresh dandelion greens and knew it would take only a few minutes to finish filling her basket. Though she knew that she and her brother were too far from the farm, Mariel caught her bottom lip between her teeth and made her decision: They would pick the greens, then hurry back. Perhaps no one would have missed them.

Holding securely to the little boy's hand, she led him toward the field and said emphatically, "You stay right here." Then she picked a few mature dandelions and gave them to Dietrich, who happily blew their seeds into the air and then tried to catch them again while she finished picking the greens that would feed her family as well as allow her father to make wine.

A sudden burst of gunfire, followed by blood-curdling whoops and yells, made her drop the basket and whirl around.

Dietrich looked up as well, his attention caught by the unexpected sounds. More shots rattled from the far side of the hill, and, startled by the noise, birds flew rapidly overhead.

"What that?" asked Dietrich.

Mariel's heart thudded in her chest, and her pulse struck a steady hammerblow in her head. But it was not enough to drown out the sound of the shots, the savage yells, and the screams of agony that she heard through the warm spring air.

"Come on!" she exclaimed, grabbing Dietrich's hand and breaking into a run. "We've got to get back to the cabin!"

When the little boy could not keep up with her, she paused just long enough to sweep him into her arms, then raced toward her family's home. Puffing with the effort, she ran up the hill and into the thick screen of trees and brush that ran along its top.

She saw black smoke and spotted flames flickering through the trees. Instinct made her slow her frantic pace, and she stopped and dropped into a crouch behind some bushes, pushing them aside to peer down at the cabin.

A shrill cry of grief and pain welled up her throat, but she caught it just in time, stifling the sound so that the marauders down the hill would not hear it over the hellish noises of the devastation they had brought to this peaceful farm.

The Jarrott cabin was ablaze, flames licking high into the sky above the log roof. Her father lay in front of the doorway, which was billowing smoke. Conrad Jarrott's bloody body was studded with arrows, and Mariel saw gunshot wounds in it as well. Two of her brothers lay facedown not far away. She couldn't tell which ones they were, but they had been shot full of arrows and were sprawled in the awkward stillness of sudden death.

Screams from inside the burning building told her that her mother and other brothers and sisters were trapped inside. She clapped her hands over her ears, but not even that shut out the nightmarish shrieks. She wanted to close her eyes, to turn and run screaming away, but instead she continued to kneel there, wide-eyed, frozen by the horror of what she was witnessing.

At least a dozen Mohawk warriors capered around the cabin, shouting and chanting in celebration of their grisly victory. Because there were no Indian bodies lying anywhere in sight, Mariel knew that any resistance her father and brothers had put up had been futile.

Her family was dead, wiped out—except for Dietrich and her.

She heard the sobs coming from her little brother and quickly clamped a hand over his mouth before a full-fledged wail could erupt. She drew him tightly against her and hissed into his ear, "Be quiet, Dietrich! Do you understand? Be quiet!" If they could stay here, hidden, until the Mohawks lost interest in their gruesome celebration and left, she and Dietrich might survive this raid.

Finally able to tear her eyes away from the horrible spectacle of her family's murder, she dropped her gaze to the ground, keeping her hand over Dietrich's mouth in case he tried to cry out again. As the screams from inside the cabin faded and then died away, the boy squirmed frenziedly. "Dietrich!" Mariel said. "Stop tha—"

Her breath froze in her throat. She saw that the Mohawks had tired of their deadly game; they had jerked the undamaged arrows from the bodies and were coming straight up the hill toward where Mariel and Dietrich were hiding.

She would not have thought it was possible for her heart to pound any harder, but it seemed about to tear its way out of her chest. She backed away from the edge of the trees, being careful not to make any sound. Her homespun dress was brown and blended into the undergrowth, and she was glad that her mother Ursula, a simple woman, had rejected her request to dye the fabric a brighter color. Dietrich wore brown breeches and a butternut linsey-woolsey shirt that would conceal him as well—at least Mariel prayed that was the case.

Once the brow of the hill was between the Mohawks and her, she stood, grasped Dietrich tightly, and broke into a run. Her steps carried her quickly down the hill and across the field at the bottom of the slope. She forced the horrors she had seen to the back of her mind. There was no time to dwell on what had happened. There was only time for survival.

Perhaps a hundred yards away was a small cave that had been dug into the hillside by Mariel's brothers Kurt and Wilhelm. It was a special, secret place, and she had overheard them whispering about it in the farmhouse's big loft that served as the communal sleeping quarters for the Jarrott children. One day, Mariel had told Kurt that she knew about the cave and persuaded him to show her where it was. He had done so only after exacting a promise from her never to tell their parents about it, and tears stung her eyes as she realized that their secret was safe now. Kurt and Wilhelm would never be punished for their boyish adventure, but perhaps it would save her life, and Dietrich's.

Knowing she had to reach the cave before the Mohawks topped the hill behind her, Mariel sprinted across the field. If she did not, they would be in plain sight, and the Indians would come after them. She saw the thicket at the base of the hill that masked the cave's entrance, and with her breath rasping in her throat, raced toward it.

Still carrying Dietrich, she tore through the bushes, ignoring the branches that clawed at their clothes and their skin, and pushed through the growth until she saw the dark oval of the cave's mouth. It was four feet tall and three feet wide, and Mariel crouched and plunged into the opening. Frantically she replaced as much brush as she could to hide the entrance.

The cave was shallow, no more than eight feet deep, and she retreated to the rear of it and knelt there in the semidarkness, panting and gulping in great breaths of air richly laden with the moist scent of the earth that surrounded her. As her eyes adjusted to the dimness, the opening of the cave grew brighter, even though the brush that hid it blocked some of the sunlight.

Dietrich began to squirm, so Mariel placed him on the floor of the cave. "Be quiet, and don't move around," she whispered sternly. "We don't want the Indians to find us."

The little boy whimpered in fear, and the sound tore at her heart. It was still beyond comprehension to her that they were the only survivors of the massacre, the only members of the Jarrott family left alive.

Just before they left Westphalia, Mariel remembered her father saying that America was a new land where one could escape the feudal legacy of Europe that made it impossible for a peasant to aspire to anything better. Conrad Jarrott had been willing to risk all their lives for that opportunity, and he had been a happy man when he and his family had settled in the Mohawk Valley. True, he was still a farmer, just as he had been in their Germanic homeland, but here the land on which he toiled was *his* and did not belong to a baron who longed for a return to the days of lords and serfs. All that was behind them, and the grateful family had stopped speaking German and learned English instead and had become full-fledged colonists of the Crown.

Now all that was over, as dead as the past they had left behind in Westphalia—as dead as Conrad Jarrott. His dream had ended in murder, blood, and flame.

Mariel tried to force those thoughts from her mind. She and Dietrich were still alive, and she had to remain calm if she wanted them to stay that way.

"Stay here," she told Dietrich, then crawled toward the cave entrance on hands and knees, not caring that the damp earthen floor made her dress muddy. She was able to move some of the branches aside and peer out.

The Mohawks were trotting through the open field, intent on whatever their destination was now that their bloody work had been done, and none of them glanced in the direction of the cave. She breathed a little easier. If they kept going, they would never notice the cave, and she and Dietrich would be safe. Then they could make their way to the cabin of one of the neighboring settlers. These were all good people around here; surely someone would take care of two orphans and see to the burying of their murdered family.

Suddenly Mariel's blood froze in her veins as her gaze fell on her straw basket, which she had dropped when the first shots rang out and was still lying on the ground, in plain sight of the Indians. If they saw it, they would know that someone else was around, and they would search the little valley, Mariel thought in horror, until they found her little brother and her.

She did not dare breathe as one by one the Mohawks ran past the thicket—twenty feet away from the opening to the cave. She prayed for Dietrich's silence and that the Indians would keep going, and it appeared that her prayers had been answered.

The first men passed by without noticing the basket, but the final warrior in the line broke stride, veered away from the others, and headed right for it. Mariel wanted to scream in frustration and fear as he stopped beside the basket and picked it up. She could see his frightening, painted face clearly as he stared in puzzlement at the dandelion greens.

The other Indians had stopped as well, and one of them called to the man who held the basket. Mariel had no way of knowing what was being said in the guttural Mohawk tongue, but the warriors seemed impatient for their companion to join them, and so with a shrug, the man tossed the basket aside and hurried back to his friends.

Too much had happened for Mariel to assume that she and Dietrich were safe. And her fear was borne out when, instead of proceeding, the man who had found the basket talked forcefully to his companions. He gestured at the basket, and Mariel knew that he had to be saying that somewhere in the vicinity at least one more of the hated white settlers was hiding.

She felt panic steal into her brain as the other raiders nodded and spread out through the field, working their way toward the hiding place where she and Dietrich huddled. This time, Mariel knew, there would be no escape.

Chapter Three

Daniel Reed was not retracing the route Quincy, Murdoch, and he had followed when they traveled west across Massachusetts several weeks earlier. Instead he rode through the villages of Pittsfield and Stockbridge. The mountains and valleys were in the full bloom of late May, and swarms of blackflies were his only annoyance. He had picked up a road that led east across the colony and followed it for several days, seeing few travelers, when he spotted a large group of men ahead of him. From the way they marched—a bit raggedly—Daniel knew they had to be a militia unit.

He rode up alongside the men and slowed his horse's pace so that its hooves would not kick up some late-spring mud. A few of the men called out to him, and he returned the greetings with a wave as he headed toward the blue-coated officers at the head of the column. As he approached them they turned their mounts, and one of the men signaled the militiamen to halt.

"Good day to you, gentlemen," Daniel greeted the officers. "Where are you bound?"

"Before I go answering that, just who would you be, lad?" The question came from one of the officers, a burly, middle-aged individual with broad shoulders, a barrel chest, and florid, rough-hewn features. His eyes, set in folds of flesh, were narrowed suspiciously.

"My name is Daniel Reed, sir, and if you think I might be a spy for the British, your concern is for naught. I've already fought the redcoats a time or two."

"Have you now?" returned the officer. "And where might that have been?"

Daniel did not want to go into the particulars of the battle in which he and a small detachment of men from Colonel Benedict Arnold's Connecticut militia had captured several wagons filled with British munitions; it was a long, complicated, and sordid story. Instead he uttered the words whose significance was instantly recognized throughout the colonies.

"Lexington and Concord," he said.

Muttering raced through the group as the men reacted to Daniel's statement. Even the officer who had been questioning him looked impressed. But the man said, "Is that so? Is there anyone who can vouch for you?"

Daniel smiled. "Samuel Adams, John Hancock, Paul Revere, Dr. Joseph Warren. There are others who know me as well."

"I'm not going to argue with famous names like those, lad," said the burly officer. "I'm Aaron Webster, duly elected captain of these boys, and I'm glad to know you. Are you headed for Boston?"

"That I am," Daniel replied. "I thought perhaps I could ride along with you if you're going in the same direction."

"Aye, and welcome you'll be." Captain Webster turned in his saddle and bellowed at his men, "Dress up those lines there! Let's get a move on, unless you plan to rest all day!"

The men moved out, and as Daniel rode with the officers, they told him that the group was made up of farmers from the Berkshire Hills in western Massachusetts, and they were bound for Cambridge, where the patriot forces were gathering.

"We got word that Boston itself is closed off," Webster told Daniel. "The bloody British have built barricades across Boston Neck and guard them around the clock. You can't get across the river anymore, either, because of the patrol boats sailing back and forth."

Daniel frowned. That was certainly unwelcome news. He had counted on being able to slip into the city. The Committee of Safety, the inner circle of patriot leadership—if any of them were still in Boston—would be waiting for his report on the campaign in upper New York, and he had personal business to attend to as well.

Once he was convinced that Daniel was not a British secret agent, Captain Webster proved to be quite talkative. With pride in his voice, he told Daniel about organizing the militia unit and being elected its commander, and as he spoke, Daniel felt an instinctive liking for the man.

That evening they camped in a field next to the road. The men pitched their tents and built cook fires beside the stone wall that marked the perimeter of a farmer's land. Daniel tethered his horse to a small bush nearby; he unsaddled the animal and was rubbing it down when he heard someone call to him from one of the nearby campfires.

"Mr. Reed, would you care to join us?" asked a young militiaman who gestured toward a pot of stew that was heating over the fire.

Daniel smiled and slung his saddlebags over his shoulder. "Thanks," he said. "I can contribute a bit of tobacco, if that would be all right."

"More than all right. Why, it'd be downright welcome, wouldn't it, boys?"

The other three men sitting around the fire chuckled and nodded. Daniel joined them, took a tobacco pouch from his saddlebag, and soon the air was filled with the aroma of pipe smoke as the men waited for the stew to cook.

"I'm Thad Garner," said the stocky young man with unruly sandy hair who had invited Daniel to join them. As he shook hands with Daniel, he continued, "These other lads are George Jennings, Benjamin Hobbs, and Fred Dary."

"Glad to meet you," Daniel said, shaking hands with them.

"And of course we know who you are," Thad Garner went on. "You're rather famous, in fact."

Daniel smiled ruefully. "I don't think I've done anything to warrant fame."

"You fought at Concord. Won't you tell us about it?" Thad asked eagerly.

Daniel hesitated. That April morning in Concord seemed almost years ago, not merely five weeks or so. His memories were a curious mixture of vague confusion and crystal-clear images, and what he remembered most vividly was the stench of burned powder, the sound of men's screams, the bright red splashes of blood, and the fear that had coursed through him during that endless day. When he looked at the faces of the men sitting with him, though they were the same age, Daniel felt old.

He knew what they wanted to hear. They wanted him to tell them that fighting the British had been a glorious adventure, a thrilling, dramatic enterprise that left one full of honor and pride and patriotism. If he told them the truth—that a man might fight out of principle but that once the battle began, survival was all he thought about—they probably would not believe him.

Instead he shrugged and said simply, "We thought the British had come far enough, so we drove them back. There really wasn't much to it except a lot of running and shooting."

"Sure," Thad said, grinning. "Not much to it." He

clapped Daniel on the shoulder. "I think you're being too modest, Daniel. You don't mind if I call you Daniel, do you?"

"Not at all." Thad had reacted just as Daniel expected, and there was no point in arguing with the young man. After he had been in battle himself, he would understand— if he lived through it.

"Are you going to join the army once we get to Cambridge?" asked one of the militiamen. "We're told that's where it's being mustered by General Artemas Ward."

Daniel had heard of General Ward of the Massachusetts Militia, and he knew that Ward was trying to mold the various companies into a real army. It was a good idea, Daniel decided. The colonists would need a unified army before this war with the British was over, but he was unsure whether or not he would join such an army; he had already been bloodied several times in the cause of freedom, and he *had* to get back into Boston.

"I'm not sure," he replied to the question. "I have some other business to take care of."

"And what would that be?" Thad asked guilelessly.

"Personal business," Daniel replied, hoping the others would not take offense at the shortness of his answer. But he was not going to tell them about his status as an agent for the Committee of Safety, and he was not going to mention the other reason he wanted to get into Boston, either.

That reason had long red hair that felt like silk when Daniel ran his fingers through it, green eyes that sometimes startled him with their intelligence and fire, and a tall, graceful figure that caused heat to build within him when he remembered how it felt to take her in his arms and kiss her.

Roxanne, he thought, the pain of missing her suddenly strong inside him. *Roxanne . . .*

"Roxanne! Roxanne, are you in there?"

The redheaded young woman turned from the nests

where she had been gathering eggs and smiled as a boy about twelve years old bounded into the barn. "Here I am, Henry," Roxanne Darragh said. "What is it?"

"Pa's looking for you," Henry Parsons told her. "He says he's got some news." As he spoke, he gazed at her with awe and infatuation. She knew he thought she was beautiful, and he was mightily impressed that she, a mere woman, had successfully fought the British.

"Thank you, Henry." She handed him the basket of eggs and patted his shoulder, which brought a blush to his freckled face. "I'll go right away."

As she left the barn and walked toward the farmhouse of Henry's father, Lemuel Parsons, the smile vanished from her face. Lemuel had taken a wagonload of lumber into Concord that morning, and if he was back so soon, the news he brought must be important.

She wondered if he had heard anything about Daniel.

It had been a month since Daniel left the Parsons farm, bound for New York with Quincy and Murdoch; Roxanne had returned to Boston a few days later, and once in the city, she had become involved in a daring plan to capture a boatload of British arms.

The success of that mission had changed her life in several ways: Her true identity as a patriot agent had been revealed, making it unsafe for her to remain at home in the city, and she had returned to the Parsons farm, which often served as a hiding place for fugitive patriots. But now the entire colony of Massachusetts had taken up arms against the British, and she no longer had to worry about being captured by roving patrols of redcoats. All the king's soldiers were bottled up in Boston.

She saw Lemuel Parsons sitting on the porch of the tidy, well-maintained farmhouse, sipping from a glass of cold tea that his wife, Lottie, had handed him. He was a thin, rawboned man with dark hair and skin like old leather. Lottie sat beside him on the well-worn pine bench next to the woodbin.

Lemuel raised his glass in greeting as Roxanne came up to the porch. "Morning, Roxanne," he said. "I heard something in Concord a while ago, and I knew you'd want to know about it."

"Don't torture the poor girl, Lem," Lottie admonished him. "Go ahead and tell her."

"Ayuh, I will. Hezekiah Wilkes was talking at the market about how our boys captured Fort Ticonderoga and Crown Point without firing a shot."

"You mean no one was killed?" Roxanne asked anxiously.

"Or even wounded any worse than a little scratch, far as I know," replied Lemuel. "I know you've been worrying about Daniel and Quincy and Murdoch, so I came straight back here to tell you about it."

She closed her eyes and inhaled deeply with relief. Concord was a hotbed of patriot activity, and she had expected to hear something about the New York campaign before now. Short of having Daniel himself deliver it, this was the best news she could have gotten.

Opening her eyes, she smiled at the farmer and said, "Thank you, Lemuel. You've eased my mind more than you can possibly know. I pray that Daniel will be returning to Boston now."

"As to that, I couldn't say, but I suppose it's likely."

"Then that's where I'll be going," she said.

Her declaration startled them. They looked at her in confusion, and Lottie said, "But it's not safe for you to go into Boston, Roxanne. The British are looking for you after what happened with that ship."

"I know," she agreed, "but I don't have any choice. Daniel was supposed to come back to Boston after the attack on Fort Ticonderoga. He won't know about the *Carolingian,* so he'll be looking for me in the city. I have to go there, or he'll never find me."

"I think you're jumping to conclusions, Roxanne,"

Lemuel told her. "When Daniel doesn't find you in Boston, he'll know to look for you here."

"There's no guarantee of that," she argued. "Besides, as far as the British are concerned, he's a fugitive, too, and has been ever since he escaped from the Brattle Street jail. Something could happen to him while he's looking for me. I have to find him, and then we'll both get out of Boston."

"That's all well and good," Lemuel said, "but how're you going to get into the city? The redcoats have Boston Neck closed off completely now, and they're patrolling the harbor and the Charles like never before."

Roxanne frowned. Lemuel was right; it *was* going to be difficult getting back into Boston. "I don't know," she said slowly. "Surely there must be some way to slip in."

"And if you're caught, you know what will happen," Lemuel said ominously.

"They wouldn't hang me," Roxanne insisted. "Not even the British would hang a woman."

"A woman who helped steal a whole boatload of guns from them and then watched while their ship was scuttled? I wouldn't count overmuch on that, Roxanne."

"Besides, even if they didn't hang you," Lottie added, "you'd be thrown in prison. I'm sure it would be just awful."

That was true enough. But it was terrible being separated from Daniel, and so Roxanne said stubbornly, "I appreciate your concern, both of you. But my mind's made up."

"I thought as much," Lemuel said glumly. "But will you do one thing for me?"

"As long as you don't try to talk me out of going."

"I'm just asking you to wait a bit. There's no way of knowing how long it will take Daniel to get back from Lake Champlain. Give it a while longer. That way it'll be more likely he's back in Boston before you risk your neck to get there yourself."

For a long moment, Roxanne considered the suggestion. She knew Lemuel was probably right, but it was difficult to be away from Daniel for even a day longer than necessary, and there was something else to consider, too. She wondered how he would feel if he reached Boston first and heard the gossip in the city, the malicious little stories about how she and Elliot Markham, the son of a prominent Tory businessman, had been lovers.

It had been a lie at first, purposely spread to cover up their activities as patriot spies. Unintentionally the lie had become the truth, and it had happened only once, a single instance when Elliot and she had let their guard down, and the strain they were under had forced them to find comfort in each other's arms.

Roxanne was sure that Daniel could understand using a lie to further the patriot cause, even such a sordid one. But would he ever understand and accept that she had actually made love to Elliot Markham—Daniel's own cousin and dear friend?

"Yes, I'll wait," she said to them. "I don't like it, but you're right. So I'll wait—for a little while."

"That's all we ask," Lottie replied. She smiled affectionately at Roxanne. "You've come to mean a great deal to us, dear, almost like one of our own children. We want you to be happy, but we want you to be safe, too."

Roxanne looked from Lemuel to Lottie. *Happy and safe* . . . That was asking a great deal, considering the way things were now. As the daughter of a printer, she had been exposed to a variety of reading matter, more than the average person, and somewhere she had come across an old saying: "May you live in interesting times." The strange thing about the adage was that it was used as a curse, and she was beginning to understand why.

Chapter Four

"Smoke up ahead," Murdoch Buchanan said quietly as he reined in his horse. He pointed at a layer of dark haze in the air. From the look of it, something fairly good sized had burned recently.

Gresham Howard brought the lead wagon to a stop alongside Murdoch. Frowning, Howard asked anxiously, "Do you think it's some sort of trouble?"

"Tha' kind o' smoke usually is," replied Murdoch, unconsciously running a thumbnail along his beard-stubbled, angular jaw.

Quincy halted the second wagon, hopped down nimbly from the seat, and left Cordelia holding the reins. He trotted up to join the men. "What is it?" he asked.

Murdoch indicated the smoke. It was on the far side of a low hill, perhaps half a mile away. *Not close enough to represent an immediate danger,* Murdoch thought, *but much too close to be ignored.*

"Tha' dinna come from a fireplace," he said. "Looks t'

me like Indian sign. Burned out some settler's cabin, would be my guess."

"We'd better go see about it," Quincy said, turning away. "I'll get my horse—"

"Stay where ye be, lad," Murdoch said sharply. "I'll take a scout around, but I want ye t' stay here with Miss Cordelia and Mr. Howard."

"But, Murdoch," protested Quincy, "if it's Indians, you might need my help."

"And so might the others," Murdoch pointed out. "Make sure your guns're loaded. I'll no' be gone long."

He heeled his horse into motion and directed it toward the hill over which thinning shreds of black smoke still hung in the air.

He trusted the boy to obey his order. No matter how much Quincy's adventurous nature dragged him into trouble, he was a good lad with common sense. Both the Reed brothers were, and Murdoch had grown to regard them as brothers.

For the past two days Quincy and he, along with Cordelia and Howard, had been following the narrow road that ran alongside the Mohawk River. At times it was little more than a path that would almost disappear, but Murdoch had no trouble picking it up again. To eyes like his, seasoned by years on the frontier, a footpath was the same as a highway.

He had enjoyed the last two days. The Mohawk Valley was good country, almost as beautiful and open as the valley of the Ohio, which to Murdoch was as close to paradise as a heathen Scotsman such as he would ever get. Massachusetts and eastern New York were too crowded for him. A place where one could ride for a mile and see two or even three cabins was too blasted civilized.

As Murdoch pointed his big, sturdy black gelding up the hill, he checked to make sure both his flintlock pistols were loose in his belt. He listened closely but heard no shots or screams or war whoops. Chances were, whatever had happened on the other side of the hill was already over.

When he reached the top of the slope, Murdoch stopped and leaned forward in the saddle to study the scene spread out before him. He saw, as he expected, the gutted, smoldering ruins of a log cabin. Part of one blackened wall still stood, but the others, as well as the roof, had collapsed.

His jaw tightened and trenches appeared in his ruddy cheeks when he spotted the motionless bodies lying on the ground near the remains of the cabin. His keen eyes made out the arrows that protruded from the corpses, and without having to examine them, he knew the shafts bore Mohawk markings.

Clucking to his horse, Murdoch got the animal moving. He glanced over his shoulder at the wagons and his companions who waited for him, but they dropped out of sight as he rode carefully down the far side of the hill. His long rifle was in a fringed sheath attached to the saddle; Murdoch slid it out and rode with it across the pommel as he descended the slope.

There was no point in checking the corpses, not with so many arrow holes in them that they looked like pincushions. It was clear from the large, bloody wounds in the bodies that the Mohawks had retrieved their undamaged arrows. Nor was there any need to sift through the ashes of the cabin. Anyone who had been trapped in there was dead now. But there could be survivors hiding somewhere in the area, so Murdoch remained watchful, and because he thought the Mohawks could still be somewhere nearby, he kept his mouth shut and did not call out.

He stopped his horse fifty feet from the cabin and sat there for a long moment, his rifle ready for use. He studied the corpses and saw that one belonged to a middle-aged man, the other two to teenage boys. There were probably other bodies in the ruins as well. A deep and abiding anger burned inside him. He had lived with Indians and had much respect and affection for most of them. He understood why they hated the white man for moving farther and farther west, forcing a proud people off the land on which they had lived for generations.

But this was wholesale slaughter, and there was no excuse for it, no wrong that could justify such an atrocity.

The song of a bird broke the silence that hung over the still-smoldering cabin, and when Murdoch looked up, he saw a sparrow hopping around in the branches of a tree. As he watched, more birds joined it, telling him the trouble here was over—the Indians who had done this were gone.

He rode quickly up the hill, waved at his companions to join him, and stayed where he was while Quincy and Howard turned the wagons toward him. The slope was gentle and the vehicles had no trouble negotiating it.

When the wagons reached the crest, Murdoch held up a hand to stop them. "I would'na come any closer," he said to Howard. "There be things down yonder tha' your daughter has no need o' seeing."

From the seat, Howard leaned to one side and peered past Murdoch. He grimaced when he saw the ruins of the cabin and the bodies. "I was afraid of something like this," he said. "You're right, Murdoch. I don't want Cordelia to see this. But those people down there deserve a Christian burial."

"Just what I be thinking. Ye and Cordelia stay here, Mr. Howard, while Quincy and I tend t' the unpleasant task."

"You're sure you want Quincy to go with you? I don't mind helping—"

"I think 'twould be better for ye t' stay here with your daughter. 'Twill no' be the first time the lad's seen dead men."

"All right. Whatever you think is best." Howard looked shrewdly at Murdoch. "I take it the Mohawks are responsible for this?"

"Aye."

The burly Scotsman urged his horse toward the second wagon, where, with anxious expressions on their faces, Quincy and Cordelia waited on the seat. Since their wagon was behind the other, the hilltop cut off their view, and they could not see the carnage.

"Is it as bad as you were afraid of, Murdoch?" Quincy asked.

"Aye, tha' it be. I need your help, lad. Untie your horse and ride down there with me." He added heavily, "And bring a couple o' spades from the wagon."

Cordelia paled, knowing full well there was only one reason Murdoch would be asking Quincy to bring spades with him. "Is there anything I can do?" she asked.

Murdoch shook his head. "Just stay here with your father and dinna come down the hill."

Quincy reached into the back of the wagon and grabbed two spades, then untied his horse and swung up on its back.

"Best take your rifle with ye, too, lad. I dinna think there be any o' the heathen savages still around, but ye canna be sure about these things."

Cordelia handed Quincy his rifle; then Murdoch and he rode down the hill. Glancing at Quincy as they approached the cabin, Murdoch saw that the lad's face was colorless at the sight of the bloody corpses. The boy kept riding, though, and his horse's pace did not falter.

"'Tis going t' be one o' the worst chores ye ever had t' do, lad," Murdoch said quietly. "If ye're not up to it, ye can stand watch whilst I do the digging."

"I'll do my share," replied Quincy, his voice shaky but stubborn. "Don't worry about me, Murdoch. I'm liable to see a lot worse than this before the war is over."

"Aye. And tha' be the hell of it."

They reined in near the cabin and swung down from their saddles. Quincy handed one of the spades to Murdoch. "Where should we dig?" the youngster asked.

Murdoch picked out a likely patch of ground, off to one side of the cabin and shaded by a big tree. "I suppose these folks'll rest as easy there as anyplace else," he said as he indicated the spot.

They had each taken several steps toward the place they would dig the graves when the crack of a shot sounded on the far side of a nearby hill. The shot was not close to them, but it was enough to tell them that there was still trouble nearby. "Get your rifle—" Murdoch began.

A scream tore through the air.

"That's a girl!" Quincy cried.

"Aye," Murdoch said, throwing aside his shovel. "Get your horse!"

They ran to the horses, mounted quickly, and raced toward the sound.

Quincy's heart hammered in his chest. The scream of pain and fear had come from the same direction as the gunshot. Quincy had no idea what Murdoch and he were riding into, but someone was in bad trouble and needed help. Neither he nor the redheaded frontiersman was the kind to stand by and do nothing.

Gripping his rifle tightly in his right hand, Quincy held the reins in his left and guided the horse up the hill behind Murdoch. The Scotsman flashed over the crest of the rise, followed a second later by Quincy. As they thundered down the far side of the slope, they spotted several Indians in a field ahead of them. The Mohawks were laughing and struggling with a young white girl who was trying desperately to get away. They shoved her back and forth among them, and each time she would try to leap out of their reach, one would grab her at the last instant and brutally jerk her back.

The sound of hoofbeats must have reached the ears of the Indians, because suddenly they quit fighting with the girl and turned to face the new threat. One of them leaned down, snatched a musket from the ground, and pointed it at Murdoch and Quincy.

Murdoch let out a howl of anger. Switching his rifle from his left hand to his right, he reached into his belt, plucked out a pistol, and cocked it even as the barrel was coming up. The back of a racing horse was no platform for shooting, but Murdoch Buchanan was no ordinary marksman. The pistol in his hand cracked and smoke blossomed from the muzzle. The Mohawk who was sighting over the barrel of his musket went flying backward—as though he had been punched by a giant fist—when the pistol ball slammed into his chest.

Quincy had his own gun ready, but not trusting his accuracy and being afraid of hitting the girl, he fired high over the heads of the Mohawks. Maybe that would be enough to scare them off, he thought, especially since Murdoch had already killed one of them.

But the Indians did not run. In fact, Quincy's heart leapt into his throat when he saw sunlight flash on the blade of a knife as one of the Mohawks lunged after the girl, who was still trying to get away.

Yanking his horse to a halt, Quincy was out of the saddle before the animal stopped moving. He brought his rifle to his shoulder, and remembering all he had been taught, first by Daniel and then by Murdoch, he cocked the flintlock, settled the sight on the back of the Indian who was pursuing the girl, and squeezed the trigger.

The long rifle bucked against Quincy's shoulder, and he was blinded for a moment by the smoke from its barrel. Then the smoke cleared, and he saw the Indian stumble, and a patch of blood spread rapidly in the middle of his back. Abruptly the Mohawk pitched forward, tumbled head over heels, then lay still.

Quincy heard Murdoch's second pistol explode and looked around in time to see the Scotsman ram his rifle into its holder. He was too close to the Indians now to bother with a long gun. He leaned over, pulled his hunting knife from its sheath, and dove off his horse onto a group of three Indians. His coonskin cap flew into the air.

With practiced speed, Quincy reloaded his rifle and fired at the remaining Mohawks who were scattering across the field. One of the Indians, his shoulder shattered by a rifle ball, staggered but did not go down. Like the others, he kept running.

Murdoch, meanwhile, was a blur of redheaded motion as he rolled over and over, locked in hand-to-hand combat with the three Mohawks he had tackled. Blood spurted and one of the Indians fell out of the tangle, his head flopping grotesquely from the knife slash that had almost decapitated him. Murdoch wound up on top of one of the warriors, and his knife rose and fell twice in an instant, each time burying its length in the Mohawk's chest. The last of his foes leapt onto Murdoch's back and wrapped an arm around the frontiersman's neck. They rolled over once, twice, and then a tomahawk rose in the air, poised to smash out Murdoch's brains.

But from behind, Quincy slammed the brassbound stock of his rifle into the Mohawk's head, and it was the Indians's skull rather than Murdoch's that shattered with a hideous sound like a breaking melon. Blood welled from his eyes, nose, and mouth, and the Mohawk fell lifelessly to the side.

Murdoch sprang to his feet, and he and Quincy stood side by side as they watched the surviving Indians flee into the trees.

"They will'na stop running for a while," grunted Murdoch. He turned to Quincy and went on, "Where's tha' lass they were after?"

Quincy's eyes searched the field for the girl, and he spotted her lying on the ground several yards away. Fearful that a stray shot might have caught her or that one of the Indians had wounded her before Murdoch and he arrived, Quincy ran toward her.

When he reached her side, he took hold of her shoulders and gently rolled her onto her back, and relief washed through him when he saw her chest rising and falling. There was no blood on her dress, and as far as Quincy could tell, she was uninjured. She must have fainted from sheer terror, he concluded.

Now that the danger was over and he was fairly sure the girl was all right, he noticed that although the young blonde's face, hands, and clothes were smeared with dirt, she was still very pretty. Quincy found himself wondering what color her eyes were.

Murdoch picked up his cap and settled it on his thatch of red hair, then went to his horse and slid his rifle from its sheath just in case the Mohawks who had fled decided to come back. He strode to where Quincy knelt beside the girl. "Is she all right?" he asked.

"I think so," Quincy replied. "She doesn't seem to be hurt. I think she just swooned."

"Aye, females'll do tha' sometimes, even the young ones." Murdoch frowned and lifted his head. "Listen! Do ye hear something?"

"What?" asked Quincy.

"I dinna ken. Just . . . a sound." Still frowning, Murdoch pointed to a hillside across the field. "Coming from over there, maybe. If ye think the lass is all right, I'll find out what it be."

"I'll stay with her," Quincy replied. "She'll come around in a few minutes."

Murdoch strode across the field toward the side of the hill where the strange noise was coming from. Now that he was close, it sounded like wailing. *A hurt animal, perhaps,* he thought. He angled toward a brushy thicket that was the source of the sound.

Using the barrel of his long rifle, he pushed some of

the branches aside. His frown deepened when he saw a dark cave mouth. The sound was definitely coming from inside the opening, and Murdoch suddenly realized what it reminded him of. "It can't be—" he muttered as he stooped and stepped into the cave, his bulk taking up the entire opening.

The next moment, a shocked exclamation boomed hollowly in the narrow confines. "A wee bairn!"

Minutes later, Quincy looked up from the still-unconscious girl and saw Murdoch striding across the field toward them. The young man gasped in surprise when he saw, cradled awkwardly in the Scotsman's left arm, a child with blond curls, whose pudgy arms were thrown around Murdoch's neck as the toddler clung tightly to the big man.

"Murdoch, what in the world . . . ?"

"'Tis a babe," snapped Murdoch. "Have ye never seen one before? I found him in a cave over yonder. He must belong t' the lass."

"I don't think so. This girl's not any more than fourteen or fifteen, and that baby has to be at least two years old. More likely they're brother and sister. Look at that blond hair on both of them."

"Aye. And I'd be willing t' wager they both came from tha' cabin on the other side o' the rise."

The little boy sniffled and spoke, his voice muffled by Murdoch's broad chest. "Bad men come," he said. "Indians. They burn my house and hurt Mama and Papa, and they chase Mariel and me."

He spoke English with a faint accent, and Murdoch grunted, "Must be Dutchies." To the boy, he said, "There, there, little one. No need t' worry now. Old Uncle Murdoch's got ye."

Despite the seriousness of the situation, Quincy had to grin. "Uncle Murdoch?" he echoed.

"And we'll have none o' your brazen tongue, lad, if ye

please," growled Murdoch. "Tha' is, if ye ken what's good for ye!"

Quincy held up his hands in mock surrender, then looked toward the hill that concealed the burned-out cabin. The sound of wagon wheels had caught his attention, and as he watched, the vehicles came into sight at the top of the rise.

Carefully avoiding the bodies of the dead Mohawks, Howard and Cordelia drove up to the small group in the center of the field. Cordelia shuddered as she glanced at the corpses, then did not look in their direction again. Howard clambered from his seat and said to Murdoch, "We heard the shooting and were worried about you. I see now you must have had your hands full."

"Aye," Murdoch agreed. "I'm sorry Miss Cordelia had t' see no' only this, but what happened back there at tha' cabin."

"It couldn't be helped," said Howard.

"Don't worry about me," Cordelia said, businesslike despite her pallor as she hurried over to Quincy and the young blond girl. "Is she hurt?"

"I don't think so," Quincy replied. "I thought she would have come around by now—"

Suddenly, the girl's eyes flew open. They were a beautiful blue, Quincy thought, but that was all he had time to notice before she sat bolt upright and screamed; she would have sprung to her feet had Quincy not grabbed her shoulders.

She screamed again and flailed her small fists at him. "Dietrich!" she cried. "Let me go! Dietrich!"

"Hold on!" Quincy said urgently. "I'm not Dietrich, and I won't hurt you!"

From the contorted expression on her face and the way she kept struggling, it was clear to Quincy that his words were not getting through to her. "Give me a hand here!" he said to Cordelia.

The young woman dropped to her knees beside Quincy and the girl. Speaking quietly but emphatically, she said, "It's all right. No one will hurt you. We're your friends, and we won't hurt you."

Quincy remembered the ordeal Cordelia had gone through a few weeks earlier, when she had been captured and raped by several members of a gang headed by her late husband. She must have drawn on her memories of her own feelings during that vile experience, because her soothing words gradually penetrated the shroud of terror that enveloped the girl. Cordelia drew her into her arms and held her tightly while sobs racked her slender body. Cordelia kept murmuring, "It's all right, no one will hurt you now."

Finally, the girl lifted her tear-streaked face and said hoarsely, "Dietrich! Where is Dietrich?"

"Would this be who ye're looking for, now?" Murdoch asked, stepping forward with the child in his arms.

"Mariel!" the little boy cried.

"Dietrich!" she exclaimed.

Murdoch leaned over, placed the boy on the ground, and Dietrich flung himself into Mariel's arms.

The reunion was a tearful one, and the others stood around for several minutes while Mariel and Dietrich hugged. Finally, Murdoch said quietly, "We'd best be getting out o' here. The Mohawks might have gone t' fetch more o' their bloody-handed clan."

"You're right," Howard agreed briskly. "Cordelia, if you'll help the young lady and her brother—"

"Of course." Cordelia took Mariel's arm and helped her to her feet. Mariel kept Dietrich in her arms as Cordelia led them to the wagon.

In a low voice, Murdoch said to Howard, "Head back t' the road, and skirt around tha' burned-out cabin as much as ye can. No need for Cordelia t' have t' see it again."

"Good idea," Howard agreed. "Are you and Quincy going to stop to take care of . . . ah . . ."

"Aye, tha' we will. We'll join ye as soon as we can."

The frontiersman jerked his head at Quincy, indicating they should mount up and be on their way. Quincy swung up onto his dun and followed as Murdoch returned to the ruins of the cabin. The spades were lying where they had dropped them, and the two men dismounted, picked up the tools, and got to work.

It was every bit as bad a job as they had expected, especially finding the charred bodies in the cabin and placing them in the big grave with the others. Both Murdoch and Quincy were covered with sweat by the time they were finished with the grisly task, and when the grave was covered up again, Murdoch picked up some big stones that had once been part of the cabin's fireplace and built a cairn at the head of the low mound of dirt. The stones were still hot to the touch from the fire, but Murdoch ignored the discomfort.

Brushing soot off his hands, he looked at the grave and said, "Well, tha' be done. We can bring the lass and her little brother here later t' pay their last respects."

Quincy took off his tricorn and wiped the sweat from his forehead onto his sleeve. "What are we going to do with them, Murdoch?" he asked.

"I dinna ken, no' yet. We'll have t' talk with the lass and find out what she wants t' do."

They mounted up and rode back to the path beside the river. As they had expected, Howard and Cordelia had parked the wagons not far away, under the spreading branches of a big tree. A campfire was burning, and Murdoch smelled corn cakes. It was still early in the day, but it was clear that they were going to be staying here for the night.

Murdoch and Quincy trotted up to the camp and dismounted, then tied their animals to one of the wagon wheels. Later, they would stake the horses out to graze in the grassy field beside the road; but now, both men wanted to find out more about what had happened.

Mariel and Dietrich were sitting on the ground near the fire while Cordelia cooked the corn cakes and Howard tended to the mule teams. Murdoch squatted on his haunches and asked the girl, "How are ye doing, lass?"

Summoning up a faint smile, Mariel replied, "I guess Dietrich and I are doing as well as we can, Mr. Buchanan."

"Ah, ye ken who I be, then."

"Mrs. Faulkner told us all your names."

Cordelia spoke up. "And I told you, Mariel, you can call me Cordelia."

"And I'm Quincy, and he's Murdoch," the young man said quickly, poking a thumb at the big frontiersman.

"Thank you, Quincy," Mariel said softly, "and you, too, Murdoch. You saved our lives."

Murdoch grunted, "Ye be more than welcome." He took a deep breath. Someone had to break the bad news to the girl, and there was no easy way to do it. He said flatly, "I have t' tell ye that if ye belonged to tha' cabin over the hill, then the rest o' your family—"

"Is dead," Mariel cut in. "I know, Mr. Buchanan— Murdoch. Dietrich and I saw the Indians. I was picking greens, and then there were these awful noises."

"I'm not sure you need to be talking about this now, Mariel," Cordelia said. "Dwelling on it isn't going to change anything."

"You're right about that. But there's no reason *not* to talk about it, is there?" Mariel lifted her head, and Murdoch saw the strength in her face, despite the pallor and the grime.

"Say what ye want t' say, lass," Murdoch told her.

Slowly, haltingly, the story of the tragic day came out of Mariel, and there was so much pain in her voice that Quincy wanted to cry out for her to stop, but he kept silent and let her recount the tale.

"I thought the Indians were going to leave, so that at least Dietrich and I would . . . would survive, but then one of them saw my basket and knew we might be hiding somewhere close by. They . . . they started searching for us, and I knew they were going to find us and kill us both." Mariel paused for a moment, swallowed hard, then went on, "So when I couldn't stand the waiting any longer, I told Dietrich to be very, very quiet—and then I ran out of the cave."

"But you had to know the Mohawks would see you!" Quincy exclaimed.

"I wanted them to see me. I thought if they caught me and killed me, they'd think I was the only one left."

In a hushed voice, Cordelia said, "You did it for your brother. You were trying to save his life."

"Yes. And then Murdoch and Quincy came along and saved both of us."

By now, Dietrich had slumped against his sister and fallen sound asleep, exhausted by the day's horrifying ordeal. The toddler was young enough that he would not remember what had happened today, Quincy thought, but Mariel would not have that luxury. The memories would always be with her.

"What will the two o' ye do now?" Murdoch asked after a few moments of silence.

Mariel shook her head. "I don't know. There are other settlers who might take us in. Martin Ulmer and his family live about a mile up the river, and I'm sure they'd help us."

Gresham Howard had come over to join the group. He said, "We'll take you to those people in the morning, Mariel, and if they can't help you, you're welcome to stay with us as long as need be."

"Thank you. I . . . I can never repay you for all your kindness."

Cordelia reached over, took her hand, and squeezed it. "There's no need to repay us," she said. "We're just glad we were here to help out." She looked at the others. "Aren't we?"

"Aye," Murdoch said. "Dinna ye worry, lass. Ye're in good hands now."

"I know." Mariel smiled wearily. "I thought the whole world had gone mad. I'm glad I was wrong."

Perhaps she had been wrong, and perhaps she had not, Murdoch thought. In a world where massacres like the one today could take place, maybe madness *did* rule.

Chapter Five

Elliot Markham, banned from the offices of Markham & Cummings, and allowed only by the good grace of his mother to live in the grand house in which he had grown up, had the bad luck to be at home when his father arrived there unexpectedly. Now he stood tensely in his father's dark, wood-paneled study and waited for the tirade to end. He knew from bitter experience there was nothing he could do to halt the angry words spilling from Benjamin Markham's mouth. Eventually Benjamin would tire of berating his son and send him out of the room with a disgusted comment about not wanting to lay eyes on him again for a while.

That was perfectly all right with Elliot. His entire world had gone to hell these past few weeks.

". . . suppose I should understand," Benjamin was saying heavily. "I sowed a few wild oats myself in my younger days."

Now *that* was something Elliot had a difficult time

imagining. As far back as he could remember, Benjamin had been a stodgy, stubborn, opinionated man who cared little about anything except the success or failure of the shipping line he owned in partnership with Theophilus Cummings.

Benjamin slumped into his big leather chair, a sure sign that the end of this lecture was near. "But to be so taken in by a . . . a traitorous trollop like that Roxanne Darragh!" He glared up at Benjamin and growled, "Are *all* your brains below your belt, boy?"

Elliot ignored the crude rhetorical question and said, "I've apologized before, sir, and I'll continue to if that's what you want. But even if I apologize a hundred times, I can't change the facts."

"Damned right you can't," snapped Benjamin. "And apologies won't pay for that shipload of munitions you helped those traitors steal or the ship they sank. Nor will they restore my reputation with the Crown. You've made me a laughingstock all the way from Boston Common to Windsor Castle!" Benjamin sat back, closed his eyes, and waved a hand at the door. "Go. Go far away. I can't stand to look at you anymore now, let alone tell you how I feel. I'll just hold it in, as always."

Elliot had to swallow the grim laughter that welled up his throat. The day his father held *anything* in would be the same day icicles formed in Hades.

Turning on his heel, Elliot stalked out of the study and slammed the heavy oak door. He found his mother standing nearby in the hall, an anxious look on her face.

"Is your father still angry?" asked Polly Markham.

Elliot grinned bleakly. "What do you think?"

She looked agitated, and Elliot knew she hated being forced to witness the continuing bad feelings between her husband and her son. But anything she might say to Benjamin would fall on deaf ears, just as Elliot's words did.

"I hate to make things any worse, but you have a visitor," she said.

"A visitor?"

"Avery Wallingford. I had Clarissa show him into the parlor."

Elliot repressed a groan of dismay. His mother knew he was upset; no need to worry her further by letting her see how much he did *not* want to be bothered with Avery Wallingford right now. "Thank you, Mother. I'll go speak to him."

"Elliot . . ." She put a hand on his arm to stop him before he went down the corridor. "A boy brought this message for you. He came a short time ago, while you were talking to your father. I hope it was all right not to interrupt the two of you with it."

He knew what she meant: She had been unwilling to stick her head into Benjamin's study for fear of being caught in the verbal cross fire. He could hardly blame her; he would not have been there himself if he could have avoided it.

She held out a folded piece of paper sealed with wax. He took it, broke the seal with his finger, and unfolded it. Penned inside, in a spidery, unfamiliar hand, were the words *Please meet me at the Red Griffin this afternoon so we can discuss a matter of mutual importance*. There was no signature.

Elliot frowned slightly, wondering who could have sent him such a message. He was well acquainted with the Red Griffin; it was a waterfront tavern of dubious reputation, and Elliot had been there more than once during his days as a wastrel and womanizer, a time that was quite recent but now seemed lost in the mists of the dim past.

He refolded the paper and slipped it into an inner pocket of his jacket. "I'll deal with this later," he told Polly, then leaned over to kiss her quickly on the cheek. "Thank you, Mother. I suppose I had better go talk to Avery now. I wonder what he wants." He added silently, *I'm sure it won't be anything good.*

He strode down the hall toward the parlor at the front of the Markham family's Beacon Hill mansion. It was one of the most impressive houses in Boston, befitting one of the city's leading businessmen. It was only his father's influence and loyalty to the Crown, Elliot knew, that prevented British officers or troops from living with them. There was plenty of room in the house, and the Quartering Act passed by Parliament several years earlier gave the military the right to take over private housing for makeshift barracks.

Elliot paused just outside the parlor door and wished he did not have to do this. He had grown to hate Avery Wallingford. They were the same age, twenty-one, and there had been a time when they were best friends, but that was in the past, too.

Elliot ran his fingers through his shock of sandy blond hair, then grasped the doorknob and turned it. As he stepped into the room, Avery smiled indolently at him. He stood beside the now-cold fireplace, an arm draped on the mantel. Even alone in the room, Avery could not resist the urge to pose, Elliot thought.

"Hello, old boy," Avery said. "So good of you to see me." He was a slender young man, a bit taller than Elliot, with a lean, handsome face and sleek dark hair. Avery was always well dressed, and today he wore cream-colored breeches, a tight brown jacket, and a silk shirt that spilled its ruffles out at his throat, just below the stylish cravat. His grin widened, and Elliot realized it would have done his mood a great deal of good to plant a fist in the middle of that smirk.

Instead he forced himself to ask in a cold but civil tone, "What can I do for you, Avery?"

"I came to invite you to my wedding. You'll be getting a formal invitation later on, of course, when Sarah and

I have set the date, but I wanted to tell you that we'll expect you to be there."

Elliot felt as if he had been punched in the stomach, and a ball of nausea rolled around inside his belly. He finally managed to swallow hard and then rasped, "Wedding?"

"Of course. You knew that Sarah and I are getting married, didn't you? I was certain my father had mentioned it to your father."

"Yes—yes, he did. I knew." Elliot forced himself to smile and wondered if he looked as much like a death's-head as he felt. "Congratulations, Avery. You're getting a wonderful girl."

"Well," Avery said, cocking an eyebrow, "you should know, shouldn't you?"

For a moment, Elliot felt control slipping away from him. He could easily have rushed across the room, hooked his fingers around Avery's skinny neck, and strangled the life out of him. Avery knew what he was doing, knew perfectly well that for years Elliot and Sarah Cummings, the daughter of Benjamin Markham's business partner, had been sweethearts. It had been assumed by everyone that sooner or later they would be married.

But all of that had changed in one shocking moment a few weeks earlier in the garden behind the Markham house. Sarah had found Elliot and Roxanne Darragh in each other's arms—

And there was no way Elliot could have explained to her that Roxanne and he were nothing more than fellow secret agents discharging their duty in the cause of liberty.

At least, at that moment that was all they were to each other. Now, Elliot did not know.

Sarah had immediately broken their engagement, and not long after, he had heard that she planned to marry Avery Wallingford, his longtime rival and the son of the city's leading banker. The news had been difficult for Elliot to accept, so difficult that he had wound up in Roxanne's arms once more—but that time the embrace was real. Their passion was not for the cause but for each other.

God, it has all gotten so complicated! Hardly a day went by that Elliot did not feel like screaming those very words.

Now he exerted every ounce of his willpower to keep his rioting emotions on a tight rein. He made himself say to Avery, "Thank you for the invitation. When do you expect the wedding will be?"

Avery shrugged his narrow shoulders. "That's hard to say. I was all for an early wedding, of course, but Sarah wanted a little time. Then, too, there's the matter of her father's plans. He wants the ceremony to be quite lavish, you know, the social event of the year and all that. Such things take time to put together, especially when everyone is distracted by this dreadful rebellion. I daresay the wedding itself won't take place until after the war is over." He plucked a snowy handkerchief from his jacket pocket and blotted an imaginary spot on his cheek. "Or perhaps I should say in no time at all, when the king's forces have drubbed those damned rebels."

"Yes, well, I wouldn't count on it being over that quickly."

"Surely you don't think an unruly mob of farmers is any match for His Majesty's finest troops?" Avery blinked in astonishment.

Elliot had to maintain his pose as a loyal Tory if he was going to continue to be any good to the patriot cause. "I didn't say that. I just meant that the rebels are stubborn, and they may not give in easily."

Avery laughed. "They won't have any choice, dear boy. They'll give in or be exterminated like the vermin they are."

"We'll see." Elliot held his hand out toward the parlor

door. "If that's all, Avery, I'm rather busy this afternoon. I have a business engagement."

Slyly Avery said, "You mean you're still involved with your father's business after that debacle in New Hampshire?"

"As you well know, Avery, I am not. My engagement is personal in nature," Elliot said quietly.

Avery must have realized how closely he was treading to the edge of actual danger, because he said quickly, "Of course, of course. Well, I must be going. I'm sure we'll be seeing each other again."

"I'm sure."

Elliot did not allow himself to relax his iron grip on his anger until after the door was closed behind Avery. Then he sighed wearily and lifted a hand to massage his aching temples. *What I need is a drink,* he told himself. *A good stiff pot of rum and a lusty wench to serve it to me.*

Perhaps he could find both at the Red Griffin—along with whoever had sent him that mysterious note.

The Red Griffin was on King Street near the Long Wharf, and a painting of the mythological beast that gave the place its name was daubed in crimson paint on the sign hung above the door. Elliot passed under that emblem and into the tavern about an hour after his unpleasant meeting with Avery Wallingford. Anger still lurked in the back of his mind, along with the guilt he felt for inadvertently driving Sarah into Avery's arms.

But he had to put such thoughts away now, he told himself. Of the two reasonable explanations that occurred to Elliot for why he had been summoned to the grog shop, the first was that the Committee of Safety had a new assignment for him and had chosen this place as a rendezvous—or else the British had proof of his role as a patriot secret agent, and he was walking into a trap.

He was dressed in an old suit that had grown slightly

threadbare in places, and the tricorn on his head was battered and stained. To enter a rathole like this dressed in expensive clothes was asking for a clout on the head or a knife slipped cleanly between the ribs when one left. Probably half the men in the room were cutpurses, or had been at one time.

Oil lamps hung from the low ceiling, and the smoky fumes they gave off mixed with the smoke from a dozen pipes to thicken the air in the room to a blue haze. The wood of the beamed ceiling was dark and oily, as were the walls. In the back of the room was a door leading to a short hall. Several cubicles opened off the hall, and the serving wenches sometimes took customers back there when the mood struck them. The bar was short; not many people sat there, preferring the tables scattered around the sawdust-covered floor or the dim booths along the walls.

Elliot chose a table in a shadowy corner, and as he made his way toward it, he crooked a finger at one of the young women in low-cut dresses who carried drinks from the bar to the customers. The serving girl, who had lank brown hair and an uninterested look on her vaguely pretty face, sauntered over to Elliot when he sat down.

"What'll you have?" she asked curtly.

"A pot of rum—and a bit more cheerful manner from you, my dear," Elliot replied.

"You can 'ave the rum," she shot back, then turned with a toss of her hips and started toward the bar.

Elliot grinned faintly. In the old days, when he had frequented places like this, he would have thought the girl was rather promising. He would have worked on her for a while, plied her with his charm—and a few coins—and wound up in one of the back rooms with her before the evening was over.

Now he had neither the inclination nor the time to waste in such pursuits. He assumed that whoever had sent him the message would recognize him. Otherwise this trip would have been for nothing, because Elliot had no idea who was looking for him.

A few minutes later the still-sullen serving girl brought the rum. She had not hurried to deliver the drink to Elliot's table, so he tossed down only enough coins to pay for the rum. Then, after a second's hesitation, he added a few more, dropping them onto the pile with a clinking sound that was all but inaudible over the buzz of conversation and laughter in the room. The girl, who had waited stolidly, now scooped up the coins with a deft motion that seemed to make them magically disappear. With another impudent twitch of her behind, she was gone.

Elliot's grin widened. *Definitely worth a bit of an effort,* he thought, *but not now—*

"Good day to you, Mr. Markham."

When Elliot finally pulled his gaze away from the serving wench's bottom, he saw a short, rotund, middle-aged man seating himself in one of the chairs at the table. "Who—" Elliot began.

"It seems that old habits die hard," the stranger cut in quietly. He went on sternly, "But considering the game you are playing, Mr. Markham, I believe it would be better if your attention was focused on something other than that young woman's physical charms."

Elliot flushed with resentment. The stranger was not saying anything Elliot did not already know, but it was galling to be reprimanded in such a fashion. "Who are you?" he demanded sharply.

"You don't recognize me?"

Elliot looked closely at the stranger but saw only a man in ragged clothes with dirt smeared on his face. He looked tired, and he wheezed a bit as he breathed. He would have looked right at home huddled in a doorway, a flask clutched in his hand as he furtively stole sips of the liquor inside. Elliot grimaced and said, "I've tossed coins to many beggars in my time. You can't expect me to remember all of them, old man."

"Then perhaps my name will mean something to you." A humorless smile stretched the man's thin lips. "It's Samuel Adams."

Elliot blinked in surprise at the audacious claim. This beggar, the leading light of the patriot cause, the most prominent member of the Committee of Safety, the firebrand who had lit the flame of revolution? Not bloody likely!

But before Elliot could open his mouth to scoff, the stranger went on, "If Daniel Reed and Roxanne Darragh were here, no doubt they could vouch for me. For that matter, you should recognize me yourself, since we met one evening in the back room of the Salutation Tavern. You brought the news that young Mr. Reed had just been arrested by the British."

Now Elliot's mouth dropped open in shock. Through the dirt and the ragged clothes, he began to glimpse the true identity of his companion.

Samuel Adams chuckled and said, "Close your mouth, boy, before someone notices you look like you've just seen a ghost."

"But . . . but you . . . ." Elliot leaned closer to Adams and hissed, "If the British knew you were in Boston—"

"They'd hang me from the nearest tree. Yes, of course they would. But they don't know I'm here, and your reaction tells me that my disguise is sufficient to prevent them from learning of my presence. I'll be sure to tell the people who helped smuggle me into the city what a good job they did."

Elliot took a healthy swallow of rum and shook his head. "I don't understand this at all," he said. "I'd heard that you were in Philadelphia, with the Second Continental Congress."

"Keep your voice down," cautioned Adams. "That's

where I've been for the past few weeks, all right, arguing with those hardheads from the other colonies and trying to convince them we've all got to act together if we want to get that fat British foot off our necks. But a matter that may turn out to be equally important in the long run has come to my attention, so I came to Boston as fast as I could."

"Something to do with . . . *me*?" Elliot asked incredulously.

"I hope so," Adams said gravely. "It's my hope that you'll agree to help us resolve this situation as quickly as possible. I know you've worked with the committee in the past, and I've also heard about that boatload of British munitions that was appropriated for the cause of liberty. That was good work on the part of you and Miss Darragh, especially since you managed to keep the truth of your involvement a secret and your reputation as a loyal Tory intact."

Elliot's hand tightened on the pot of rum. He was unsure just how much Sam Adams knew about that operation. It had been set up by Benjamin Tallmadge and Robert Townsend, two former classmates of Daniel's at Yale who had formed their own intelligence and espionage web to assist the patriots. The network run by Tallmadge and Townsend was operating independently of the Committee of Safety because it was rumored that there was a traitor, a British agent, somewhere in the inner circle of the committee. Daniel and Roxanne had been convinced of that, and Elliot had no reason to doubt it.

If Adams wanted to know about Tallmadge and Townsend and their activities, Elliot wondered how much it would be prudent to tell him. He knew that Samuel Adams was not the traitor, but would it be wise to reveal *any* information to a member of the committee?

"Thank you for the compliment, sir," Elliot said, stalling for time to try to figure this out, "but I really didn't do much—"

Adams waved a hand to cut off Elliot in midsentence.

"That's not why I asked you here," he said, "and considering the circumstances, the less you tell me about the details, the better. You see, what has been rumored for quite some time is now a certainty. We are being betrayed by one of our own."

The pudgy little man's face was almost comically grave, and such a dramatic statement in such a shrill voice might have been humorous under other circumstances. But Elliot did not feel at all like laughing. Instead he said, "I've heard the same rumors. Daniel and Roxanne are convinced of it."

"So am I, now," Adams replied heavily. "As you may know, there is a loosely knit organization reaching out from here in Boston all across Massachusetts and into some of the other colonies, all for the purpose of passing along vital information to our fellow patriots. Too much of that information is finding a home in British hands. Last week, a certain gentleman here in Boston—who shall remain nameless—was ready to pledge his loyalty and his considerable funds to our cause. This man, whose identity was known only to the members of the inner circle, was visited by a British major named Kane and warned that if he aided us in any way, he would be risking not only his own life but that of his family as well. You understand, this gentleman is a prominent man, and it was vital that his support for our cause remain a secret. Following the visit of Major Kane, he severed all his ties with us and will no longer have anything to do with the battle for freedom."

Adams leaned closer to Elliot and went on, "When I heard of this matter, I knew there was no longer any doubt. Someone in our midst is passing our secrets along to the British, and whoever he is, he must be stopped!"

Elliot mulled over what Adams had just told him. "I agree this is an important matter," he said after a moment's thought, "but what's my connection with it?"

"Quite simple, really. We want you to catch this spy."

Once again Elliot frowned in confusion and astonishment. "Me?" he finally said. "What in heaven's name makes you think I could catch the man?"

"You're an outsider of sorts," Sam Adams told him. "Oh, I know you've assisted us before, but you don't really know any of us that well. Your involvement with the committee came about indirectly, through young Reed and Miss Darragh. So you have no preconceived notions. You can go into this investigation suspecting all of us equally."

"Even you?" Elliot asked quickly.

Adams smiled. "Even me. Although I would hardly be calling on you to locate this traitor if I were indeed he, now would I?"

Elliot sighed, took another swallow of rum, and shook his head. "Not unless you're playing a much cleverer game than I can comprehend." With his brow furrowed in thought, he leaned back in his chair and regarded Adams. "You're sure you trust me with this assignment? After all, my father is one of the leading Tories in the city."

"That didn't stop you from helping to capture that ship full of munitions, now did it, hmm?"

Elliot said nothing.

"Perhaps it demonstrates some measure of how desperate we are that we're willing to trust a relatively unknown quantity like yourself, Mr. Markham," Adams went on. "We're not certain just how much damage this traitor has already done to our cause, but one thing *is* certain: He cannot be allowed to continue with his perfidy. We must put a stop to his activities—or to *him*."

A chill went through Elliot. Was Adams actually advocating that the traitor be killed once his identity was discovered? Adams did have a reputation for ruthlessness in the name of the cause in which he so passionately believed.

"I'm not a killer, Mr. Adams," Elliot said hoarsely. "If that's what you want—"

"No, no!" Again Adams waved off Elliot's objection. "You misunderstand me, Mr. Markham. All I'm asking you to do is poke around a bit to see if you can ascertain the identity of this spy. If you're successful, then you can give his name to the proper people, and the matter will be taken care of, I assure you."

"Well . . . I suppose I can dig around some," Elliot said reluctantly, his sense of responsibility winning out over the misgivings he had about this assignment.

"Excellent!" Adams beamed. "Now, give me some money."

"What?"

"You said it yourself—I look like a beggar. We've been sitting here talking for several minutes now, and I don't wish any of this, ah, establishment's other patrons to have any suspicions about the subject of our discussion. It should look like I've been cajoling you for a handout the entire time."

Elliot nodded in understanding and dug in the pocket of his coat. He tossed down a few shillings, and Adams greedily scraped them up off the table. He stood and tugged at the filthy cap on his head, saying in a voice loud enough for those at nearby tables to hear, "Thank you kindly, sir. You're a gentleman and a scholar, you are."

"You've got what you wanted," Elliot snapped, taking up the act. "Now go on with you and leave me be."

"Aye, sir." Adams scuttled away and left the room through the rear door. The hallway there led to an alley, as well as the rooms where the serving girls plied their secondary trade.

Elliot leaned back and sighed. The past twenty minutes seemed like a dream. Samuel Adams, disguised as a beggar? Elliot Markham, unlikely spy, was to become Elliot Markham, even more unlikely sleuth?

But it had actually happened, Elliot realized, and now he was committed to ferreting out the identity of the British informant in the inner circle.

He had a feeling this was a quest that could lead him down stranger paths than any he had walked before, and he feared these paths might end in death.

Chapter Six

Daniel could have ridden at the head of the column of militiamen with Captain Aaron Webster and the other officers, but after the warm welcome he received from volunteers Thad Garner, George Cummings, Benjamin Hobbs, and Fred Dary, he preferred to stay with his newfound friends. He led his horse and walked alongside Thad as they marched toward Cambridge.

In the following three days Daniel learned that Thad and the others were farmers from the Stockbridge area and were very curious about the battles at Lexington, Concord, and Fort Ticonderoga. The men regarded Daniel as a hero and would not let go of that notion, no matter how modestly he downplayed his part in the events.

On the afternoon of the third day, they arrived in Cambridge, and when the militiamen reached the Harvard College Yard, they found troops gathered in front of Holden Chapel, Hollis Hall, Harvard Hall, Stoughton Hall, and Massachusetts Hall. Daniel looked up at the impressive four-story brick buildings and remembered the hours he had spent in each of them, listening to his professors' lectures on law, philosophy, and the natural sciences. Those days seemed so simple—and so far in the past.

"Look at that," Thad Garner said, awestruck. "Did you ever see such a place?"

"As a matter of fact, I spent a year here reading for the law," Daniel told the young farmer.

"Go on with you. Is there anything you *haven't* done, Daniel Reed?"

"Plenty," he replied, thinking of Roxanne.

He tore his thoughts away from the lovely, redheaded young woman and went on, "Captain Webster's motioning for us to keep marching."

When Daniel and the men reached a large open area near the Charles River, they saw a scattering of tents that appeared to be a military camp. Webster rode up to the largest one, swung down from his horse, and spoke to a blue-coated officer who had just stepped out of the canvas tent. Behind Webster, his troops came to a halt.

A man with thinning white hair and a slender frame also emerged, and he was followed by an elderly, white-haired officer, who seemed to Daniel to be more robust than his companion. The men spoke with Aaron Webster for several minutes, and then the burly captain turned to his followers and bellowed, "Look sharp, laddies, and listen close. These are your new commanding officers, General Artemas Ward and General Israel Putnam!"

General Ward stepped forward and said in a thin voice, "Welcome to Cambridge and the Massachusetts Provincial Army, men." He paused momentarily as he was seized by a bout of coughing, and Daniel realized that General Ward was ill.

"As you may know," he continued, "at this very moment the Second Continental Congress is meeting in Philadelphia, and we await their pleasure. Until such time as we receive instructions from them, Major General Putnam and I, as well as our fellow officers, will do our best to train you men into an efficient fighting force. The British are going to be bloody well sorry they started this fight, gentlemen!"

Though they were voiced in weak tones, the words spoken by General Ward drew a cheer from Daniel and the men. Ward stepped back then and deferred to Major General Israel Putnam. Daniel had heard of the man, known affectionately to his troops as "Old Put." He was a veteran of the French and Indian Wars, and now, around the age of sixty, looked and sounded vital enough to saddle up and ride into battle.

Putnam put his hand on the hilt of his saber and said, "I hope you men have come to work and fight, because you'll be obliged to do both before this war is over. That's all I've got to say."

The men gave another cheer, and Captain Webster ordered them to fall out. "Camp where you will," Webster bellowed. "But any man who abuses the hospitality of the citizens of Cambridge will answer to me, do you understand? Report to Harvard College Yard in the morning, and we'll begin our drills. Dismissed!"

Daniel turned to Thad and the others and said, "Why don't you fellows come with me? I have an apartment not far from the college, and while it may be a bit crowded with all five of us staying there, it'll be better than camping."

"Sounds good to me, and mighty generous of you to offer it," Thad replied. "Come along, boys."

They walked quickly to the side street near Harvard, to the apartment over the stationer's shop where Daniel and Quincy had stayed in more peaceful times. The rent on the flat had been paid through the end of the year, and though it seemed to Daniel that he had been away for years, merely two and a half months had passed since he and his brother had fled from Cambridge.

Daniel walked into the shop, and when the landlord looked up, he stared in disbelief at him. "Is that you, Mr. Reed?" he asked after a moment.

"It is indeed," Daniel told him. "Is my apartment still empty, Mr. Gidden? The rent *was* paid up, you know."

"Aye, the rooms are vacant, and all your belongings are still there." The landlord frowned darkly at Daniel. "The way you disappeared like that, son, I would've been justified in selling off your possessions and renting the apartment to someone else."

Daniel did not want to explain why he had been forced to leave Cambridge so abruptly a few months earlier, so he said simply, "I'm glad you didn't, sir. My friends and I have come to join the Provincial Army, and we need a place to stay."

"Well, why didn't you say so? You're welcome to the apartment, lads, for as long as you need it." Mr. Gidden grinned. "Which probably won't be for long. It won't be any time at all until the army's run those damned lobster-backs out of Boston. Then you can stay in a fine house in the city."

Daniel didn't respond to the landlord's confident claim. He was worried that too many supporters of the patriot cause felt the same way—that the war with England would be a short and victorious one.

But he knew from experience that the British would not give up easily. As General Putnam had said, the next few weeks would bring more than their share of both work and battle.

As soon as he could, within two days of arriving in Cambridge, Daniel rode to Charlestown Neck and across the narrow strip of land to the heights of Bunker Hill, where he could gaze across the Charles at the city of

Boston. Several lookouts were posted at the top of the hill, and as Daniel swung down from his saddle, one of them called out to him, "Have you come to relieve one of us, matey?"

"I'm afraid not," Daniel said. "I was just wondering about the British patrols on the river."

"Thinking about trying to slip across into town?" asked one of the men. He laughed harshly before Daniel could answer. "I'd forget that idea if I were you, lad. That's a quick way to get killed. The damned British aren't letting as much as a gnat across the Charles."

That claim had been made before, but Paul Revere had used a small boat to slip across unchallenged at night, and Daniel thought he could do the same thing.

His intent must have been plain to see because one of the sentries said, "Don't try it, my friend, even on the darkest night. Our officers have studied the waterfront through their spyglasses, and the British have guard posts set up every hundred yards or so. And they have patrol boats tacking back and forth from this side of the peninsula all the way 'round to the other. You'd wind up getting shot—or hung, if the British feel like a more elaborate entertainment."

Daniel shivered. Pinned down as they were on the Shawmut Peninsula, he was sure the British felt as if their backs were against the wall, and he had no doubt they would execute anyone they believed was a spy.

He thought about his cousin Elliot Markham, somewhere in the city, and he hoped he was being very careful if he was still working with the Committee of Safety.

"What about Boston Neck?" asked Daniel.

"What about it? It's barricaded, closed off just like the rest of the city." The guard who had answered Daniel's question suddenly looked at him through eyes narrowed by suspicion. "Why are you so curious about getting into

Boston, boy? Could it be that you're a redcoat spy trying to get some information to them about our forces?"

"Not likely," Daniel said grimly. The opposite was true, in fact, but he did not want to tell that to these men. "You see, there's a girl over there . . ."

One of the men snorted in disbelief as Daniel's voice trailed off. Holding their rifles tightly, the sentries closed in around him. "If he *was* a redcoat spy, he'd lie about it, now wouldn't he?" one said.

"Aye, he would," responded another. "Mayhap we better try to beat the truth out of him. We'll find out why he's so damned curious!"

Daniel glanced around. They had cut him off from his horse, so he would have to fight if he wanted to get away from here; outnumbered or not, the last thing he wanted was to get into a fracas with his fellow patriots.

"What's going on here?" a stern voice asked sharply as a tall man on horseback topped the hill.

Daniel looked up at the handsome, well-built rider and felt a surge of relief as he recognized Dr. Joseph Warren, one of the members of the committee's inner circle.

"Hello, Doctor," Daniel said. "It's good to see you again."

"Daniel Reed? Is that really you?" Dr. Warren leaned down from his horse and shook hands with Daniel. "I thought so when I caught a glimpse of you riding across Charlestown Neck, but I followed you to make sure. When did you get back in the area?"

Before Daniel could answer, one of the sentries demanded, "Do you know this man, Dr. Warren?"

"Indeed I do," he replied. "And I'll vouch for him unequivocally, no matter what the trouble is."

"No trouble," Daniel said. "Just a simple misunderstanding."

"Well, get your horse and come along," Warren said

with a look that made the guards turn around and hurry back to their posts. "We have a great deal to talk about."

Daniel swung up into the saddle and trotted his mount down the hill alongside Dr. Warren's horse. "I arrived in Cambridge only days ago with a group of militiamen from western Massachusetts."

"Ah, yes, Captain Webster's group. Good sturdy yeomen all, from the looks of them. I saw them this morning when I passed by the camp." Warren lowered his voice, even though there was no one nearby to hear them. "How went your mission to New York, Daniel?"

"Quite well, though not exactly what we'd planned," Daniel replied. "It's fortunate you came along when you did, Dr. Warren. Not only did you save my neck from the guards, but you can help me figure out a way into the city so I can deliver my report to the committee."

Warren sighed. "I'm afraid that's not going to be possible for a while," he said. "No one goes in or out of Boston anymore. The only reason I'm not there is that I was in Cambridge on business when the British slammed all the doors. But I hope to be back soon, once we've retaken the city."

Despite the bold words, Dr. Warren did not sound confident of the outcome. Daniel twisted in his saddle and peered past the hill and the river. He could faintly see the roofs of the buildings in Boston.

"Did you happen to speak to Miss Darragh when you were in the city?" Daniel asked, keeping his tone impassive.

"Not for several weeks," replied Warren. For an instant, the physician seemed to be on the verge of saying something else, but he fell silent, and when he spoke again, he said, "I believe Roxanne may not be in the city, but as to her whereabouts, I really couldn't say."

Daniel stared at him in surprise. "Not in the city?" he

repeated. "But where else could she be? I know she planned to return there."

"And she did. Dr. Church brought her back to Boston, in fact, and she was working with your cousin, young Markham, gathering intelligence for us. But then—" Warren shook his head. "She seems to have disappeared. For all I know, the British have captured her. I hate to be the bearer of this news, Daniel, but I believe you have a right to know the truth."

He felt as if someone had plunged a knife into his belly and cruelly twisted the blade. *Roxanne gone? Disappeared? Perhaps in the hands of the British?*

"I have to get over there," he said raggedly.

"It's impossible," Warren told him again. "General Ward has issued strict orders that no one is to attempt to sneak into Boston. When the fighting begins, we're going to need every man we have, Daniel. If Roxanne *is* in trouble, you can do her more good by staying here and helping us."

Daniel knew Dr. Warren was right, but every instinct cried out for him to rush to Roxanne's side. He sighed heavily. "So what do I do in the meantime?"

"The same as the rest of us. You get ready to give the bloody British the fight of their lives!"

Reluctantly, Daniel returned to the encampment and, praying that Roxanne was safe at Lemuel Parsons's farm in Concord, vowed to go there as soon as there was a break in the training routine. Meanwhile he would work doggedly to turn himself into a first-class soldier.

The days turned into weeks, and Captain Aaron Webster, new to the military, drilled his men unmercifully on Harvard Yard. Daniel learned that prior to leading the militia, the officer had been a farmer like the others—albeit wealthier and with more extensive holdings—and many of the men still called him squire. General Ward assigned an experienced lieutenant to Webster's command, and with the help of the junior officer, the squire turned the men into a disciplined fighting force. It didn't matter that only the officers had uniforms; the important thing was that the ragtag army was feeling and acting like a unit.

Although Daniel had never officially joined either the militia or the Massachusetts Provincial Army, that did not matter under circumstances like these. All that counted was whether a man was willing to fight and die for the cause in which he believed.

The training went well, and by the middle of June, the Provincial Army looked like a bona fide military force, even if it could not march as crisply as the British regulars it would oppose. Morale was high, but so was impatience. The men had not left their farms and families simply to march around Harvard Yard. They had come to fight redcoats, and the time for that was drawing nigh.

Anticipation dominated the encampment in Cambridge, and generals Artemas Ward and Israel Putnam were well aware of it as they sat in Ward's tent and sipped from glasses of sack. Ward was propped up on his bunk, and from time to time, he was racked by coughing that the sherry did little to ease.

"I thought certain we would have received word from the Congress by now," he complained as he leaned against the pillows stuffed behind his back. "Orders of some sort should have been forthcoming. What the devil are they *doing* down there in Philadelphia?"

Putnam felt sympathy for his ailing colleague Ward, and he thought the man should have been in bed in his own house, recovering from his illness, rather than leading an army. Although he was older than Ward, Israel Putnam was still ambitious enough—and honest enough—to feel that command would be better off in his hands rather than Ward's.

"I'm afraid you're going to have to do *something,*

Artemas," said Putnam. "With every day we wait, the men grow more restless. Besides, we're just giving the British a chance to strengthen their own positions."

"I know. But I've always been a cautious man, Israel—"

"Caution can be dangerous at the wrong time," Putnam ventured, daring to speak up in the privacy of Ward's tent.

Ward shrugged his narrow shoulders, then coughed again. He was still struggling with the spasm when the entrance flap of the tent was thrust back and an officer entered, snapped to attention, and saluted the two generals.

"I hate to barge in here like this, sirs, but we've just received an important dispatch from one of our agents in the city," he said.

"That's quite all right, Colonel Prescott," Ward answered weakly, holding out his hand for the paper held by the colonel. "Let me see it."

Colonel William Prescott, the regiment commander of the Massachusetts Provincial Army, gave the dispatch to Ward, who read it and handed it to Putnam.

"So the British are planning to cross the Charles, eh?" Ward mused. "Their objective must be Bunker Hill and Breed's Hill."

"Undoubtedly," agreed Putnam. "Whoever controls those hills controls Boston. Cannon emplacements there could bombard the city and bring it to its knees." Putnam had recommended just such a tactic some time ago, but General Ward had not acted on the suggestion.

Colonel Prescott took off his black tricorn and said, "If I may be so bold, General Ward. If you will give me a thousand men to take across Charlestown Neck, sir, I'll fortify those heights and occupy them this very night. The British will get quite a welcome if they try to take Farmer Bunker's and Farmer Breed's hills!"

"I concur, General Ward," agreed Putnam.

"Very well," Ward said, looking gaunt and tired. "You will have your thousand men, Colonel Prescott."

"As long as some of them are *my* men, Colonel," growled Putnam. "I'll put myself and all my volunteers under your command."

Though the concession was difficult for the wily old Indian fighter, so great was Putnam's desire to participate in the coming battle that he was willing to relinquish command to Prescott. The colonel looked faintly embarrassed, but he agreed. "Thank you, General," he said to Putnam. "I'm sure we'll be able to work together on this. We'll need to talk to Colonel Gridley, the engineer, to plan the fortifications. Do you have any suggestions as to which companies would best complete our force?"

"Captain Thomas Knowlton's men are ready to fight," Putnam said, "and there's a bunch from western Massachusetts under the command of a squire named Webster. They seem to be good lads."

"Knowlton and Webster it is, then," Prescott agreed. "And may God be with us all!"

Roxanne was in the farmhouse cook room, helping Lottie Parsons with supper, when they heard hoofbeats in the yard outside. The women looked each other and frowned. Lottie wiped her hands quickly on a cloth and said to Roxanne, "You go fetch Lem. I'll see who our visitor is."

Roxanne ran out the back door of the house, and as she approached the barn, she saw a musket leaning against the open door. Lemuel did his chores with the weapon close by now. He was not expecting trouble, he said whenever Lottie asked him if it was necessary, but a man was a fool not to be cautious in times like these.

Lemuel came out of the barn as Roxanne hurried up. "Someone just rode into the yard," she told him breathlessly. "Lottie went to see who it is."

Lemuel snatched up the musket and said anxiously, "She shouldn't have done that. Come on!"

As she followed him, she was glad the children were inside studying the lessons Lottie had given them earlier. She hoped they stayed there.

Lemuel relaxed when he rounded the corner of the house and saw Lottie talking to a man on horseback. The visitor wore rough work clothes, similar to Lemuel's, and had a battered tricorn pushed to the back of his head. A lock of brown hair hung over his forehead.

"Howdy, Lem," he called.

"Evening, Chris. What brings you here?"

Roxanne recognized Christopher Gannett, whose farm was located between the Parsons place and Concord. Gannett crossed his hands on the pommel of his saddle and leaned forward on the back of the old plow horse that did double duty as his mount. "A pair of riders just brought the word to Concord whilst I happened to be there," Gannett said. "The British are going to attack Cambridge tomorrow."

"No!" exclaimed Lottie. "Are you sure?"

"Sure as sure can be, Lottie, and I'll be heading for Cambridge first thing in the morning to join the militia already there!"

Roxanne saw Lemuel and Lottie exchange worried glances. As word of the patriot forces streaming into Cambridge reached the surrounding countryside, there had been much discussion in the Parsons household in the past weeks. Lemuel had vowed more than once that he was going to join them, but so far Lottie had talked him out of it. However, with a battle against the British imminent, it would be impossible for her to dissuade him.

As for Roxanne, she had intended to be in Cambridge by now anyway, looking for a way into Boston, but Lemuel and Lottie had convinced her it would be foolhardy. Even if

Daniel *had* returned to the area, she was doubtful that he had been able to enter the city.

But if that were the case, why hadn't he come to the Parsons farm to look for her? There was no time to worry about that now; she had a more pressing decision to make.

Lemuel reached up, shook hands with Gannett, and said, "Thanks for bringing the news, Chris."

"What about you, Lem?" the farmer asked bluntly. "Are you going?"

Lemuel glanced once more at his wife, hesitated, then said firmly, "Ayuh. I'll be there."

Gannett grinned, waved, wheeled his horse, and rode out of the farmyard.

"Are you sure about this, Lem?" Lottie asked, breaking the tense silence.

"I don't see that I have much choice," he said, his lean face solemn. "It's my duty as a militiaman and a patriot."

"But you've already done your part! You fought at Concord. The scar on your arm left by the ball from the Brown Bess is proof enough that you're a patriot." It was the same argument she had used before to keep him at home.

But Roxanne understood how Lottie felt. She knew from experience what it was like to watch a loved one go off into danger, not knowing if he would return. She had worried about Daniel for months now.

"This war's a long way from over. I can't let the other fellows do all the fighting," Lemuel said stubbornly. "Roxanne knows what I mean, don't you?"

"Indeed I do," she replied.

"Roxanne doesn't have children who are depending on her," Lottie said sharply. Instantly she looked contrite. "I didn't mean any offense, my dear."

"I know that," Roxanne assured her. "And you're right, I don't know what it's like to leave a home and a family behind me—other than my parents, of course. They're still in Boston."

"I'm sure they're probably fine," Lemuel said. "Your father's the best printer in the whole town. The blasted redcoats'll leave him alone as long as he stays neutral."

"That's a choice you and I no longer have left to us, though."

"Aye. That's why I'll be going to Cambridge in the morning."

Lottie caught her bottom lip between her teeth but did not say anything, sensing that it would no longer do any good to protest. Lemuel's mind was made up.

So was Roxanne's. "I'll be going with you when you leave," she said.

"What?" Lemuel and Lottie asked the question in unison.

"I'm going to Cambridge, too. Maybe Daniel is there with the militia."

Lemuel looked dubious. "That's not likely. Besides, you heard what Chris said. There's going to be fighting."

"That's why I'm going," Roxanne insisted. "There are bound to be injured men, and volunteers will be needed to tend to them."

"You've never done any nursing, Roxanne," Lottie pointed out.

"Then it's time I learned." Suddenly the anxiety was too much for her. "Don't you see? I've been on this farm for weeks, not knowing if Daniel, Quincy, and Murdoch are alive or dead, not knowing how Elliot is, not knowing anything! I've got to become involved in this war again. You understand, don't you, Lemuel?"

"Aye, dear girl," he said quietly. "Indeed I do."

"Well, I don't," Lottie said, a faint trace of bitterness tingeing her voice. "But I know I could talk until I'm hoarse and not change the mind of either one of you! I wish this war would just go away and let us live our lives in peace!"

"It's not going to happen unless we make it happen," Lemuel told her, taking her into his arms and patting her on the back. "But I'll be safe, Lottie. You have my word on that." He looked at Roxanne. "There's not going to be any talking you out of this, is there?"

"No, I'm afraid not."

The farmer sighed. "All right. You can go with me to Cambridge, but you'll have to ride horseback because I want to leave the wagon here for Lottie and the children."

"I've ridden a horse before," Roxanne said with a faint smile.

"What you do once we get to Cambridge is your own business. I'll be too busy to look out for you."

"I wouldn't have it any other way," Roxanne assured him.

"So it's settled." Lemuel glanced at his wife. "Isn't it, Lottie?"

She nodded sadly. "I wish it could be some other way, but I know it can't. You'll do what you have to do, Lemuel, just as all the rest of us will in these dark and bloody times."

"Aye." Lemuel hugged her tightly again, then looked at Roxanne and forced a smile. "I hope you find Daniel and bring him back here when the fighting is over. He's a fine young man."

"Yes, he is," Roxanne agreed softly. But would Daniel feel the same if he found out about what had happened between Elliot and her? There would be time to worry about that, Roxanne told herself sternly, *after* the battle.

Dr. Benjamin Church sat at a small desk, his coat and wig off, his collar open. Sunlight slanted into the bedchamber through a gap in the gauzy curtain over the single window. The only sounds in the room were the scratching of the doctor's pen as he wrote on a piece of paper spread out before him and a soft snore from the woman in the rumpled bed on the other side of the room.

Church was anxious to leave. He was a fastidious man, and the leftover signs of a night of passion vaguely offended him. That was why he had risen while the doxy called Maureen was still sound asleep. He would prefer to be gone from the tiny apartment she maintained in a less than elegant section of Boston before she awoke. This letter had to be written before he could leave, however.

After a few minutes of scrawling words on the paper, Church put the pen aside and looked over what he had written to make sure it was all right. Once he was satisfied with the wording, he could transcribe it into the cipher that he used, and give the letter—ostensibly a jumble of meaningless gibberish—to Maureen to deliver for him.

My dear Major Kane, Church read to himself, *it has come to my attention that a certain farm near Concord owned by one Lemuel Parsons is being used by the insurrectionists as a hiding place for the leading members of their movement. The traitors also store supplies there from time to time.*

Church pursed his lips as he read on: The rest of the letter gave directions to the Parsons farm. For quite some time now, Church had known the rebels were using it as a hideout, ever since he himself had gone there to pick up Roxanne Darragh and bring her back to Boston. In the scheme of things, this was not very important information, but Major Alistair Kane, Church's contact within the British army, had been pressing him for more revelations about the patriot cause. Perhaps this would satisfy him.

It would take a while for the message to reach the major. Maureen was only the first link in a long, convoluted chain of agents that would ultimately deliver the enciphered letter. Such elaborate precautions were necessary to make certain that no one could trace the information to Dr.

Benjamin Church, the renowned patriot leader—and double agent in the service of the British.

Satisfied with what he had written, Church took another sheet of paper and quickly rewrote the message using the cipher Major Kane and he had worked out. He was almost finished when he heard the bed squeak behind him as Maureen shifted around.

She yawned and asked, "What're you doin', luv?"

"I have another letter here for you to deliver," Church told her without turning to look at her. "You must take care of the matter today."

"Sure, sure, don't I always? Come over 'ere and give us a kiss good mornin'."

Church forced a pleasant look onto his face. For all her sluttish ways, Maureen was a dependable courier, and he had to keep her happy if he wanted to retain her services—in all capacities.

She was sitting up in the bed, her red hair frowsy and disheveled. The sheet had fallen down to reveal her large, pendulous, blue-veined breasts with their huge brown nipples. Looking at her, Church felt an immediate response, even though he was impatient to leave the apartment and get on about his business. Maureen was coarse and vulgar, but he had to admit that she was good at what she did.

He handed her the folded letter, which he had sealed with wax. The original was folded and tucked away safely in his pocket. As soon as he got home, he would toss it into the fireplace and dispose of it permanently.

"Deliver this to the usual person," he told her curtly.

Maureen reached up for him. "What about that kiss?"

Church bent over and brushed his lips across hers. She grabbed the back of his head with her hand and pressed her mouth hard against his. When she finally took it away, Church was pale and breathing a bit harder than he had been earlier.

"You could stay, you know," Maureen suggested.

"No, I think not," Church said firmly. "I've things I have to do today, and so do you."

"You're sure?"

God, how he despised the whine in her voice. "Positive," he answered curtly.

She shrugged her naked shoulders. "Well, all right, then. Don't forget to leave me a few coins. A girl's got to eat, y'know."

"Of course." Church put on his coat, wig, and hat and fastened his collar, then dropped several coins on the desk. "Good day," he said formally as he went to the door.

"And a bloody good day to you, too," Maureen said and lay back on the bed pillows.

As he shut the door behind him, Church hoped she would not lie there all day. It was important that the message get started on its way to Major Kane. It was vital that the farmer called Parsons and his family and whatever rebels were hiding at the place be captured and interrogated by British troops.

Church put those thoughts out of his mind. He had more pressing matters to consider, such as how he was going to continue to keep both Maureen and his wife satisfied financially until he got his next packet of blood money from Major Kane.

Chapter Seven

With the sun barely up on the morning after Murdoch and Quincy rescued Mariel and Dietrich Jarrott from the Mohawks, the assembled travelers walked over the hill and down to where the Jarrott family had been laid to rest. Even though Dietrich was too young—and too sleepy—to fully comprehend what was going on, he clutched his sister's hand tightly and tears rolled down his pudgy cheeks as Gresham Howard said a prayer over the grave.

Murdoch placed the birch marker he had made the night before by the stones at the head of the earthen mound, then took off his coonskin cap and said, "These were good folks, and may the Lord welcome them t' their rest." He bowed his head and continued for a moment in a mellifluous language that Quincy had never heard before, and he concluded by saying, "I never learned the German tongue, but there's a prayer for ye in me native Scottish Gaelic, Conrad Jarrott. God rest ye and yours."

Quincy looked at Mariel's wan, tear-streaked face and wanted to say something comforting to her, but the words would not come to him. Although he had seen more violent death than any sixteen-year-old boy should have, the emotional aftermath of it was new to him, and he was glad when Cordelia put her arm around Mariel's shoulder and gently led the girl away. Slowly the group returned to the wagons and left the grave behind.

With Murdoch and Quincy taking the lead on horseback, the travelers set out once more along the Mohawk River and headed for Martin Ulmer's farm. The man had a wife and a large brood of children, and Mariel was certain the Ulmers would be more than happy to take in little Dietrich and her. The sun had not risen very high and mist still hung under the trees along the river when they came within sight of the Ulmer homestead.

Murdoch reined in sharply and tried to motion the others back, but it was too late. Mariel clapped her hands over her mouth to stifle a scream when she saw the burned-out rubble—all that was left of the Ulmer cabin.

"Stay here," Murdoch said to Gresham Howard, then jerked his head at Quincy and heeled his horse into a trot. Quincy rode alongside him, long rifle held at the ready.

There were no arrow-riddled bodies outside the cabin, but Quincy saw several huddled shapes in the ashes and felt his stomach lurch. Murdoch nodded and said, "Aye, 'tis going t' be another bad job, lad. Go back t' the wagons and get the shovels, and we'll get started."

Quincy wheeled his horse and galloped back to the others.

"Any survivors?" Gresham Howard asked quietly.

"I don't think so," Quincy answered. "It looks like the whole family was inside the cabin, and I don't see how anybody could have lived through that fire."

Howard grimaced. "I was afraid of that. The Mohawks

probably came through here first, before they hit the Jarrott place. Probably hit all the farms along the river."

Quincy looked at the second wagon and saw that Mariel was crying, her face buried in her hands as sobs shook her slender body. Dietrich huddled beside her, and although Cordelia was doing her best to comfort them, Quincy knew she was not going to have much success. Too much had happened; Mariel's world was never going to be the same, and now she had been dealt another blow by the grisly discovery they had just made.

Howard got the shovels and handed them up to Quincy, who then rode back to join Murdoch. They made quick work of the grave digging and by midmorning had gently lowered the charred remains of the Ulmer family into the ground.

"I dinna like this," Murdoch said as he began to shovel dirt into the opening.

Quincy snorted as he joined in the task. "Who would?"

"Tha's no' what I mean. The Mohawks go out on a raid every now and then, but they've been quiet for a good while. Now they've gone t' killing again. Something must be stirring them up."

"You think we're going to run into more trouble?"

The big frontiersman shrugged his brawny shoulders. "If the Mohawks be up in arms, we'll be damned lucky not t' have a fight on our hands before we get t' the Allegheny."

Quincy leaned on his shovel. "Should we turn around and go back the way we came?"

"Too far around," Murdoch said. "Besides, I dinna want t' tackle the Appalachians with the wagons. This way, instead o' the mountains, we'll climb only gentle hills. Mercifully, most of the land along here is flat."

"I don't like taking Cordelia and Mariel into danger," Quincy declared grimly. "If the Mohawks hit this place, too, Mr. Howard said they may have gotten the other farms on this stretch of the river. We're going to have to take Mariel and Dietrich with us."

"Right ye are, lad. We'll walk light, keep our eyes and ears open and our powder dry. Tha' be all we can do."

When the burying was done, Murdoch waved the wagons forward, and for the second time that morning, prayers were said over the dead. As the unofficial leader of the group, Murdoch went to Mariel when the service was concluded and said, "Ye and the bairn will be coming with us now, unless there be some other neighbors around here ye wish us t' look for."

"There's no point in that, is there?" Mariel asked in a whisper. "They're all dead—everyone in the valley, all our friends and neighbors."

"We don't know that," Quincy said.

"We certainly don't," agreed Howard. "We'll do whatever you want, my dear. But I speak for all of us when I say you're welcome to travel on with us if you'd like."

"Thank you. I think Dietrich and I would like that."

"I want go home," piped up Dietrich.

Mariel knelt beside him and put her hands gently on his shoulders. "We can't do that, Dietrich," she said softly. "We're going to have to find a new home now, and these people are going to help us. Do you understand?"

Dietrich frowned, deep in thought. "New home?" he finally said.

"New home," said Mariel.

The boy smiled, and Mariel pulled him into her arms and held him close.

After a moment, Murdoch quietly broke the poignant silence. "We'd best be moving again."

Mariel looked up at him. "We're ready," she said.

As the travelers made their way westward over the next few days, Mariel remained nervous, jumping at any unexpected sound and never letting Dietrich stray too far from her side; considering what she had been through, it was understandable that she was acting this way. Quincy's heart went out to her and the little boy, and he wished he could help them get over their fear.

Mariel remembered her father mentioning a distant cousin who had also immigrated to America and had intended to seek land somewhere along the Ohio River.

"'Tis a long stream, lass," Murdoch replied when she told them this around the campfire one evening, "but we'll find tha' relation of yours if we possibly can. We have no firm destination once we get out t' the frontier, so looking for him won't take us much out o' our way."

"Thank you, Murdoch," Mariel said warmly. "I—I don't know what Dietrich and I would have done if you hadn't come along."

"Ye'd have managed somehow," Murdoch replied in a gruff voice, feeling uncomfortable at what he thought he saw in the girl's blue eyes.

Quincy saw the same thing and did not know what to make of it. Murdoch was in his mid-thirties, a good twenty years older than Mariel. What she was feeling for the frontiersman had to be a simple case of hero worship.

After all, thought Quincy, *he* had been in the thick of the fight against the Mohawks, too. It was not as though Murdoch had saved Mariel and Dietrich single-handedly, even if that was how Mariel was acting now.

Cordelia sat down beside him and handed him a bowl of the stew she had made for supper. "What are you so worried about?" she asked as he slowly spooned the hearty concoction into his mouth.

"Who said I was worried?" he replied between bites.

"Well, you look like something's bothering you."

Quincy glanced across the fire at Mariel, who sat gazing at Murdoch, with her knees drawn up under her chin. Then he turned his head and looked at Cordelia and saw the concerned expression on her lovely face. She was worried about him, he realized, and that meant she had to care about him. Just the thought seemed to make his heart swell in his chest.

"I'm fine," he said firmly. "Nothing wrong with me."

"I'm glad to hear it," Cordelia said. She smiled warmly at him.

Quincy felt better then. Murdoch might have some wide-eyed little girl mooning over him, but Quincy had a mature, beautiful woman for a friend—and maybe someday something more.

Not that Mariel disliked him, Quincy discovered over the next few days. She often talked to him and told him what her life had been like in Westphalia, that her father had been a flax farmer in a fertile area called Hellweg. But there was little opportunity for his children to better themselves and so the family had come to the new world to settle in the Mohawk Valley. When she talked about her mother and father and her brothers and sisters, Quincy saw tears glisten in her eyes, and he wanted to tell her that she did not need to dwell on those memories. But reminiscing about her family seemed to make Mariel feel better, as if it lessened the pain of her grief.

They passed the settlements of Fort Johnson and Stone Arabia, and it was while they were replenishing their supplies at a small trading post in the latter community that they learned the full extent of the Mohawks' rampage.

"They came out of the west," an old-timer told them as he sat on a stool next to the trading post's cracker barrel and whittled a piece of wood. "Must've been a hundred of them or more, broken up into raiding parties of a dozen or so braves in each one. They stayed away from the towns, but they hit all the outlying farms and massacred everybody they could find. I'm telling you, folks around here didn't sleep much for a fortnight or so. Bloody Mohocks," he said, giving the tribe's name its original pronunciation.

After arching a stream of tobacco juice into a nearby spittoon, he went on, "I'm guessing they've all pulled back to where they came from, and folks are resting a mite easier now. But those savages'll be back. Mark my word on that. Here, little miss, this is for you." The old man held out what he had been whittling to Mariel. When she took it, they saw that the old-timer and his knife had transformed a willow branch into a flute.

"Thank you," Mariel said, somewhat embarrassed by the attention.

The old man gestured to her with a gnarled hand. "Play it," he commanded.

"I—I don't know how."

"It's simple enough. Put your fingers over the holes and move them back and forth whilst you blow on the other end."

Mariel positioned her fingers awkwardly and brought the carved instrument to her lips. Still reluctant, she blew softly into it.

Gentle notes trilled out from the flute, and Mariel jumped a little and took it away from her mouth for a second. The old-timer motioned for her to continue, and she took a deep breath and began playing again.

This time as she moved her fingers, she mimicked the motions the old man was making, and the notes took on a melodious sound, even though they formed no real tune. Mariel's companions were watching her, and as the sweet sound of the flute filled the air inside the log building, the trading post's other customers paused to look and listen as well. If she was still embarrassed by the attention, she did not show it. Instead she seemed caught up in the music, and she swayed gently back and forth in time to the notes that floated into the air. Beside her, Dietrich squealed with glee and clapped his hands.

For a moment, all the hardships and dangers faced daily by the settlers seemed to vanish. Men and women clapped work-roughened hands, and smiles appeared on faces made leathery by the elements. Out here, people relied on their neighbors, but the feeling of kinship inside the trading post grew even stronger as they listened to the music. It provided a warmth that penetrated deeper than any that came from the cast-iron stove.

Of course, it did not last. Mariel played the whittled flute only for a few minutes, and then people went on about their business, relinquishing the feelings that had gripped them only seconds earlier. After all, they had things to do, supplies to load on wagons, chores waiting back on their farms.

But in their minds, the memory would linger of a pretty young girl who had played a flute carved by an old man and united them all, if only for a few minutes. It was a memory that could be retrieved in the middle of a hard afternoon clearing rocks from a field or plowing or chopping wood or churning butter or carrying water or spinning wool, and it would help these people remember why they had come here in the first place.

It was the sound of freedom.

They would be turning south by southwest soon, before they reached the village of Oneida. So far there had been well-marked roads and paths most of the way, but once they veered off from their westerly direction, they would be traveling across open country. The going would be slower, Murdoch warned them. Still, he expected to make fairly good time if they did not encounter any trouble, and they could reach the Allegheny within a week or ten days, two weeks at the most. From there it would be a simple matter to head downriver to Pittsburgh. There the Allegheny joined the Monongahela—the "river with sliding banks," as Murdoch explained the Indian name—to form the mighty Ohio.

This is certainly pretty country, Quincy thought more

than once as he drove the second wagon or rode ahead with Murdoch on horseback. The road wound between thickly wooded hills and large, flat meadows, and it curved around clear lakes so blue it hurt the eyes to look directly into their depths. The June warmth had fields of flowers blossoming in the valleys. Quincy had to admit it: This New York country was almost as beautiful as his native Virginia.

It was the beguilement of the scenery, Quincy supposed later, as well as the fact they had not seen further signs of Indian trouble, that led them to let their guard down. If it had not been for Murdoch . . .

The road followed a ridge that ran alongside the Mohawk River, which was little more than a stream off to the right about a hundred yards, at the bottom of a gentle open slope. To the left the ridge fell away more steeply, and the hillside was covered with brush. Farther away from the river, to both north and south, rose larger hills that were blue-gray in the sunlight due to the pines mantling them.

Murdoch was in the lead as usual, with Gresham Howard at the reins of the first wagon, and Quincy brought up the rear with the second wagon. Cordelia was riding with her father today, while Mariel and Dietrich perched on the seat beside Quincy. "Have you known Murdoch for long?" Mariel asked, leaning slightly to the side so that her gaze could follow the rugged frontiersman as he rode ahead of the wagons.

"I've only known him for a few months," Quincy replied, somewhat irritated that Mariel was asking about Murdoch. "But we've been through so much together, it seems as though we've been friends for years."

"Will you tell me about it? Every time I start asking questions, Murdoch won't talk to me."

Perhaps he's embarrassed by the fact that a mere child is infatuated with him, Quincy thought. But aloud he said, "Murdoch's been living on the frontier for several years. He only came east on a visit. From what he's told me, people keep to themselves more out there. I imagine that's all it is."

"I hope so," said Mariel. "I'd hate to think he didn't like me."

Quincy rolled his eyes and turned his head to hide the insincere smile that seemed stuck on his face. Surely Mariel saw that she was making a fool of herself.

He was so preoccupied that he did not notice that Howard had brought the lead wagon to a stop. When he saw that the vehicle in front of him was not moving, Quincy hauled back quickly on the reins, using all the strength in his wiry young body to manhandle the mule team to a halt.

Murdoch had waved Howard to a stop, and now he brought his horse alongside the man's wagon. "What is it?" Howard asked anxiously. "Is something wrong?"

"Just a bad feeling," replied Murdoch, "like something's about t' happen, even if it hasn't started yet." He slid his long rifle out of the fringed sheath on his saddle and turned the horse in a slow circle; his keen eyes scanned the hillside.

Suddenly he threw himself out of the saddle and shouted as he fell, "Get down! Get behind the wagons!"

An arrow flew out of the brush and whistled through the space Murdoch's body had occupied an instant earlier. The big black gelding shied, spooked by the flurry of movement, and as Murdoch landed in the road, he rolled clear of the dancing animal's hooves. He came up on his knees, lifted the rifle smoothly to his shoulder, and steadied the weapon. Smoke and flame belched from its muzzle as Murdoch fired.

A shriek of mortal pain sounded in the brush, then died away in a hideous gurgling noise. By this time, Quincy had leapt down from the seat of the wagon and was holding out his hands to Mariel, but out of the corner of his eye he saw a limp figure roll into view from behind one of the bushes. The buckskin pants, the bare bronze-hued chest, and the upthrust row of hair down the center of the man's head identified him as a Mohawk, and the blood cascading down his chest from his throat—torn open by Murdoch's rifle ball—told Quincy the Indian was dead—or soon would be.

Mariel screamed when an arrow thudded into the seat beside her. She snatched up Dietrich and all but threw the boy at Quincy, who staggered back a step but hung on as he caught him. Mariel leapt off the wagon and stumbled as she landed beside Quincy. He handed Dietrich to her and said, "Stay on this side of the wagon! Get down behind the wheel!"

As they crouched there, the wagon protecting them from the attacking Mohawks, Quincy pulled his pistol from his belt and ran to the front of the vehicle. For the moment, the mules stood stolidly, but there was no telling when they might bolt. As he peered over the animals he saw another Mohawk waving a tomahawk and howling out his killing frenzy burst from the undergrowth and rush toward the wagons.

Quincy aimed his pistol over the backs of the mules and shot him.

The Indian tumbled backward, and the tomahawk dropped from his lifeless hand as soon as Quincy's ball took him in the chest. Quincy tucked the pistol away and reached for his rifle, which was still lying on the floorboards beneath the wagon seat. As he did so, an arrow glanced off the bench and peeled away a long splinter of wood. The splinter, stinging like a bee, embedded itself in the back of Quincy's hand. He ignored it until he had the rifle gripped firmly, then used his other hand to pluck out the splinter and cast it aside. A drop of blood welled from the wound, but he paid no attention.

He had been in enough battles by now that the natural fear and panic he felt in the face of danger were shunted into the far recesses of his mind. If he kept his wits about him and remained calm, he knew he might come out of this alive. If not—well, at least he would have taken one of the enemy with him.

Meanwhile, Gresham Howard and Cordelia had lunged for shelter behind their vehicle. Howard had his old musket ready in his hands, but when he peered around the wagon, he could not find a target. Arrows thudded into the sideboards of the wagon, ripping its canvas cover and making it worth a man's life to stick his head out too far.

Murdoch scrambled past the mules, his empty rifle still in his hands, and when he reached Howard and Cordelia, he thrust the weapon at the blonde.

"Reload!" he snapped, handing his powder horn and shot pouch to the startled young woman. She stared at him for an instant, then, as though she had been jolted out of a sound sleep, grimly took up the task of charging and priming the flintlock rifle.

Murdoch pulled his pistols and crouched behind one of the mules. At that moment, an arrow buried itself in the neck of one of the lead pair, and the animal screamed and thrashed as it went down. Murdoch dropped the pistol from his right hand, leapt forward, and snagged the harness before the team tried to bolt and became entangled with the body of the dead mule.

Once Murdoch had settled the mules, he scooped up the pistol he had dropped, glanced at it to make sure dirt had not plugged the muzzle, then downed another Mohawk with its ball. For a few moments all was chaos atop the ridge, but with Cordelia reloading for them, the two men were able to keep up a steady rate of fire into the brush.

Behind the second wagon, Quincy saw a flash of red in the bushes, and as he lifted his rifle to his shoulder, he stared in disbelief when a white man came into view—a white man wearing a red coat, white breeches, black boots, and a black hat.

A British soldier!

There was no time to gape at the unexpected sight of a British regular fighting on the same side as a band of Indians known for their ferocity. The soldier had a Brown Bess musket in his hands, and he was aiming the weapon right at Quincy.

By a split second Quincy fired first, and as the redcoat reeled to the side from the impact, the ball from his musket screamed harmlessly off into the air. The soldier fell to his knees, the weapon slipped from his fingers, and he pitched forward on his face and lay still.

Ignoring the nausea in his belly, Quincy reloaded. As he did so, the Mohawks charged the wagons, and he saw two more British regulars. Behind them, down the slope, he saw a white man waving clenched fists in the air and shrieking at the Indians, "Kill them! Kill the heathens! Kill them all!"

Quincy blinked in surprise at the sight of the tall, gaunt man wearing a white shirt, black broadcloth coat, and a black hat with a round crown.

"Strike them down, Lord! Smite the evildoers! Rend their flesh from their bones with your divine vengeance!"

Turning his attention from the man in the black suit in time to see another Indian lunging toward him, Quincy, with no chance to reload, grabbed the only weapon close at hand. He tore free one of the arrows that had stuck to the wagon seat and thrust it blindly in front of him. The Mohawk ran right into it, and the sharp head at the end of the feathered shaft embedded itself in the soft flesh of his belly. He stumbled past Quincy, pawing futilely at the arrow, until he tripped and fell, and when he landed, the ground drove the shaft all the way through him. The arrowhead ripped through his back.

Quincy whirled around, looking for another enemy, but the Mohawks were gone. He saw Murdoch and Howard firing into the brush where the Mohawks had lurked in ambush, and Cordelia, her face pale and streaked with blood, was handing the two men their guns as fast as she could reload them.

Mariel! Quincy thought suddenly. *Where were Mariel and Dietrich?*

The sound of sobbing led him to look underneath the wagon. The brother and sister were huddled there, and because it was probably as safe a place as any for them, he told them to stay there while he ran up to the lead wagon to join Murdoch, Howard, and Cordelia.

"The savages be on the run," Murdoch said. He grinned. "Likely they had a wee bit more trouble killing us than they expected."

Quincy looked down the hill and saw that the Mohawks were retreating so fast they were already out of rifle range. The scarecrowlike man in the black suit was with them, and from the way he was waving his arms around, he was still haranguing them. If he was urging the Mohawks to turn around and continue the battle, however, his exhortations were not doing any good. Clearly, the Indians wanted no part of any more fighting. As Quincy and the others watched, their attackers vanished into the woods.

There were half a dozen Mohawks stretched out on the ground, all of them dead. With them were the three British soldiers. Quincy pointed to the redcoats and asked, "What were *they* doing here?"

"Looked t' me like they were doing their damnedest t' kill us, just like the Indians," Murdoch replied grimly. "And I'd like t' know who tha' other white man was. I could'na hear everything he was saying, but from what I did hear, he sounded like some sort o' preacher."

"That's what I thought, too," agreed Howard.

Cordelia shuddered. "He was howling like a lunatic. I never heard such."

There was a little blood from a scratch on Cordelia's hand, and there were several patches of blood on Murdoch's buckskins, but Quincy could not tell if the gore had come from him or from some of the dead Mohawks killed in hand-to-hand fighting. When he looked down at himself, he saw that his shirt was splashed with crimson, but as far as he knew the only wound he had sustained had been from the splinter in the back of his hand.

They had been lucky, very lucky, he realized. The Mohawks had underestimated the amount of resistance they would put up, and when the battle had proved more costly than the Indians had anticipated, they had broken off the fight. If they had kept it up, Quincy knew, eventually they would have overpowered their intended victims by sheer force of numbers.

"We'd better get moving," Murdoch said. "I want t' be in some place easier to defend than this if those Indians decide t' come back."

Quincy hurried back to the second wagon. Mariel and Dietrich were still underneath, and when he bent over and held out a hand to them, Mariel flinched away from him. "No!" she cried hysterically.

"It's all right," Quincy told her in a calm, soothing voice. "It's only me, Mariel. It's Quincy."

"Quincy?" she whispered.

"That's right. Come on out now. The fighting's over."

Dietrich squirmed out of Mariel's arms and scooted out from beneath the wagon. Quincy scooped him up and said, "You're all right now, Dietrich. There's nothing to worry about."

That was a lie, of course, Quincy thought. There was plenty to worry about, but it would not do any good to frighten them more.

Slowly, Mariel emerged, too, and when Quincy looked her over, he could see that she was disheveled and terrified but unhurt. Dietrich had come through the battle unscathed, and he grinned as Quincy placed him on the wagon seat.

"We've got to get moving again," Quincy said. "Murdoch wants to find a place where we can fort up if we have to."

Mariel nodded slightly, but she barely seemed to hear what he was saying.

Murdoch and Howard, meanwhile, had been unhitching the dead mule from its harness. The carcass was too heavy to drag out of the way, so they led the surviving members of the team to the edge of the road and around the fallen animal.

"What about those dead men?" Cordelia asked quietly, gesturing to the bodies of the Mohawks and the British soldiers.

"They would've left us where we fell, had the situation been turned around," replied Murdoch. "I will'na waste time and sweat burying them."

"I agree," said Howard. "They were merciless killers, Cordelia. Don't bother feeling sorry for them."

A shudder ran through the young woman. "Believe me, I wasn't. I'd just as soon get out of here as quickly as we can."

When they had traveled another two miles, Murdoch pointed out a cluster of large rocks with a clearing in the center large enough for the wagons and the mules. Howard and Quincy angled the vehicles toward the natural fort. Even though there were still a few hours of daylight left, none of them felt like pushing on any farther.

"We'll spend the night here," Murdoch announced. "If the Mohawks come back, we'll have another hot welcome ready for them."

The Indians did not reappear, however, and by that night, Mariel and Dietrich had calmed down enough to drop off to sleep after a hearty meal of stew and corn cakes. Cordelia retired to the wagon to join them, and Murdoch, Quincy, and Howard sat beside the fire. The older men had pipes going, and the familiar smell was comforting to the group. Quincy had learned not to look directly at the flames so that he would not have to wait for his eyes to adjust to the darkness in case of trouble, and when he finished gnawing one last corn cake, he asked, "Where do you think those British regulars came from?"

"Down from the north, would be me guess," replied Murdoch. "There were probably more than just the three of them, too. I bet they brought guns and ammunition with them, t' give t' the Indians."

"Good Lord," breathed Howard. "You mean you think the British are arming the savages and trying to rouse them against the settlers?"

Murdoch nodded grimly. "Tha' be what I think, all right. And a smart move by the British it is."

Quincy mused, "If this is just the start of it—if the British can get the Indians to attack the colonies from the west while we're trying to deal with the British threat from the east—"

"Aye," Murdoch said. "If they do tha', this war isn't going t' last long. And when 'tis over, the redcoats will have won."

Chapter Eight

"**F**all in! Fall in your ranks!" The stentorian voice of Captain Aaron Webster boomed across the section of the encampment where his company of militiamen was staying. Daniel, on a twenty-minute rest break, drowsed under a tree on this warm, humid Friday evening. He sprang immediately to his feet. Thad Garner was stretched out on the grass nearby, and he rubbed his eyes as he sat up.

"What is it?" asked Thad anxiously. "What's going on?"

"I don't know," Daniel replied, "but the captain's ordering us to form up into ranks. We'd best step lively." He held out a hand, grasped Thad's wrist, and helped his friend to stand.

Daniel was frustrated by his inability to get away from his rigorous training schedule for even so much as a morning to ride to Lemuel Parsons's farm in Concord to get word of Roxanne. He had been denied permission each time he asked because Captain Webster had told him war was imminent. As far as he was concerned, this alarm had better be a frontal attack by the redcoats, or he was going to leave without permission.

As they headed toward Captain Webster, who was still bellowing, Ben Hobbs, George Cummings, and Fred Dary joined them as well. "Do you think it's the British?" George asked.

"I hope so," Fred answered before anyone else had a chance to reply. "I'm getting damned tired of sitting around Cambridge and waiting."

"Aye," agreed Ben. "It's time we let those lobster-backs know we mean business."

More than one company was forming up, Daniel saw as he and his companions entered Harvard Yard. Another group of militiamen led by an officer Daniel recognized as Captain Thomas Knowlton was also gathering. Daniel and his friends fell in line with their group, and as they did so, Daniel spotted several officers approaching on horseback. He recognized General Israel Putnam, Colonel William Prescott, and Colonel Richard Gridley, the Provincial Army's chief engineer. With them was Dr. Joseph Warren, and although Daniel wanted to wave to the physician, he restrained the impulse. Whether he was an official member of this army or not, he intended to follow military discipline. He stood at attention, his rifle on his shoulder, and stepped out smartly with the others when Webster ordered the men to parade.

For the next hour, the officers watched while the men drilled. Satisfied with what they saw, General Putnam and Colonel Prescott spoke approvingly to Captain Webster and Captain Knowlton.

However, not everyone was pleased. From his place beside Daniel, Thad grumbled in a low voice, "I don't think we're going to do anything but march back and forth. And it's getting on toward suppertime!"

Daniel's empty belly and the position of the sun in the sky told him it was around six o'clock, the time when the army would normally be taking its evening meal.

It was clear there would be no supper today. Following the orders of their commanders, the men knelt, and a local minister from Cambridge appeared to say prayers in a loud, ringing voice. Daniel felt a chill as the black-coated preacher called on the Almighty to aid and protect the valiant patriots assembled before him.

There was going to be trouble, Daniel knew, and he was not the only one to sense that. He heard muttering in the ranks that contained overtones of both apprehension and anticipation, but it was stilled by the shouted commands of the officers, who got the men on their feet and marched them along behind Putnam, Prescott, Gridley, and Warren.

"This is it, isn't it?" Thad said with only slight tension in his voice to betray his growing nervousness. "There's going to be a battle."

"Yes," said Daniel solemnly. "I think so."

The sun was setting when they marched out of Cambridge toward Charlestown Neck, and more soldiers joined them along the route. From the way General Putnam placed himself at their head, Daniel knew they were from Old Put's personal command. In addition, a column of wagons fell in behind them.

A thousand strong, the soldiers tramped the four miles from Cambridge south across Charlestown Neck as the shadows of night closed in. Looking off to the right, Daniel could see the lights of the buildings in Charlestown itself, and beyond them, across the Charles River, was Boston.

Daniel wondered if Roxanne was there somewhere, sitting in a room illuminated by a lamp that was only a faintly flickering dot of light from this distance. He had spoken to Dr. Warren twice during the past two weeks, and on each occasion the doctor had had no information to offer regarding Roxanne's whereabouts.

Are we going to invade the city? Daniel asked himself. Surely not; there were only a thousand of them, and the British had at least six thousand troops in Boston; an attack on the city would be suicidal.

The army did not veer toward Charlestown but continued marching straight ahead until Daniel saw Bunker Hill, the tallest of the three heights on the peninsula, rising in front of them. He knew that south of Bunker Hill and somewhat smaller was Breed's Hill, and off to the west, closer to the town, was School Hill. All three, but especially Bunker and Breed's Hills, offered a commanding view of the city across the river.

Daniel, Thad, George, Ben, and Fred marched at the front of their company and, in the clear moonlight, had a good view of the mounted officers who were leading them up Bunker Hill. Dr. Warren had fallen back a bit to ride with Captain Webster, but General Putnam, Colonel Prescott, and Colonel Gridley rode without hesitation to the grassy summit of the hill. They stopped, and Prescott turned and ordered the troops to halt. Webster relayed the command in a voice that carried to each man but was softer than they were used to. Knowlton did the same. Sound carried well across water, and it was clear to Daniel that the officers in charge of this operation did not want to alert the British to their presence.

While the soldiers waited, the officers atop the hill conferred at length. Dr. Warren spurred forward to join them, and even though Daniel was only thirty yards away, he could not make out what they were saying. He could only tell that the discussion was serious.

After a few minutes, Colonel Prescott left the group and rode over to Captain Webster. Daniel heard him say, "I need a detail of six men to serve as forward sentries, Captain."

"Aye, sir," said Webster. He turned in his saddle and called softly, "Garner, Cummings, Reed, Dary, Hobbs, Farnsworth! To the front!"

Daniel and the men detached themselves from the ranks and marched forward.

Webster continued, "You six go with Colonel Prescott and follow his orders. Keep your wits about you, boys, it's liable to be a long night."

Holding their muskets and rifles at the ready, Daniel and his fellow militiamen walked to the top of Bunker Hill. Prescott waved them ahead until they had descended ten yards down the far side of the slope. Then the colonel called, "That'll be far enough, men. Keep an eye out for anything moving on these hills, and on the Charles, too, if it's coming this way."

Suddenly Daniel realized what they were doing. He had enough knowledge of rudimentary military tactics to know that whoever held the high ground possessed the advantage, and the commanders of the Provincial Army were worried that the British would try to take control of these hills.

But, Daniel thought, *if the patriots can hold these heights, a few cannon placed up here could lob cannonballs right into the heart of Boston.*

His hunch was confirmed a moment later when he heard Colonel Prescott say, "We can construct our redoubt right here, gentlemen. There's plenty of time before dawn for the needed excavations. Correct, Colonel Gridley?"

The engineering officer, deep in thought, did not answer for a moment. Then he said, "It'll take a while for the British to mount a response once they see what we're doing, so I think there will be ample time to complete our preparations before we have to engage them."

General Putnam cleared his throat and said, "If I might make a comment, gentlemen?"

"Of course, General," Prescott said quickly. "We're relying on your experience to guide us."

Daniel sensed a certain tension between the two senior officers, and he understood why when Old Put went on, "No, no, Colonel, you're in charge of this operation, and I'm just a volunteer like everyone else. But it seems to me that the best course of action would be to fortify Breed's Hill. That way we can keep the British from getting so much as a toehold on this peninsula."

"Hmmm," mused Prescott. "What do you think, Gridley?"

Daniel could almost see the mental shrug the engineer gave as he replied, "It's up to you, sir. Breed's Hill is shorter and commands less of the field. However, it *is* closer to the river and to Boston itself."

"If we give the redcoats Breed's Hill, they can sit there, hold us off, and set up cannon to bombard Cambridge," Putnam said. "Of course, that's just speculation on my part."

Speculation, Daniel thought. He chuckled grimly. The old fox was trying to run this show without making it look as though he was being disrespectful of Colonel Prescott's authority. And it was clear to Daniel that the approach was working, because after a few more minutes of discussion, Prescott said firmly, "Breed's Hill it is. Colonel Gridley, ride over there and begin laying out the entrenching lines. The rest of the men will follow with the wagons and tools."

"Yes, sir," Gridley said.

"I want to hold some men back here," Putnam put in. "Just in case the British try to flank our fortifications on Breed's Hill and get behind us. If they do that, we'll catch their bloody hides in a cross fire!"

That made sense to Daniel. He did not get to hear any more of the discussion, however, because Colonel Gridley rode up alongside the other sentries and him and said, "You men come with me. You'll function as the advance guard while I'm busy with my own tasks."

Gridley held his horse back a bit, but Daniel and the others were still forced to trot at a good pace to keep up with him. A long saddle of land bridged the gap between Bunker Hill and Breed's Hill, so the men did not have to descend all the way to the level of most of the Charlestown peninsula to reach the top of Breed's Hill. From this summit, the land sloped all the way to the Charles River, and there were small roads between the hill and the river, as well as some stone fences. Other than that, the approach to the summit consisted of open fields.

For the next hour, while Colonel Gridley rode back and forth making drawings on a scrap of paper with a piece of charcoal, muttering arcane pronouncements to himself, the rest of the militiamen marched across the saddle between the hills, followed by the wagons. When the vehicles arrived, Daniel was not surprised to see that they were loaded with picks, shovels, and spades, and when Gridley was finally satisfied with the plans he had worked out, he conferred again with Colonel Prescott and General Putnam, who had also ridden to Breed's Hill.

Daniel estimated it was around midnight when the entrenching tools were passed out to the men and the order was given. It was a simple one.

Dig.

And so they drove their shovels into the soft earth at the top of Breed's Hill and tossed the dirt in front of them to erect an earthen barrier before the trench that was taking shape.

It was backbreaking labor, and despite the hardships he had gone through in recent months, Daniel was not accustomed to intense physical work, especially a never-ending task such as this one. For every shovelful of dirt flung out of the trench, there were a thousand more waiting to be lifted. To make it worse, the night was hot and still, almost airless. Within a quarter of an hour, Daniel's shirt was soaked with sweat and a nagging ache had settled into his lower back.

Thad Garner and the other friends Daniel had made stood shoulder to shoulder with him in the trench. Their shovels rose and fell, and the trench sunk gradually into the earth as the breastworks rose. Colonel Gridley had laid out a rectangle roughly fifty-five yards long and forty-five yards wide, perched squarely atop the summit of the hill. Once the trench was complete and packed with men, they could lay down a withering fire across the slope in front of them, using alternating volleys to keep up a continual rain of lead.

General Putnam galloped back and forth between Bunker Hill and Breed's Hill in order to supervise the placement of forces being held in reserve on Bunker Hill as well as to check on the progress of the redoubt atop Breed's Hill. Colonel Prescott, worried that the unavoidable noises of digging would drift across the Charles and alert the troops in Boston, spent much of his time close to the shore, watching for any sign of British response. Daniel heard enough of the conversations between the officers to know what was going on, but stuck in the hole he could not see anything but dirt. He tried to use his sleeve to wipe perspiration off his forehead, but his shirt was too wet.

There was no water to drink, but when the men took short breaks, they sipped rum from flasks passed around by the officers. Under the circumstances, they sweated out the liquor immediately, and no one got drunk. On the other hand, the rum did little to quench their thirst.

No one was willing to give up, and so the digging continued as the stars wheeled through the velvety black sky, but to the east, the darkness began to pale.

Dawn was coming. A new day—Saturday, June 17, 1775—was at hand.

* * *

The heavy features of General Thomas Gage were set in a threatening scowl when he stalked into his office and tossed his summer-weight cloak at the rack in the corner. The garment missed and fell in a heap on the floor, but Gage paid no heed to it. He did not even notice as his adjutant quickly picked up the wrap and hung it on one of the hooks. Gage was occupied with more pressing matters.

He walked behind his desk and slammed a fist down on its top. "How?" he thundered. "How could those damned rebels sit up there on Breed's Hill all night without anyone noticing?"

Gage did not expect an answer to the question, but he got one anyway when Gentleman Johnny Burgoyne strolled into the room. "Someone did notice," Burgoyne said. "There's talk among the men who were standing sentry duty that they heard noise from there commencing around midnight and lasting all night." Burgoyne smiled humorlessly. "None of them saw fit to mention that fact to a superior officer, however."

Staring at Burgoyne as if he did not believe what he was hearing, Gage took a moment to digest it, then bellowed, "My God, what idiots! I'll have every man jack of them flogged!"

General Henry Clinton hurried into the office. In contrast to Burgoyne, who was his usual impeccable self even after being roused at five o'clock in the morning for this hastily called meeting, Clinton was just pulling up his suspenders and had his uniform coat draped over his arm. In response to Gage's furious declaration, he said, "You'd better wait on that flogging, General. You may well need those men before the day is over, to help rout out that insidious nest of traitors."

Gage sat down heavily in his chair and motioned for Burgoyne and Clinton to take seats as well. General Howe had not yet arrived, but there was no time to waste—they would simply proceed without him.

"Well, gentlemen," Gage said grimly, "what course of action shall we undertake to meet this latest threat?"

Clinton snapped, "We can do what we should have done weeks ago—occupy Bunker Hill."

"To do that, we'll have to drive the rebels away from it," Burgoyne pointed out. "And that won't be easy."

From the doorway of the office, General William Howe snorted his disagreement. "Nonsense!" he said as he stalked into the room. "That so-called Provincial Army will be no match for His Majesty's troops."

Burgoyne made no reply, but his eyes flashed angrily as Howe took his seat. Although the four men were experienced, dedicated officers, loyal to the Crown, it was inevitable that a trace of jealousy and friction would exist between them. It was strongest in Clinton, but none of them was immune to it.

"General Clinton is correct in one respect," Howe went on. "We should have already had Charlestown Peninsula under our control."

"What about Dorchester Heights?" Burgoyne asked. "There is as much danger to the south as to the north, in my judgment."

"And so we made no moves in either direction," muttered Clinton.

Coldly Gage said, "I don't believe there is any need to cast aspersions on anyone's judgment. What we must do now is decide how we shall meet this new development."

"Attack, of course," Clinton said. "I'd suggest a flanking maneuver. We can send our boats around to Charlestown Neck, put the troops ashore, and secure the neck itself. That cuts the peninsula off from the mainland."

"Indeed it does," said Burgoyne, "but what about the rebels already *on* the peninsula? We cannot ignore them.

For all we know, they're already hauling cannon up the hill to send a few balls whistling directly at us."

Gage shook his head and picked up a paper from his desk. "This intelligence report from Dr. Benjamin Church via our old friend Major Kane tells us that the rebel forces have few cannon, and none in the Charlestown area is close enough to pose any danger to us at the moment."

"Major Kane is a good man," Howe admitted, "but even he can make mistakes. The last thing I want to do is leave a nest of those traitors dug in atop the hills."

"I agree," Gage said. "I propose we make a start immediately by ordering the warships in the Charles to fire several rounds each at the fortification the rebels are constructing up there. Perhaps that will be enough to make them think twice and leave the vicinity."

"It's a good start," Burgoyne agreed. "But I wouldn't count on the rebels fleeing, General. I think they are made of sterner stuff than to allow a few cannonballs to shake their resolve."

Gage stood up and turned to the window that overlooked Boston Harbor. "We'll see," he said. "We'll just see about that."

It was well before dawn when Roxanne awoke. She had slept only fitfully, and there was a fine sheen of perspiration on her forehead as she sat up in bed. She did not know if she perspired because there was little air stirring in the attic bedroom of the Parsons farmhouse—or if, as usual, she was worried about Daniel.

She did know that she was ready to start for Cambridge at this very moment, had it been possible. As it was, by the time she dressed and went down the ladder and then the stairs to the ground floor, she found Lemuel and Lottie already in the kitchen, and she was grateful for that.

"Sit down and have some breakfast," Lemuel told her.

He was seated at the table, cleaning his musket, while Lottie tended to the pans on the wood stove.

Roxanne heard the crackle of frying bacon and smelled hotcakes, and though she thought she would be too nervous to eat this morning, her stomach suddenly told her she was ravenously hungry.

She noticed there were only three places set at the table, despite the fact that the children would be getting up soon to tend to their chores. When she remarked on that, Lottie said, "We decided to let them sleep a bit later this morning, Roxanne. They won't be up before you and Lem are gone."

With a frown, Roxanne began, "Are you sure—"

"Of course we're sure," Lemuel broke in, a forced grin on his lean face. "No need to make a big fuss. I'll be back tonight, or tomorrow at the latest. Let the youngsters get a little extra sleep. It won't hurt them this once."

Roxanne smiled slowly in understanding. They were going to pretend there was no possibility that Lemuel might not return. By assuming he would be safe, perhaps they could make it so.

Lottie dished up platters of bacon and hotcakes, then poured mugs of warm cider for her husband and Roxanne.

"Aren't you going to eat?" Roxanne asked her.

"I don't really feel like it right now," Lottie said quietly. "I'll eat later, when the children are up."

For a few moments Lemuel ate in silence, then commented cheerfully, "Maybe when we come back tonight, we'll have Daniel with us."

"That would be wonderful," Lottie said, smiling at Roxanne. "I'll pray that it's so."

"So will I," Roxanne murmured as she looked down at her plate. And yet she was unsure. It had been so long. Even if she *did* find Daniel, would he still want her? That would depend, she knew, on just what he had heard about her—and Elliot.

For now she could not worry about that. Perhaps, like Lottie and Lemuel, she should simply pretend that everything was going to be all right, and it would be. Yes, that was it. She and Daniel would soon be back together, and everything would be fine.

If she said that to herself often enough, she might begin to believe it.

"My God, look at that!" Thad Garner breathed.

He had paused in his digging and scrambled up the earthen parapet to peer at the Charles River. The sun was creeping above the eastern horizon now, and it cast a reddish-yellow light over the waters of the Charles.

Hearing the surprise in his friend's voice, Daniel clambered to the top of the breastworks, too. All along the front edge of the fortification, men did the same as startled comments alerted them to the fact that something was happening. When Daniel reached the top and looked over, he saw what was causing the commotion.

Eight British warships were lined up in the river, starboard sides toward Breed's Hill, and their decks were beehives of activity. In the next instant, accompanied by flashes of fire and billowing puffs of smoke, the sailors manning the starboard batteries opened fire. The roar of the cannon thundered across the water and up the hill.

"Get down!" bellowed Captain Webster. "Get down, blast you!"

With a yelp, Thad twisted around and slid down the hill of dirt into the trench. Daniel was right behind him. They staggered as they landed, then caught their balance. All along the front of the fortification, men were doing the same thing. For the moment they had forgotten their duty and were talking excitedly. Anxiety crackled in the air.

"Get back to work!" Colonel Prescott shouted as he strode through the ranks. "Pick up your shovels and keep digging!"

The firm command made some of the militiamen, including Daniel and Thad, resume their task, but others looked as though they were on the verge of bolting from the redoubt and fleeing back across Charlestown Neck to the mainland.

Having leapt onto his horse, Colonel Prescott appeared at the rear of the fortification and called out, "Don't worry about a few British cannonballs, lads!"

That is easier said than done, Daniel thought, what with six-pound shot whistling overhead. This was the first time he had been subjected to cannon fire, and he flinched every time one of the balls passed close by. He fought down his fear and tried to concentrate on the job at hand: driving the shovel into the earth, lifting the dirt, and flinging it onto the breastworks.

So far they had been lucky. The balls from the naval bombardment had either fallen short of the summit or passed beyond it, but that changed abruptly. When Daniel straightened up to empty his shovel, he saw the most hideous thing he had ever witnessed in his life. A soldier who was standing only a few feet from Colonel Prescott was hit in the head by one of the cannonballs. The man's skull exploded, covering the startled Prescott with a grisly shower of blood, brains, and bone fragments. Incredibly, the headless body continued to stand for a few seconds, gouts of blood bubbling from its neck, a shovel still clutched in hands that did not realize they were dead. Then the corpse toppled over and flopped around in a manner that turned Daniel's blood to ice. He knew the horror he had just seen would remain imprinted on his brain forever.

Some men screamed at the sight; others, like Thad Garner, bent over and retched uncontrollably. Some simply stared, like Daniel, hardly able to credit what their eyes had seen.

Coolly, Colonel Prescott wiped away as much of the gore as he could from his face, then leaned over and cleaned his hand on his horse's neck. As he straightened, he snapped, "Everyone back to your posts and back to work! Captain, have a detail bury that man!"

"Aye, sir," replied Webster, but even the burly squire was pale and shaken by what he had just seen.

Daniel was thankful that Webster did not choose him for the burial detail. He forced himself to look away from the gruesome spectacle and went back to digging, glad to have something to do, something to occupy his mind. That way he did not have to think about how easily the dead man could have been any one of them, even he.

The cannonade from the British warships had shattered the calm of early morning, and all across Boston, people leapt out of their beds, dressed quickly, and hurried out to see what was happening. Cannon smoke in the air over the river rapidly drew the citizens' attention. They headed for rooftops and second-story windows, as well as hills and any other heights they could attain, in order to find a good spot to watch the battle. And it was clear, even to those unschooled in military matters, that a fight was going to break out. The cannon on the ships were merely firing the first shots.

Soon, the British battery located on Copp's Hill, directly across the river from Charlestown, joined in the offensive. The cannon roared continually as generals Gage, Howe, Clinton, and Burgoyne approached the British gun emplacement from the rear with their entourage. The four officers watched with grim satisfaction as the shells arched over the Charles River and peppered Breed's Hill.

Howe lifted a spyglass to his eye and studied the patriots' position. When he lowered the glass, he said, "As far as I can tell, they're still digging. You were right, General Burgoyne. They show no signs of running."

"These Americans don't," Burgoyne said. "I've never seen a more stubborn people."

"Well, stubbornness won't stop a cannonball nor a bayonet," Clinton said crisply. "I say soften them up with some more cannon fire, then go in and rout the traitors."

Howe nodded and a bit reluctantly said to Gage, "General Clinton is correct, sir."

"Very well." Gage's face was mottled with anger and frustration. He had been trying to deal with this crisis for months, and now, open warfare was the only solution remaining to him. He went on, "General Howe, you'll be in charge of this operation."

Howe nodded curtly, and if he felt any reluctance, he did not show it. The generals knew he harbored some sympathies for the colonists; Burgoyne shared those feelings as well. Besides, as Whigs, they were politically opposed to the Tory leaders of Parliament whose actions had helped bring about this conflict. But first and foremost, all four men were soldiers of the Crown, and none of them would contemplate for an instant shirking his duty.

For a moment, however, a black look passed across Henry Clinton's face. He had been hoping that the leadership of this mission would fall to him. Once the rebels had been defeated—as he was certain they would be—the commander of His Majesty's forces would have another shining mark beside his name. Clinton swallowed his disappointment, though, and said nothing.

Gage turned to Clinton and Burgoyne and continued, "You two stay here and observe. I'm going back to my office. General Howe, the field is yours."

"Thank you, sir," Howe murmured.

"How many troops will you need, and what will be your plan of attack?"

After a moment of thought, Howe replied, "Give me two thousand men, sir. That should be more than an ample number. As for my plan of attack—well, head on is usually best, is it not?"

Gage and Clinton smiled in agreement, while only

Burgoyne looked dubious at hearing the simple plan. "I don't mean to doubt you, General," he said to Howe, "but are you sure that's wise?"

His wide mouth set in a grim line and his dark features taut, Howe waved a hand at Breed's Hill across the river. "Those men over there are farmers and shopkeepers, General. What chance will that rabble have against crack British troops?"

"None," Gage replied before Burgoyne could say anything. "None at all." He shook hands with Howe. "Good luck, General."

"Thank you, sir." Howe smiled faintly. "But luck will have nothing to do with the outcome of this battle."

Gentleman Johnny Burgoyne merely cocked an eyebrow and hoped that Howe was right. If he was not, then heads might roll—including those of four illustrious generals.

Chapter Nine

In the western reaches of the New York colony, in land that belonged to the Iroquois Nation, Murdoch, Quincy, and their companions slowly covered the distance to the point southwest of Lake Ontario where they would turn south. Several days had passed since the fight on the ridge with the Mohawks and the British soldiers, but the hope that they would not run into any more Indian trouble had proved to be a futile one.

The countryside was, as Murdoch put it, "damn near crawling with bad-intentioned Mohawks."

Not a day had passed that the big frontiersman did not spot some Indian sign, usually the tracks of moccasined feet along game trails. Twice they had been forced to hide out when Murdoch saw some warriors running across the distant hills. Both times the travelers had pulled the wagons as far off the path as possible and sat in silence until Murdoch was convinced it was safe to continue. Once, war-painted Mohawks had passed within two hundred yards of the hidden party, and after they were gone, Murdoch had scowled and said, "Lucky thing the wind was blowing toward us. If it had'na been, they'd have smelled us for sure."

A campfire at night was out of the question; the flames would draw too much attention in the darkness. The travelers settled for cold camps and colder suppers—salt pork and corn cakes that were no longer fresh. As they sat beside the wagons on the third evening after the ambush, Cordelia asked quietly, "Would it be better if we turned back?"

Murdoch shrugged his brawny shoulders. "Could be. But from what we've seen, the Mohawks are up in arms all the way t' Schenectady. Granted, an unusually large number of them seem t' be heading west, but we'd still be likely to run into a war party or two, even if we head back east."

Gresham Howard chewed on his pipe, which was unlit because Murdoch had warned him that the smell of burning tobacco carried for long distances. Not moving his teeth from the stem, he said, "Going back isn't the answer. Once we get to the Ohio Valley, things are more settled, aren't they, Murdoch?"

"There are some settlements that are big enough t' be called towns. But there's still plenty of Indians and Indian trouble from time t' time. I figure we'll be safe enough in Pittsburgh, though."

Quincy had been listening intently to the conversation, and he spoke up now and said, "What about Mariel and Dietrich? They've got a stake in this decision, too."

"Aye," said Murdoch, looking over at the girl in the gathering darkness. "What do ye say, lass?"

"Whatever you think is best is all right with Dietrich and me, Murdoch," Mariel replied without hesitation. "You know that."

Murdoch cleared his throat sheepishly. The girl was too conspicuous in the way she felt about him, he thought. She kept her eyes on him whenever he was around, and she ignored Quincy, which Murdoch knew irritated the young man. But he had more important things on his mind than a girl mooning over him and making Quincy jealous.

Howard turned to his daughter and asked, "What about you, Cordelia? How do you feel about going on?"

She took her time before answering but finally said, "If there's going to be danger either way, I'd rather go ahead. I've been looking forward to starting over in the Ohio Valley, and I don't want to give up now."

Murdoch looked at Quincy and said, "We've heard from everyone save ye, lad. What do ye think?"

"Well . . ." Quincy frowned. "I wouldn't mind going back. You know I didn't want to leave Daniel. But I'm anxious to see the frontier for myself, too. What Cordelia said makes sense—if there's trouble either way, let's keep going."

"'Tis settled, then. We'll push on. Tomorrow or the next day, we'll be heading southwest, toward the Allegheny. Ought t' be in Pittsburgh in less than a week."

Before the dew had dried from the grass the next morning, they were on their way again, following the open fields along the southern side of the river, seldom straying more than a few hundred yards from the stream and only when the terrain warranted. Midmorning they approached a thinly wooded hill that rose steeply beside the river, then dropped off sharply to form a rugged bluff. The wagons would have to skirt this hill by cutting through a pass that would put the hill between the stream and them.

Murdoch frowned. Quincy was riding alongside him, and when he saw the expression on the Scotsman's face, he asked, "What's wrong, Murdoch?"

"I dinna like the looks o' that pass up ahead. It would be a good place for an ambush, if the Mohawks were of a mind t' try such a thing again."

"You think so?"

"Aye."

"Then what should we do? Can we go around it some other way?"

"No' without going over some rough country." Murdoch reined in, gestured for Howard and Cordelia to bring the wagons to a halt, then rasped his thumbnail along the line of his jaw as he studied the landscape. Something nagged at him, an instinctive feeling that something was wrong.

A flock of birds suddenly erupted from the trees on the hillside to the south. Murdoch stiffened in the saddle when he saw them. He yelled over his shoulder, "Get those wagons turned around! We have t' get out o' here!"

Howard cursed and hauled in on the reins with his left hand while he used the right to crack the whip over the mules' ears. "Come on, you jugheaded beasts!" he called. "Move!"

Murdoch turned to Quincy and snapped, "Go tie your horse t' the back o' Cordelia's wagon and help her! She'll need a hand with the mules."

Quincy wheeled his mount around, galloped to the wagon, tied his horse to it, and jumped up onto the seat, relieving Cordelia of the reins. He was not sure what was going on, but it was clear that Murdoch expected trouble.

And trouble started moments later when Murdoch saw Indians with drawn bowstrings dart out from behind the trees on the hillside. Arrows cut through the air toward the travelers. The range was too far for the missiles to carry all the way to them, but the attack prevented them from trying to outrun the Mohawks to the pass.

As he jerked his horse around, Murdoch whipped his long rifle from its sheath and waved it at Howard and Quincy. "Head downriver!" he called to them. "Dinna look back!"

Although he was greatly outnumbered, he was going

to hold off the charging Mohawks as long as he could. He had already counted as many as two dozen warriors.

"Murdoch!"

The shout from Quincy made Murdoch pull his horse around again, and as he did, he saw the Mohawks coming toward them from downstream. He grimaced. *Boxed in.* They were trapped as neatly as could be, with the river to the north, rugged hills to the south, and painted warriors coming at them from east and west.

Murdoch knew the Mohawks must have been watching them for quite a while now, just waiting for the right moment to strike.

The Indians who had come up behind them were getting too close, and Murdoch wanted to slow them down a little. He brought the rifle to his shoulder, thumbed back the hammer of the flintlock, and settled the sight on the chest of one of the Indians. He pressed the trigger and the blast of black powder made his horse shy, but the shot went true. The man who had been his target flew backward when the heavy ball struck him in the chest.

"Head for the top of that bluff!" Murdoch called to Quincy and Howard. "'Tis the only place we might be able t' stand them off!"

If they could reach the top of the rise, the Indians would not be able to come at them from the river; the bluff that fell to the water was too steep and rugged for that. And if the wagons could achieve the advantage of height, the defenders might be able to hold off the Mohawk attack—for a while.

Their only hope, Murdoch knew, was to make the price of victory so high that the Indians would not want to pay it.

Quincy and Howard lashed at the mules with the reins and whips and got the wagons turned around again. They careered across the open field next to the river and bolted up the hill. Cordelia, Mariel, and Dietrich had retreated to the rear of Quincy's wagon, and Murdoch silently prayed that the two young women were loading the spare rifles and pistols. They were going to need all the weapons they could get to repel the Mohawks, who screamed wildly as they closed in.

The Indians were within arrow range now, which meant they were in range of Murdoch's pistols, as well. He slid the rifle back into its sheath and tugged out one of the pistols. Using his other hand on the reins to control the plunging horse, he yanked the animal around so that he faced the advancing Mohawks. The two groups of Indians had come together to pin their victims' backs against the river.

An arrow tore past Murdoch's head as he cocked and fired the pistol. One of the Indians spun to the ground, his shoulder shattered by the lead ball. Murdoch tucked the gun back in his belt, then reached across his body to pluck out the second pistol. Hesitating just long enough for his horse to settle down again, he took aim and fired. Another Indian fell to the ground.

His mount was getting too skittish for him to keep up such marksmanship forever, so he kicked the horse into a gallop and followed the wagons up the slope.

They were almost at the top of the rise. Quincy and Howard had been forced to veer around several clumps of trees, but now they had to haul back on the reins to keep the mules from plunging off the edge of the bluff that overhung the river. They swung the vehicles around so they would be parallel to the rim, then brought them to a stop.

Murdoch galloped up as the others leapt from the wagons and ducked behind them. He yanked his rifle free, dropped out of the saddle, and let the horse run behind the wagons where Quincy caught its dangling reins and whipped them around one of the wheels. He untied his mount and led it behind the wagon as well.

Murdoch took off his powder horn and shot pouch and

handed them to Cordelia along with his rifle. Pleased by his confidence in her, she said, "The rifles in the wagon are already loaded."

"Good. 'Tis certain we're going t' be needing them." He reached behind the wagon seat, picked up one of the weapons, handed it to Quincy, and got one for himself. Howard already had a rifle. Murdoch ran to the rear of the wagon. "Make your shots count. We got t' break the back of this attack and break it soon, else the heathens'll overrun us."

Coolly, the three men ignored the arrows falling around them and lined up their shots. Murdoch was at the left end of the barricade formed by the wagons, Quincy was in the center, and Howard had stationed himself at the right end of the line.

Murdoch fired, and the weapons belonging to Quincy and Howard exploded in the same instant; the three reports came so close together they sounded like one. Two of the Mohawks fell with the loose-limbed sprawl that signified death. A third staggered but stayed on his feet, then limped toward them, his thigh creased by one of the shots.

Cordelia could not handle all the reloading by herself. Murdoch looked around and saw Mariel, tightly clutching Dietrich, huddled beside one of the wagon wheels. He leaned over, caught the girl's arm, and tugged her to her feet with surprising gentleness for a man of his size.

"Ye've got t' help reload," he told her. "Stay here with me and let Cordelia go help her father."

Mariel stammered, "I—I c-can't—"

"Aye, ye can," insisted Murdoch. "If ye don't, we may all die, even the bairn. Ye can do it, Mariel, I know ye can!"

Her face pale with fear, she forced herself to nod. "I'll try," she said, her voice so small and hollow Murdoch barely heard her.

By this time, Cordelia had his rifle reloaded, and as

she handed it to him, he took the powder and shot back from her and passed them to Mariel, who told Dietrich to stay where he was. "Go help your father," Murdoch told Cordelia, who got up and ran toward the other wagon, bending low to offer a smaller target as she crossed the open area between the two vehicles.

"Quincy!" Murdoch called. "Ye'll have t' handle your own reloading!"

Quincy rammed a ball down the barrel of his rifle, primed the flintlock, lifted the weapon to his shoulder, and calmly shot down another Mohawk. Disguising his fear with a smile, he glanced at Mariel and saw that she was reloading Murdoch's weapons. The young man felt a surge of pride in her. She had to be terrified, but she was conquering her fright long enough to help them fight off the charge.

But Murdoch knew they were going to need more help than that. There had to be at least forty rampaging Mohawk Indians in the war party. Six men had fallen, either dead or wounded, but that still left nearly three dozen warriors. They would not think about withdrawing until half their number was cut down, and even if every shot hit its target, Murdoch knew that would be impossible to accomplish.

The brave Scotsman had never been one to quit, though, no matter what the odds. He took the brace of loaded pistols that Mariel handed to him and turned to face the Mohawks with an expression of defiance on his craggy face. "Come on, ye red devils!" he roared as he fired both pistols.

Another Mohawk went down, but one of Murdoch's shots had missed, and he let out a curse of frustration. He spun and slapped the pistols into Mariel's waiting hands, then snatched up one of the loaded rifles leaning against the wagon.

The Indians were not charging toward them in the same foolhardy manner as before. Some were using the trees on the hillside for cover, hiding behind the trunks and

peering around only long enough to aim and shoot their arrows at the wagons. That made it more difficult for Quincy
and Howard to pick out a target, and they missed some of
their shots, too. They were in no danger of running out of
ammunition, Murdoch knew; Gresham Howard had
brought along enough powder to supply a small army. But
now that the Mohawks were being smart and using the trees
for cover, the chances of being able to drive them off had
dropped considerably.

Suddenly Murdoch spotted a flash of movement in the
trees and recognized the same white man who had been
goading on the Mohawks in the previous fight. There was
no mistaking the tall, gaunt figure in black. The man ran
right out into the open and shouted to the Indians, "Fear
not, my brothers! The hand of the Lord small protect you,
and the unbelievers shall not smite you down!" He waved
something in his hand, and after a second Murdoch realized
the object was a black book—a Bible.

Murdoch raised the butt of the long rifle until it sat
comfortably against his shoulder and sighted on the chest
of the raving preacher. His finger twitched on the trigger
but stopped short of the pressure needed to fire the rifle.
The man in black was an enemy, but he was still a man of
God. Murdoch had never killed a preacher in his life, and
he was not sure he could start now.

The preacher exhorted the Mohawks to charge, but,
wisely, they held back. One of the Indians, a tall, broad-
shouldered, hulking warrior, leapt from behind the trees
and grabbed the preacher's arm. Murdoch switched his aim
to the Mohawk and squeezed the trigger just as the man
yanked the preacher into the shelter of the woods. One of
the feathers from the Mohawk's scalp lock jerked as the
rifle ball nicked it, but that was the only damage done by
the shot. The burly warrior tossed the preacher deep into
the cover of the trees, then plunged in after him.

"Damn!" Howard called. "I wish one of us could have gotten that big fellow. I'll wager he's the leader."

"Him or that crazy white man," agreed Quincy as he reloaded his rifle. "Is there any way we can make a break out of here, Murdoch? They've really got us pinned down now!"

"Aye, tha' they have," Murdoch said as he took his reloaded pistols from Cordelia. "But there's nowhere we can go, no' with tha' cliff behind—" As he spoke, he glanced over his shoulder at the bluff, then broke off in midsentence when he saw a pair of Indians scrambling over the rim. As they came to their feet, they plucked tomahawks from their belts and lunged at the defenders.

Murdoch spun around smoothly, and both his pistols cracked at the same time. One of the Mohawks staggered and blood welled from a wound in his chest; then he vanished soundlessly over the edge of the bluff. The other managed to stumble forward even though the ball from one of Murdoch's pistols had bored into his temple. Then he pitched forward, dead before he hit the ground.

"Behind us!" shouted Murdoch, grabbing a rifle and handing his pistols to Mariel. More warriors swarmed over the rim. Murdoch had been convinced the bluff was too steep to climb, but clearly he was wrong.

His rifle boomed and the shot knocked another man back into empty space to plunge screaming to the river. Quincy and Howard fired, too, and knocked down a pair of Mohawks. Howls of rage from the opposite direction made Murdoch look around again, and he saw that the Indians who had been protected by the trees were charging now that the attack from the rear was under way.

They were doomed, and Murdoch knew it. But by God, they would go down fighting!

The wagons had been pulled up so close to the edge of the bluff that the Mohawks were climbing on them in a matter of seconds. There was no time to reload, no time to do anything but fight off the attackers by using the rifles as clubs. Murdoch sprang forward to meet the Mohawks and, holding his gun by its barrel, whipped it around and brought down three of them before it was torn out of his hands. Then he fought with his fists and, with a mighty uppercut, knocked one of the Indians off the cliff.

The Mohawks were swarming over the wagons. Cordelia and Mariel screamed when painted warriors grabbed them, and although Quincy fought furiously, he suffered knife slashes as he struggled against them. Next to the other wagon, one of the Indians snatched up a fallen rifle and drove the butt of the weapon against Gresham Howard's head. When he slumped unconscious to the ground, Quincy tried to leap to the man's side, but an Indian's fist slammed into his face, and he collapsed, dazed and no longer able to fight. He waited for a knife to thrust into his vitals or a tomahawk to crush his skull, ending his life—but neither of those things happened.

A tomahawk did rake the side of Murdoch's head, staggering the big frontiersman. He tried to regain his balance as he turned to face the opponent who had struck him from behind. He caught a glimpse of the huge warrior who had pulled the man in black into the trees, but before Murdoch could launch a blow of his own, the tomahawk in the Indian's hand rose and fell again. Bright lights exploded behind Murdoch's eyes, and he felt himself falling. His hands pawed feebly at the Indian, who shoved him away with a contemptuous look in his fierce eyes.

That was the last thing Murdoch saw before darkness claimed him.

He was not unconscious for long, however. Awareness rolled back in on him, bringing with it a pounding pain in his head. He blinked his eyes against the light and tried to sit up, but a foot came down heavily on his chest and pressed him against the ground.

"You stay," a harsh voice growled. "Move again and I kill you."

"Ah, the sinner is awake," said another voice, high and reedy. "Let him sit up, Sagodanega. He cannot harm us now."

The foot did not leave Murdoch's chest immediately. He looked up and saw the hulking warrior standing over him, clearly enjoying the feeling of power. Wearing the same sneer of disdain Murdoch had seen moments earlier he slowly lifted his foot.

When Murdoch sat up, the world spun crazily around him for a few seconds. The hammering in his head got worse, and he thought he was going to be sick. Then his eyes focused on the other captives. Huddled beside the wagons, they were surrounded by Mohawks brandishing knives, tomahawks, and bows at the ready. There were a few British Brown Bess muskets in evidence as well, but Murdoch could not recall any shots being fired by the attacking Indians, and he wondered if perhaps they were low on ammunition.

Cordelia sat on the ground with her father's head pillowed in her lap. Murdoch could see Howard's chest rising and falling and knew the man was still alive. Quincy was sitting nearby, shaking his head groggily. Beside him sat Mariel and Dietrich, looking as though they were afraid to move. Murdoch observed gratefully that no one seemed to be hurt too badly.

He wondered why Howard, Quincy, and he were still alive. It was clear that Cordelia and Mariel had been spared so they could be turned into slaves or sent to one of the lodges where warriors slaked their lusts with captive females. And there was a great likelihood that Dietrich would be adopted by one of the Mohawk families and eventually made a member of the tribe. But there was no reason as far as Murdoch could see why the men had not been killed.

The preacher strode over and glowered at him. He

shook the Bible in his face and shouted, "Thou hast trans-
gressed, sinner, and must pay the price, fearsome though it
may be. The Lord shall strike down all evildoers!" And
then he laughed—a piercing giggle that sent an icy shiver
down Murdoch's spine.

The man is mad, thought Murdoch, *utterly and completely mad.*

None of the Mohawks joined in the man's laughter,
and it ceased abruptly after a moment. He clutched the
Bible to his scrawny chest and went on in a normal voice,
"I am the Reverend Jason Sabbath, and these noble savages
are my flock. Who might you be, stranger?"

"Me name is Murdoch Buchanan," the buckskin-clad
Scotsman stated, deciding to humor the man. "We did'na
come here looking for trouble, Reverend." The honorific
threatened to stick in Murdoch's throat, but he managed to
get it out.

Sabbath knelt in front of Murdoch. He was as gaunt as
he had appeared to be from a distance, with hollow cheeks
and large eyes below a tousled shock of grayish-brown
hair. He said, "Then why did you come here, Brother
Buchanan?"

There was a faint English accent in Sabbath's voice, as
though he had been raised in England but had spent many
years in the colonies. He watched Murdoch with genuine
interest.

"We're just traveling through these parts," Murdoch
answered. "We did'na mean to offend ye or your friends."

Sabbath's mood changed in the flickering of an instant. He bounded to his feet, let out a wolflike howl, and
danced a little jig. When he finished, he pointed the Bible
at Murdoch like a gun and shouted, "The Lord giveth, and
the Lord taketh away! Blessed be the name of the Lord!"

"We kill them now?" asked the big Mohawk called
Sagodanega.

Sabbath shook his head. "Not yet, Chief. Jehovah

wreaks His vengeance in His own time and place. Bind them up so that we may take them with us. We'll take the wagons, too."

Despite his brutal features, there was a gleam of intelligence in the Indian's dark eyes, and Murdoch wondered why he willingly followed the orders of a madman. He had a feeling Sagodanega had his own reasons for cooperating with Reverend Sabbath; the Mohawk chieftain struck Murdoch as a man who did not do anything without its benefiting him in some way.

Turning away from Murdoch, Sabbath went to where Mariel and Dietrich sat with their heads down and their terrified gazes fixed on the ground. The preacher extended a bony hand and commanded, "Give me the boy."

Mariel tightened her arms around her brother. "No!" she cried. "Leave us alone!"

A hideous grin stretched across Sabbath's face. "I must do the Lord's work," he declared in a ringing voice. "Give me the boy, I say!"

Quincy started to his feet. "Leave them alone!" he exclaimed.

Murdoch said urgently, "Quincy, no!"

It was too late. One of the Mohawks stranding nearby lashed out with his tomahawk and slammed it into Quincy's left shoulder. Only the fact that the Indian had used the flat of the stone head, rather than the cutting edge, saved Quincy from a mortal wound. As it was, he let out a gasp of pain, then slumped to his knees and clutched at his shoulder. His left arm hung limp and useless at his side, momentarily deadened by the blow.

Sabbath leveled a finger at Quincy and proclaimed, "If you interfere with the holy endeavors once more, you shall be struck dead!" He followed that with another giggle.

Indians would not harm an insane person, Murdoch knew, for they considered such individuals to be touched by the spirits. That was probably part of the explanation for

Sabbath's presence among these Mohawks. And in his more lucid moments, perhaps he possessed a cunning that Sagodanega and the Mohawks were putting to good use.

Sabbath turned to Mariel and Dietrich, impatient to have his way. He leaned over, took hold of Dietrich's arm, and pulled the toddler out of Mariel's grasp. She had to let go of the little boy or risk hurting him. Tears of anger, frustration, and fear rolled down her cheeks as she watched Sabbath pick up the boy.

"Don't worry, lad," Sabbath said to Dietrich, who was sobbing and squirming in his arms. "We'll teach you to be a good Christian. You'll forget all about your time with these heathens."

Dietrich howled, "Let me go!"

Sabbath tightened his grip on the boy. "Tie the others and bring them along, as I told you," he snapped at the Indians, then strode away, carrying Dietrich.

Under the supervision of Sagodanega, the Mohawks found a rope in one of the wagons, cut it into smaller lengths, and used it to tie Murdoch's and Quincy's hands. Gresham Howard had still not regained consciousness, but they rolled him over onto his stomach, jerked his arms behind his back, and bound his wrists. Then several of the Indians picked him up and tossed him into the back of the lead wagon. Cordelia was tied up as well, along with Mariel, and Murdoch and Quincy had no choice but to look on in helpless anger as the warriors took advantage of the opportunity to run their hands over Cordelia's womanly curves and Mariel's budding figure. Both young women were lifted into the lead wagon with Howard.

Murdoch and Quincy were forced to climb awkwardly into the second wagon, and once they were inside, their ankles were lashed together. Cramped and uncomfortable, they lay on the floorboards. Under the circumstances, Murdoch was grateful that the Mohawks had used rope to tie them up, rather than strips of rawhide. It might be possible to work some play into the rope, whereas rawhide bonds would have stubbornly resisted such efforts.

He could hear Mariel crying in the other wagon and wondered where Sabbath had taken Dietrich. Then the wagons lurched into motion and it was impossible to hear much of anything over the creaking of the wheels. There was no one on the driver's bench, so Murdoch knew the Mohawks must be leading the mules by their harness. He could tell they were heading west.

Heading west—but into what? How long would Sabbath and the Mohawks let them live? Murdoch had no idea, but for now they were still alive, and survival was all that mattered.

Chapter Ten

By midmorning the heat on Breed's Hill was so fierce, Daniel despaired of ever being cool again. But for the time being, the bombardment from the British warships and gun emplacements inside Boston had tapered off to an occasional blast.

That was probably because the British had finally realized how little good they were doing with their cannon. The earthen breastwork in front of the patriot redoubt was a thing of crude beauty, so thick and firmly packed that not even a direct hit from a cannonball could penetrate it. Along with Thad and the rest of his friends and fellow militiamen, Daniel lay just beneath the crest of the man-made barrier, the barrel of his rifle poking over the top. From here he was able to view the preparations the colonists had made during the long night and morning.

The redoubt atop Breed's Hill was complete, and another defensive line had been established off to its left, toward the Mystic River, which ran along the northern side of the peninsula. Men also crouched behind a stone wall topped by two wooden rails that ran all the way down to the shore of the Mystic. Reinforcements had come up during the morning, hurrying across Charlestown Neck from Cambridge. They numbered around six hundred, so now there were sixteen hundred men dug in on Breed's Hill and its environs.

Not a great number, considering the British had at least six thousand men in Boston, Daniel thought. But he believed that when the British came, he and his fellow patriots would be able to give a good account of themselves.

"Daniel!"

Daniel looked around and saw Dr. Joseph Warren striding through the crowd of soldiers in the redoubt. Warren was dressed resplendently in civilian clothes. Few of the men around him wore uniforms, but he stood out because of the quality of his garb rather than its lack of military styling. He grinned boyishly and extended a hand to Daniel when the young man slid down from the parapet.

"Hello, Doctor," said Daniel, shaking Warren's hand. He wondered how the physician managed to look so fresh and eager; after all, Warren had been up most of the night like the rest of them.

"Not only doctor any longer," Warren said proudly. "You're looking at Major General Warren, my boy. Newly appointed, I must add."

Daniel was not sure what to say, so he settled for, "Congratulations, Doctor—I mean, General."

Warren waved a hand. "We're old comrades, Daniel, no need to stand on formality. How are you and your mates doing?"

"All right, I suppose. We all got a bit nervous during that bombardment."

"Everyone did, except perhaps Colonel Prescott. The man has an incredible amount of nerve. I saw him pacing back and forth atop the breastworks during the height of the cannonading."

Daniel had seen the same thing, but he had thought Prescott had taken leave of his senses. Perhaps Warren was right; the colonel had merely been trying to set a good example for his men.

Another newcomer entered the fortification, and his presence caused a stir among the soldiers. Daniel and Warren looked over to see a tall, spare, white-haired officer striding among the men, shaking hands with them and offering words of encouragement. In a low voice, Warren said, "That's General Seth Pomeroy. He fought the French and Indians along with Prescott and Old Put. We have a distinguished group of commanders here today, Daniel."

"Including yourself, sir."

Warren shook his head at the compliment. "I'll never be in the same military firmament as they. But I'll do my best, as I'm sure everyone else will, too." He looked around and quietly continued, "I know these men, Daniel, perhaps not individually, but I know what stuff they're made of. They may not look like much, some of them, but inside they're titans! They won't run. They won't desert the field of honor so long as breath remains in their bodies!"

Daniel thought Warren was overestimating the fortitude of most of the militiamen. Young though he was, he had already learned that wars are not won by heroes, but rather by badly frightened men doing their jobs despite their fear. But he had to admit that Warren's words were stirring, and there was a place for that as well.

A great booming noise rolled across the Charles, and Daniel tensed. "The bombardment's started again!" he exclaimed.

"Aye!" agreed Warren, clapping Daniel on the shoulder. "And when they think they've pounded us enough, then their regulars will come at us."

Daniel knew Warren was right. The standoff might

continue for a while longer, but the end had to be in sight. Before many more hours passed, men would be fighting and dying on Breed's Hill.

Roxanne and Lemuel heard the noise before they reached the outskirts of Cambridge. It sounded as though every church bell in town was ringing. But not even the pealing of the bells could completely drown out the low, continuous rumble that sounded like distant thunder—though there was hardly a cloud in the sky.

Reining in her horse, Roxanne asked anxiously, "Lemuel, what's that sound?"

"I think you probably know as well as I do, Roxanne. It's cannon fire."

Her heart was pounding, and if she had not known better, she would have said it was beating in time with the distant bombardment. She had no way of knowing if Daniel was up there somewhere, facing the British guns; but whether he was or not, there were hundreds or thousands of other patriots risking their lives.

"Come on," she said to Lemuel as she heeled her horse into a trot. "We'd better hurry."

The farmer rode alongside her as they entered Cambridge. The streets were almost deserted, but after they had ridden for several blocks, Lemuel hailed an elderly man and asked, "Where can we find the army headquarters?"

"Keep goin'," the man told them. "Ye might find somebody at Harvard Yard, if they haven't all gone down to the sea already. There's goin' to be a battle yonder on Breed's Hill."

"The militia's already gone over there?"

"The Provincial Army, they call themselves now," the old-timer reminded Lemuel. "Ayuh, that's where most of 'em have gone."

"Thanks." Lemuel spurred ahead, and Roxanne followed close behind. The old man watched them and with a gnarled hand scratched at a tuft of white hair on his head and wondered why a pretty, young redheaded girl was racing toward a battle.

At Harvard Yard, they found a small caravan forming up. In the center of the group were a pair of six-pound cannon mounted on wheels. Lemuel spotted someone he recognized from the battle at Concord. They had been members of the same militia company on that bloody April morning.

"Arch!" called Lemuel. "What's happening?"

The harried militiaman shook hands quickly and said, "Good to see you, Lem! We're taking these cannon to Breed's Hill so our boys can shoot back at the damned lobsterbacks! Come along and give us a hand, why don't you?"

"That's what I'm here for," Lemuel replied solemnly. Then he turned and said, "You'd best find a safe place to wait out this battle, Roxanne. You'll be all right here in Cambridge. There's never been a British cannon that could reach the four miles from here to Boston!"

She knew he was concerned for her safety, but her fiery nature, held in submission for much too long, made her respond sharply, "I didn't ride all this way to cower in a hole like a rabbit, Lemuel."

With that, she wheeled her horse around and kicked it into a gallop toward Charlestown Neck.

She saw many soldiers heading in the same direction, and most of them gave her puzzled stares as she galloped past them, her long red hair streaming out behind her. Something called her on, some unfathomable instinct that insisted she had to be present for this battle, or at least as close as she could reasonably come.

She was not the only one who hoped to witness the impending conflict. Nearly all the citizens of Cambridge were streaming toward Charlestown Neck, some on foot, others on horseback or in carriages. There was something in the air, almost a festive mood. People were laughing and excited as they hurried to find a good spot to watch the battle.

Her belly was tight with dread. She had seen the results of war firsthand and knew it was not to be taken lightly, as these people were behaving. War was a grim, bloody business, not something to be celebrated.

But they would learn. Roxanne feared they would learn all too well before this very day was over.

On Copp's Hill, across the Charles River in Boston, Henry Clinton and John Burgoyne watched the summit of Breed's Hill through spyglasses. "Howe's taking his bloody time about it, isn't he?" grumbled Clinton without lowering his glass.

"The boats should soon be leaving from the Long Wharf and the north battery," Burgoyne replied. "But it's going to take a while to ferry all those men across the Charles."

General Howe had settled on the Fifth, Thirty-eighth, Forty-third, and Fifty-second Regiments of His Majesty's Light Infantry and Grenadiers. At this moment, the soldiers were boarding forty transport boats that would carry them across the Charles to the Charlestown Peninsula.

Suddenly Burgoyne exclaimed, "My God, look at that!"

"What is it?" Clinton asked sharply.

"See that smoke rising from Breed's Hill? I think *they're* shooting at *us*!"

Indeed, smoke was floating in the air above the patriot redoubt, and though it was impossible to hear the sound of the colonists' cannon due to the constant roar of the British weapons, both generals heard the unmistakable whistling of cannonballs overhead. There was a crash behind their position, and Burgoyne spun around and saw a commotion in one of the streets beyond Copp's Hill.

"They overshot us!" he cried.

Clinton looked nervous. "Perhaps we should consider withdrawing and setting up another observation post elsewhere," he suggested.

"Nonsense!" Burgoyne said with a brash laugh. "We've got the best seat in the house right here, General, and I intend to make the most of it." He knew Clinton was being prudent rather than frightened, but he felt a prickling of contempt for his fellow officer.

"All right," grumbled Clinton, "but don't blame me when a cannonball takes your head off, General!"

"Wouldn't think of it," Burgoyne replied lightly.

No more shots came their way, however, and the brief exchange was forgotten. The boats carrying the troops came into view; the oars flashed as the vessels sliced through the waters of the Charles toward Breed's Hill.

"*Now* we'll see something," Clinton said. "Those upstart rebels are going to wish they'd never started this war!"

"Here they come!" Thad Garner peered over the parapet and said in a shaky voice, "My God, how many of them are there?"

Daniel tried to count the ships that were crossing the Charles and gave up after twenty. There were at least twice that number. "They'll probably bring two thousand men, perhaps more. But we're situated well, Thad. No matter how many men they have, it's not going to be easy for them to take this hill."

The cannonading was still going on, and Thad's voice was barely audible over the pounding roar as he said slowly, "Daniel, I'm scared. I didn't know it would be like this."

"I'm scared, too," said Daniel, "as scared as I've ever been."

"You?" Thad sounded dubious.

"It's all I can do not to run," Daniel confessed. He was

stretching the truth, but only a bit. His nerves had been pulled taut by the long night of hard work and the morning-long bombardment, all the while waiting for the British to attack. At this moment, he would have gladly seized the opportunity to be somewhere—anywhere!—else.

"Well, we can't run," Thad mused. "We'd be letting all the others down."

Daniel glanced along the line of men. He saw George Cummings, Ben Hobbs, and Fred Dary nearby. Captain Webster was there, too, and farther away he spotted Colonel Prescott, Dr. Warren, and General Pomeroy. General Putnam was somewhere around, even though Daniel could not see him at the moment. And surrounding them were the members of the Provincial Army, men who had come here for one reason and one reason alone: to fight for freedom. There would be no running away on this hot, late spring afternoon.

Below, the British boats were landing.

"Hold your fire!" Colonel Prescott called emphatically. "No one shoots until the order is given!"

Daniel understood the logic of the command. They had a limited amount of ammunition, and wild firing before the British came within easy range would waste valuable powder and shot.

He wondered what had happened to the two cannon. The guns had sent a few rounds toward Boston, then had been withdrawn and sent toward the left flank. Daniel had no idea why. If those cannon had been here at the summit, they could have been fired into the crowd of redcoats who were swarming off the transport boats.

The British were taking their time about unloading, and as the regiments formed up into ranks on the shore, the boats turned around and headed back across the Charles.

Daniel expected the troops to advance immediately, but they just stood at attention, sweating profusely in their heavy red uniform coats. From their tall hats and the insignia on their uniforms, he was able to identify soldiers of the Light Infantry and Grenadiers. *His Majesty's finest,* Daniel thought bitterly. *Wouldn't German George be proud of them if he could see them right now, these young men he had sent to kill—and die—in his name?*

"Why don't they come *on*?" Thad asked hoarsely. "Why don't they get it over with?"

Daniel squeezed his friend's shoulder. "Hang on," he said quietly. "Just hang on, Thad."

Suddenly a pair of loud, resonating reports sounded from the left end of the entrenchment that ran down to the Mystic River. Daniel saw that the two cannon that had been firing earlier at Boston had been redeployed there. The cannonballs flew over the British troops on the beach and splashed into the Charles, throwing up great spouts of water. While none of the redcoats were hurt, they began to mill about, unnerved by the cannon fire.

Daniel gasped as he looked at the patriot soldiers manning the cannon. He had not gotten a good look at them earlier, but now he thought he recognized one of them as Lemuel Parsons. Daniel raised himself higher, trying for a better view, but at that distance, it was difficult to be sure of anything, especially with so much smoke in the air.

If that was Lem, he might know something about Roxanne, Daniel thought. Several times during the two weeks he had been in Cambridge, he had thought about riding to the Parsons farm near Concord, but something had always prevented him from going. Now it was too late. Like all the men, he had to hold his position.

Still, the sight of the man had Daniel's heart racing faster than the thought of the impending battle. When all this was over, he was going to find Lemuel, Daniel vowed, and if that was unsuccessful, he was going to Concord, the Provincial Army be damned!

The gunners' aim was abysmal, and although none of the rounds fired from their cannon hit anything but the river, the explosions kept the British troops jumpy. That was worth something in itself, Daniel supposed as he watched the transport boats return to the same spot where they had unloaded their human cargo earlier. This time, along with more soldiers jumping from the boats and splashing ashore, there were several light field pieces being unloaded. These short-range cannon would offer support for the waves of British troops that would soon be marching up the hill.

"They're coming," Thad said, an edge of hysteria in his voice. "They're coming."

The redcoats had formed into two long lines that stretched from the mouth of the Mystic River almost to Charlestown, which was all but deserted. Most of the citizens, fearful of being caught in a bombardment, had fled days earlier, and nearly all who had stayed behind had taken advantage of the morning's respite to gather a few belongings and race across Charlestown Neck to the mainland.

From the parapet, Colonel Prescott surveyed the British lines, then turned and called urgently, "Colonel Robinson! Major Wood!" The officers hurried up to Prescott, who went on, "Each of you take a detachment with all speed to Charlestown. The British must not be allowed to sweep around us on that side! Harry them all you can and, for God's sake, don't let them proceed unimpeded!"

"Yes, sir!" the junior officers cried in unison, then raced off to gather their men and follow Prescott's commands.

Daniel's position was close enough for him to have heard every word of the exchange, and as he studied the field of battle, he saw why Prescott was worried. The patriots' left, if not as well protected as the redoubt atop the hill, was at least fairly secure behind the short trench and the stone fences. The right side was a different story. Although the British had been forced to stretch their own lines rather thin in order to encompass as much territory as they had, it was a daring maneuver that could quickly show results if a regiment or two managed to get behind Breed's Hill. General Putnam had some men in reserve on Bunker Hill but too few to protect the forces on Breed's Hill from an attack from the rear. And the men on Breed's Hill could not swing around to catch any flanking troops in a cross fire without exposing themselves to the frontal attack that would be going on at the same time.

No, Daniel realized, the patriots who were now running toward Charlestown to try to head off the British on that side had to stop the redcoats, or the men on Breed's Hill were doomed.

British fifes and drums began to play, and the sound carried eerily up the hill, filling in the abrupt silence that fell when the bombardment ceased. Banners were unfurled and fluttered in the occasional breeze that swept the peninsula. The redcoats, carrying packs that weighed one hundred twenty-five pounds and included a blanket and enough food for three days, as well as their weapon that weighed another fifteen pounds, lowered their muskets and, with fixed bayonets held proudly in front of them, trudged steadily up Breed's Hill.

Thad brought his musket to his shoulder. The barrel quivered as he aimed at the oncoming sea of red. The young militiaman was about to fire when Daniel's hand closed on his arm. "Wait!" Daniel whispered. "The order hasn't been given yet!"

As if to echo Daniel's warning, General Israel Putnam galloped up and swung down from his saddle with the agility and grace of a much younger man. He strode to the top of the earthen parapet and joined Colonel Prescott. As Old Put walked among the men, he called in a loud voice, "Hold steady, lads! Don't fire until you can see the very whites of their eyes!"

Palms sweating on the stocks of their weapons, Daniel and the patriot soldiers obeyed the command.

Time seemed to stretch out. Seconds became minutes, minutes hours. Steadily, inexorably, the British closed the distance between them. At first it was nearly five hundred yards, then four hundred, three hundred, two hundred . . .

Suddenly they were in front of Daniel, mere rods away, so close he could indeed see their eyes. Thus far there had been no shooting other than the far-off rattle of sniper fire from the companies dispatched to Charlestown. Daniel felt as though he couldn't breathe as he stared at the redcoats from behind the barrel of his rifle. Then a great muffling silence settled over him, as if cotton had been stuffed in his ears.

But through the stillness he heard one of the officers—he was never sure which one—shout stridently, *"Fire!"*

A huge, ragged volley rang out along the line as the patriots pressed the triggers of their weapons. Daniel heard the blast of his rifle, felt it kick back against his shoulder. Smoke instantly filled the air in front of him, issuing not only from the muzzle of his own gun but also those of hundreds of other defenders. The British, in their bright red coats and shiny white breeches that made them perfect targets, had walked right up to the patriots' guns.

And now, as the breeze shredded the gun smoke and carried some of it away, the men who wielded those guns saw what damage they had done.

The carnage was unimaginable. British soldiers lay everywhere, their lives smashed away by the heavy lead balls of the colonists' rifles and muskets. The wounded men writhed on the grassy slope and shrieked out their agony, while a British general, a tall man with a dark complexion, stood dumbfounded in what had been the front rank of the advancing army. Some bizarre providence had spared him. He turned slowly, looking over his shoulder at his slaughtered men, and the color drained from his face like water from an urn.

For a long moment, the Americans seemed as stunned by what had happened as the British who had survived the deadly volley. But the patriots regained their wits before the redcoats, and a second wave replaced the first. Daniel was one of hundreds who slid down from the top of the parapet to reload his rifle while another militiaman scrambled up to take a turn. Another volley shattered the afternoon air, and more of the British went down like wheat before a scythe. The fifes and drums were no longer playing, but a cheer from the Americans took their place.

Daniel glanced at Thad. The young farmer seemed calm now, although he was still pale. He finished reloading his musket, gave Daniel a grin, and said, "Let's get back up there!"

Daniel followed him up the breastworks. When they reached the top, they saw that the British were in full retreat, pulling back as fast as they could and throwing only a few stray shots toward the patriot forces. Daniel and Thad fired into the chaos, but in the confusion there was no way of knowing if their shots hit anything.

Some of the men tried to leap out of the redoubt and pursue the British, but the officers stopped them. Daniel understood that to go out into the open would have meant giving up the advantage they held, and he was ready to stop Thad if the younger man got caught up in the frenzy. But Thad stayed where he was, reloading after his second shot.

The firing was heavier toward Charlestown now, as British troops engaged the men who waited on the edge of town. Someone in Boston must have noticed what was going on there, because incendiary shells suddenly came screaming across the Charles to land among the deserted buildings and scatter their fiery payload. Within minutes, many of the structures in Charlestown were ablaze, sending a thick, black column of smoke into the sky. Luckily, the wind carried it away from the men on Breed's Hill.

Daniel watched as the British officers screamed commands and threatened their men with sabers or pistols to prevent the British retreat from becoming a full-fledged rout. When the patriots saw what was going on, they waved their hats in the air and called out insults to the redcoats. The scent of victory was in the air, and it was a heady perfume for the Americans.

But Daniel knew it would not be that easy. The British troops were too well trained, too disciplined to break and run and keep running, and he was not surprised when, fifteen minutes later, the redcoats rallied to mount another advance, this time with General Howe in the forefront.

If they had learned any lessons from their first encounter with the patriots, they showed few signs of it. Their pace was still slow and deliberate, and they marched in the open, not even attempting to use the meager cover on the hillside. This time, however, they did open fire sooner, and some of the men defending the redoubt, the trench, and the stone fences were hit.

Daniel's nose stung from the acrid powder smoke that filled the air, and his ears rang from the deafening explosions that surrounded him. He loaded, fired, reloaded, and fired, until he was carrying out the movements with little conscious thought. He had to blink several times to bring himself to the full realization that the British were retreating again.

Twice the crack troops of His Royal Highness King George III had come up the hill. Twice they had been sent packing by a mere rabble of farmers and shopkeepers.

The British batteries opened fire and were joined by a salvo from the gun emplacements on the warships that stood offshore. Daniel grabbed Thad's arm and slid to the bottom of the fortification for cover.

"Daniel!" Thad cried, shaking his powder horn. "I'm about out of powder and shot."

As he looked at the other men, Daniel realized the same was true of them. He was running low on ammunition as well. They all were. *This might be our undoing,* he thought. They had not had a tremendous amount of powder and shot to begin with, and they had expended a great deal in repelling the first two British attacks. A third British surge would use up the rest of the patriots' ammunition.

"There's nothing we can do now but keep fighting," Daniel told Thad. "The redcoats won't be in any mood to let us surrender, not after the losses we've hit them with."

Thad passed a shaky hand over his face. "You're right," he said. A fatalistic tone entered his voice. "Let the bastards come! They'll never forget the price they'll have to pay for this hill!"

Daniel extended a hand and summoned up a grin. "It's been a pleasure to fight beside you, Thad Garner," he said, meaning every word of it.

Thad hesitated only an instant, then took Daniel's hand and shook it firmly. "We're going to win this war," he said.

"No doubt about it," agreed Daniel.

Then, as the bombardment ceased, they turned and scrambled to the top of the parapet to meet the third British charge. This time, however, the volley that rang out from the hill's defenders was ragged, and the redcoats, who had finally been ordered to drop their heavy packs, must have sensed the dwindling opposition. Instead of the slow, stately advance of the first two attacks, they broke into a run, and a few men howled out their anger as they charged the redoubt. This time the curtain of lead thrown up by the patriots had too many holes in it, and the British poured through.

Daniel managed to get two shots off before the wave of redcoats crested the parapet and rolled over the patriots.

One of the Light Infantrymen crashed into him and sent him rolling down the slope. The redoubt had been breached on three sides, and a bloody melee filled the long excavation. This was hand-to-hand fighting at its most brutal, with pistols, bayonets, swords, knives, and fists. Daniel had no time to reload, so he wrapped his fingers around the hot barrel of the gun and used it as a club.

This was madness, sheer madness, and Daniel gave himself over to it willingly. He knew he was going to die, but before he went down, he would take as many redcoats as he could with him. He slammed the butt of his rifle into the center of a British soldier's face and felt the man's bones crack under the blow. A bayonet cut at his arm and another slashed his thigh, but he barely felt the wounds, neither of which was deep. He swung the rifle again, caving in the skull of another redcoat. A warm sticky wetness coated his left cheek, but he had no idea if the blood was his or someone else's.

Whirling around, he laid low several more redcoats, until the stock of his rifle shattered. He dropped it, snatched a pistol from his belt, and fired at point-blank range into the face of a trooper who lunged toward him. Daniel dodged the falling body, flung the empty pistol at another redcoat, and jerked his knife from his belt.

Somehow, through the welter of screams and shots, he heard one particular cry that cut into his soul like a knife. He spun around to see Thad Garner slumped forward over a British bayonet that had been thrust through his belly. Thad's mouth opened and blood gushed from it as he pawed feebly at the musket. The redcoat ripped the bayonet free and let Thad fall.

That was the last thing the soldier ever did, because in the next second, Daniel Reed's knife slashed across his throat. Daniel let out a hoarse cry as he swung the blade with such force that steel grated on bone with an impact that shivered up Daniel's arm.

Thad lay on the ground, coughing up blood, and Daniel went to one knee beside him. "Thad!" he cried, grasping the young militiaman's shoulders to turn him over. Thad's shirt was sodden with blood.

"Daniel—" Thad said, and again, Daniel heard him somehow over the tumult. "I never . . . I don't want . . . Oh, God! It hurts!" Life faded from the eyes that stared up at Daniel, and he thought Thad was gone, but Thad whispered, "Don't give up."

"I won't," Daniel promised. "I never will."

Thad could not hear him, and Daniel knew it. His friend was dead.

Alerted by his instincts, Daniel tightened his grasp on his knife and rolled out of the way in time to avoid an attacking redcoat's sword, and then, with a swift uppercut, he stabbed the soldier in the groin. The man let out a high, thin scream and collapsed, dropping his saber on ground that had become muddy with blood. Daniel snatched it up and bounded to his feet.

A few yards away, he saw Dr. Joseph Warren, the newly appointed major general. Warren's once-resplendent clothes were disheveled and streaked with blood, and there was a fierce look on his handsome face as he lashed out and thrust his sword at the British soldiers who surrounded him. Suddenly a pistol cracked, and Warren staggered. A red-rimmed black hole appeared in his temple, and he crumpled to the ground, his life snuffed out by a redcoat's shot.

"Retreat! Retreat!"

The shouted order came from Colonel Prescott, and his men responded immediately. Those who were able flung themselves over the edges of the redoubt and ran for their lives toward Charlestown Neck.

If anything, the retreat was more chaotic than the battle had been. Using the British saber he had picked up, Daniel hacked and slashed a path through the crush of redcoats until he found himself beside Prescott, one of the last men to leave the redoubt. Fighting shoulder to shoulder, they made their way out of the excavation. Some of the Americans who had already fled but who still had powder and shot turned to provide a covering fire for the rest of the retreating patriots, and its accuracy drove the redcoats back into the fortification they had just overrun.

Daniel glanced to the north as he and the other survivors ran toward Bunker Hill. The stone fences had not been breached, but the men who had been defending them were falling back in order to avoid being trapped by the enemy troops who had taken the redoubt. The devastated patriot force was converging on Bunker Hill, but the men there were also in retreat.

Daniel wiped blood out of his eyes and off his face and realized it was not his. His own wounds were the scratches on his arm and thigh, and neither slowed him down.

British troops harried the Americans and chased them from behind every fence and wall as the retreat continued from Bunker Hill. While only thirty men were killed in the redoubt, many more casualties were sustained in the retreat.

Daniel's powder horn still held powder and there were shot in his shot pouch, so he picked up a fallen musket, checked the barrel for fouling, then loaded the weapon and fired toward the onrushing redcoats.

Nearby, General Putnam still sat astride his horse, supervising the retreat. Old Put's face was livid with fury and disappointment. He looked at Daniel and called out, "Give me a hand here, son!"

Daniel hurried over to him, and Putnam dismounted.

The general strode up to a deserted field piece and slapped its barrel. "Ever loaded one of these?" he asked Daniel, who shook his head. Grinning savagely, Putnam went on, "Well, you're about to learn!"

Following Putnam's instructions, Daniel helped the elderly general load the cannon, and then they turned it until its barrel pointed at the British. "Stand clear!" Putnam called, then yanked the firing lanyard.

The cannon boomed, and Putnam shook his fist at the British. "Have a last taste of that, you devils!" Then he turned to Daniel and shouted, "Let's get out of here."

Daniel was more than willing.

The running battle lasted all the way to Charlestown Neck, and although the firing tapered off, it did not cease until all the patriots had been driven off the peninsula. The British stopped there to organize a defense on Bunker Hill, but they could have pursued the fleeing Americans all the way to Cambridge. As it was, the defeated patriot forces left behind the burning buildings of Charlestown and the peninsula—firmly in British hands. It was only later that the defeat came to be regarded as a victory. Over a thousand British troops had died, while fewer than four hundred and fifty militiamen had been killed. The British had won. They had captured Breed's Hill and Bunker Hill—but only at a staggering cost.

Daniel Reed knew none of that. All he knew was that he had not slept for over thirty-six hours, had not eaten in over twenty-four, and had had nothing to drink except a little rum. He remembered crossing Charlestown Neck with the British in hot pursuit, but of the stumbling, staggering journey back to Cambridge he recalled little.

He was alive, he knew that. But Thad Garner was dead. Daniel had no idea what had happened to George and Ben and Fred. They had probably been killed, too, he thought, just like Dr. Warren. It was hard to believe the dashing young physician was gone.

Daniel looked around and realized he was in Cambridge at a makeshift hospital where the wounded were being treated in the street. He was not hurt badly enough to take medical attention away from someone else, but he was tired. Lord, he was tired! Slowly he trudged over to a vacant building with a recessed doorway. His legs felt like lead, and it required all his strength to plant one foot in front of the other. As he came up to the building, he caught a glimpse of himself in the grimy front window: He looked like a scarecrow, dressed in bloody, tattered clothes, his face dark with soot, dirt, dried blood, and beard stubble. His cheeks were gaunt, and his eyes were large and haunted. He looked like a ghost himself, he thought, a ragged, filthy ghost.

Exhausted, he slumped to the ground in the doorway. He had to rest for a few minutes, and he leaned back against the wall, closed his eyes, and told himself sternly that he would not fall asleep. After what he had seen today, he never wanted to sleep again. If he did, he knew his slumber would be filled with the most hellish nightmares a man could have.

But there was no holding back sleep. A black, stygian darkness cradled him, and Daniel went willingly into its embrace.

Chapter Eleven

By the time the wagons came to a stop, it was dusk, and Murdoch was unsure if he would ever walk again. He had not been able to feel his feet for the past hour; the bonds around his ankles were pulled tight, as were those of the other captives.

Unseen inside the wagon, he had been straining against the ropes that tied his hands, and as he had hoped, they were looser now.

At this rate, he thought grimly, *I'll probably free meself in another two or three days.* It was time he didn't have.

Glad that he was not being bounced around any longer, Quincy asked, "What do you think they're going to do with us now, Murdoch?"

"I dinna ken, lad. But remember—if all they wanted t' do was kill us, they could've done it before now."

Murdoch tried to make his words sound reassuring, but in truth he took little comfort from them. The big Mohawk,

156

Sagodanega, seemed to do whatever the Reverend Jason Sabbath told him to, and it was impossible to predict what a madman like Sabbath would do next. He might stand over them and read Bible verses while the Mohawks tortured them to death.

Sabbath's cracked voice came from outside. "Get them out of the wagons," he called. "We'll camp here."

Some of the Mohawk warriors climbed into the wagons, grabbed hold of Murdoch and Quincy, and with some grunting and groaning on the part of the braves who had to heft Murdoch's massive form, carried them out and dropped them unceremoniously on the ground.

Awkwardly Murdoch worked himself into a sitting position with his back propped against one of the wagon wheels. Quincy did the same, then looked around. "Mr. Howard!" he exclaimed when he saw Gresham Howard sitting by the other wagon with Cordelia and Mariel beside him.

"Be ye all right?" Murdoch asked Howard.

"It feels like all the imps of hell are jumping up and down in my head," he replied. "But I can see straight and clear, so there's no permanent damage done. This old skull of mine is pretty thick."

Echoing Quincy's question, Cordelia asked worriedly, "Murdoch, do you know what they're going to do to us?"

"I have no idea, lass," he answered honestly. "It dinna look like they plan t' do anything right now, though."

Sabbath had chosen a small valley between two wooded hills as a stopping place, and Murdoch studied the scene around them. The Mohawks seemed oblivious to anything but setting up camp for the night. Some of the warriors were building a campfire, while others drifted off into the woods, probably after the small game that came out at this time of the evening: Unwary rabbits would venture out of their burrows to get a drink and graze on some sweet grass as the day's light faded away and would wind up roasting on spits over the campfire.

The afterglow in the sky from the setting sun and the stars that were visible where the sky was turning blue-black allowed Murdoch to determine that they had veered south during the journey. The river was probably several miles away by now. If they kept going in the same direction, they would be right in the middle of wild country inhabited only by the Mohawks and other members of the Iroquois Confederation. He had planned to skirt that territory to the north and west.

Well, it dinna work out tha' way, now did it? Murdoch thought. *So what in the name of me sainted mother are we going to do now?*

That was up to the mad Reverend Sabbath.

The man in black came over to the captives and smiled beatifically down at them. "Are you all comfortable?" he asked.

Gresham Howard growled, "What do you think, you damn-blasted—"

"Tha' be enough," Murdoch cut in sharply as he saw the expression change on Sabbath's face. The truth was the last thing the lunatic reverend was interested in. Murdoch went on hurriedly, "We're fine, but we'd feel better if ye could untie some o' these ropes. They're a wee bit confining."

Sabbath looked sad and shook his head. "Alas, I cannot do that, brother. I fear Chief Sagodanega would be quite upset with me if I released the five of you." His voice went down to an intimate whisper as he continued, "I think the chief has something special in mind for you."

A shiver went down Murdoch's spine as he thought about what that something special might be.

But before he could say anything else, Mariel cried raggedly, "Where's Dietrich? What have you done with my brother?"

"The little boy is fine," Sabbath assured her. "You have no cause to worry about him. On the contrary, you should be happy that he will be raised as a good Christian, rather than a heathen."

"But we're not heathens," said Mariel, her voice thick with anguish. "We're Lutherans!"

Sabbath waved away that distinction. "The child is better off," he said curtly. "He is with some of my red brothers at the moment, being taught the ways of the woodland."

"You—you let those savages take him off into the forest?" Mariel screamed.

Sabbath's gaunt face tightened with anger. "I'll not stand here and bandy words with you, you little Dutch slut! Be silent!"

Murdoch sighed. Sabbath was off again, and there was no point in trying to talk sensibly to him until he calmed down.

Mariel's lips quivered in anger and fear, but she did not say anything else. Sabbath glowered self-righteously at her for a long moment, then turned and stalked off. Finally, Mariel managed to say to the others, "I—I'm sorry. I didn't mean to make him angry."

"Dinna worry about it, lass," Murdoch told her. "Tha' man listens t' the skirling of his own bagpipes, and what we say t' him matters naught."

"He's crazy," muttered Quincy.

"Aye, lad. Tha' be what I said."

The Mohawks returned from their hunt, and Murdoch spotted Dietrich with them. The little boy was stumbling along in a daze, but he seemed to be unhurt. He was carrying the bloody carcass of a rabbit and being prodded along by one of the warriors. Mariel sobbed when she saw him; whether from relief or horror Murdoch could not have said.

Soon the smell of roasting meat filled the air, and the response from their bellies reminded the prisoners it had been a long time since they had eaten. None of them had much of an appetite, but the body signaled its need for food anyway.

One at a time, the hands of the captives were freed long enough to be tied in front, rather than behind their backs. During the few seconds that his hands were free, Murdoch thought about grabbing for a knife or a tomahawk, but the prudent side of his nature won out. He knew he would get himself killed if he tried something like that.

With their hands lashed together, they were able to pick up the bones the Mohawks tossed to them. Most of the meat had been gnawed off, but at Murdoch's insistence, the prisoners managed to strip small bites off each bone. It was disgusting fare, but it was enough to keep them from passing out from hunger.

After the paltry meal the huge warrior called Sagodanega swaggered over to the wagons and looked down at the prisoners. He crossed his arms and sneered at the frightened captives. Suddenly he thumped his chest with his fist and announced proudly, "I am Sagodanega, war chief of the Mohawks! My name means Fist of the Spirit World! It is my destiny to bring my people together and lead them to victory over our enemies! The enemies of the Mohawks will drown in their own blood, and their women and children will wail long into the night!"

"Talking English quite well, aren't ye?" Murdoch commented with a grim smile. "I'd wager the reverend over there taught ye most o' tha' speech, dinna he?"

Sagodanega glared at the big frontiersman. "Shut mouth," he growled. "White man not talk!"

"Whatever ye say, Sagodanega. But I'd sure like t' ken what ye got in mind for us."

The war chief smiled, but it was not a comforting sight. "You find out," he said. He turned, knelt beside Cordelia, and reached out to touch her blond curls. She flinched away from him, but there was only so far she could go, backed up against the wagon as she was. His fingers tangled in her hair and jerked her toward him, and he reached out and grabbed her left breast, squeezing and kneading it cruelly through her dress. He laughed and repeated, "You find out."

Then he stood and stalked away, leaving Cordelia trembling in fear and humiliation. Quincy and Howard were both livid with rage, but neither of them said anything.

Grateful that the men had kept quiet in order to keep them all alive, Murdoch thought he saw an opportunity. Sabbath was standing beside the campfire, watching them, as he had been all through Sagodanega's brutal display. Murdoch called to him, "Could I talk t' ye, Reverend?"

"What is it, Brother Buchanan?" Sabbath asked, clutching his Bible and frowning.

"Ye saw what tha' red brother of yours just did, Reverend. Surely a man of God cannot approve o' such behavior?"

"Sagodanega is a man of lusty appetites, prey to all the weaknesses of the flesh which all men are heir to."

"But not ye," Murdoch said.

Sabbath smiled and patted the thick black book in his hands. "I have the help of the Lord in my struggle, and I shall continue trying to bring that help to Sagodanega and his comrades as well. All things are possible with the Lord."

"Amen," muttered Murdoch. "But ye dinna intend t' allow him t' do as he pleases with these women, do ye?"

Sabbath glanced at Cordelia and Mariel. "They're heathen women, harlots, Jezebels. I'll not clash with my brother Sagodanega over them if he wishes to take them. But I *will* speak to him, Brother Buchanan, to try to make him see the error of his ways."

"Thanks, Reverend. Tha' be all I'm asking."

When Sabbath had walked away and rejoined the Mohawks around the campfire, Cordelia asked shakily, "You don't really think he can control that—that monster, do you?"

"I would'na be so sure which one is the monster," Murdoch replied softly. "But aye, I think Sagodanega will do as Sabbath asks—for a while, anyway. And we can't ask for more right now."

"We've got to get out of here, Murdoch," Quincy said.

"Aye. But right now, I'd try t' get some rest. It may be a while before we get a chance t' do anything, and we'd best be rested up."

"How can you even think about sleeping when we're in the hands of these—these savages?" demanded Howard.

"A man sleeps when he can, even in the midst o' trouble," Murdoch advised. "They will'na do anything tonight, but if it'll help, I'll keep one eye and one ear open, and if anything starts t' happen, I'll wake the rest o' ye right away."

"Murdoch's got a point," Quincy spoke up. "I know it'll be hard, but I think we should do as he says."

Reluctantly the captives stretched out on the ground, their hands and feet still bound. The night would probably be cold, and the damp earth made a hard bed, but the day had been long and exhausting, and Murdoch was not surprised when the others dozed off quickly. Their slumber would not be restful, but it was better than nothing.

He let his mind drift, too, and settled down into the half-asleep, half-alert state that every woodsman learned in order to stay alive in the wilderness.

Murdoch could not have said how long he had been resting when he snapped to his senses. It had been a while, he saw, because the campfire had burned down, and most of the Mohawks were asleep around the faintly flickering flames. The forest around them was quiet; most of the animals had moved away from the ominous scents of man and fire.

But Sagodanega sat cross-legged near the fire, and beside him was the Reverend Jason Sabbath. They talked in low voices, and Murdoch decided that was what had awakened him. If he listened closely he could understand most of what they were saying.

" . . . do something about Brant," grunted Sagodanega in his usual surly tone.

"Of course we'll do something about Chief Brant," Sabbath answered quietly. "We'll have no choice if we intend to go ahead with our plan."

"Mohawks listen to Sagodanega. Brant better . . . knows what is good for . . ." Sagodanega was gnawing on something as he talked, and Murdoch lost several of the words. But he had heard enough.

Murdoch knew that the man they were talking about was Chief Joseph Brant, leader of the Mohawk Nation. He had never met him, but he had heard a great deal about him. Brant was of mixed blood, perhaps only half Mohawk, perhaps less, but he embraced the Mohawk people and their ways and had risen to the leadership of the Mohawks even though he was not a hereditary sachem. He had been educated in New England and lived a good many years with Sir William Johnson, who before his death had been England's proconsul to the Indians of North America. It was rumored, Murdoch knew, that Johnson was actually Brant's father, when in truth Brant's sister Molly, who was the Englishman's common-law wife, had taken Joseph, her brother, to be raised and schooled by Johnson.

From what Murdoch had heard tonight, it sounded as if Sagodanega and Sabbath were plotting against Brant. It was none of his business, Murdoch thought to himself, but any wedge driven into the Indians' opposition to the white settlers might come in handy in the future.

Such an intertribal feud had nothing to do with the situation in which Murdoch and his companions found themselves. They had merely had the bad luck to run into a band of warriors under the command of Sagodanega, who had a lust for conquest—as well as female captives.

"We shall bide our time until we get to Oswego," Sabbath went on. "That will be the moment to strike, when we have proven your prowess, Brother Sagodanega, by exhibiting our captives to your illustrious comrades."

Murdoch blinked in surprise. He had not stirred since coming awake, and it was clear that Sabbath and Sagodanega thought he was asleep. Doing his best to keep his breathing deep and regular, Murdoch continued eavesdropping on the preacher and the war chief. It did not take long for him to realize that he had been wrong about there being no connection between the captives and whatever it was Sabbath and Sagodanega were planning for Joseph Brant.

Oswego—Murdoch knew the name. It was a Mohawk settlement on the southeastern shore of Lake Ontario, and Murdoch wondered if all the other bands of Mohawks that had been roving through this territory were bound for the same place.

What the devil have we stumbled into? Murdoch asked himself.

As the Scotsman watched, Sagodanega tossed aside the rabbit bone he had been chewing on, stretched, and lay down on his side by the fire. He was asleep almost immediately, and snoring. Beside Sagodanega, Reverend Sabbath drew his knees up, rested his arms on them, bowed his head, and began to pray. At least Murdoch assumed that was what he was doing as he watched Sabbath through slitted eyes. After a few minutes the preacher's head sagged even more, and Murdoch suspected he was asleep, too.

Not a bad idea, he decided. Sabbath and Sagodanega intended to keep them alive until they reached Oswego, and that knowledge eased his mind a little. Of course, the Mohawks probably would not hesitate to kill them if they caused trouble or tried to escape, but for the time being, it might be best to play along with their captors.

However, it would also be a good idea to get away from the Mohawks sometime *before* they arrived at Oswego. If it was difficult to escape from three dozen warriors, it would be even harder if there were a few hundred—or more—gathered on the shores of the great lake.

Murdoch eased back into slumber, still curious about what the Mohawk chieftain and the preacher were planning. One thing was certain: Whatever it was, it would not be good for Murdoch and his friends, or any other settlers in New York.

The constellations had wheeled on in the sky toward morning, and it was the darkest hour of the night when Mariel Jarrott stirred on the ground next to the wagon. She had slept the deep, dreamless sleep of exhaustion, and she was groggy. She had no idea what had disturbed her, but she knew she was stiff, sore, and cramped from sleeping tied up on the ground. A chill had worked its way into her bones. She opened her mouth to let out a moan of discomfort, but a hand closed roughly over her lips, cutting off any sound she might make.

She stiffened and her eyes flew open. The darkness was thick and relieved only by a faint glow from the embers of the campfire, and she could barely make out the figure looming over her. She could distinguish enough to be sure he was one of the Mohawks, but that was all.

That was enough. There could be only one reason the man was there, and as he brought his face closer to hers, she could see the leer that pulled his lips back from his teeth. His free hand came up and closed over her small right breast.

Mariel's instincts screamed at her to thrash away from the man, but she knew it would do no good. He was the guard who had been left on duty while the other Mohawks slept, and even if they had been awake, they would not have helped her. Her terror-stricken mind told her all she could do was submit. If she did that, perhaps he would let her live.

But something deep inside her rebelled. She remembered the burned-out cabin and the bodies left behind when the Indians were finished slaughtering her family. She remembered fleeing through the woods, hiding in the cave with Dietrich, and then letting the Indians chase and catch her so that Dietrich would have a chance to get away. She could hear their harsh laughter as they toyed with her, shoving her back and forth, almost letting her escape before cruelly jerking her back again. She remembered the crash of guns and the acrid stench of black powder from the two battles with the Mohawks since she had joined Murdoch, Quincy, Cordelia, and Howard. The fear, the sheer terror she had felt, still danced its evil jig inside her. But mixed with that fear was anger.

It was all too much. She had had *enough.*

The Mohawk's hot, foul breath filled her nostrils. He still had one hand on her mouth to stifle any outcry she might make, and the part of Mariel's brain that was still rational knew he wanted to keep her quiet so that the other Indians and Sabbath would not know what he was doing.

He shifted his free hand from her breast to her legs and pulled up her skirt and her petticoat so he could reach the bare flesh of her thighs. Once again his fingers dug painfully into her, but she did not struggle. She lay motionless as he pressed his body against hers, and she could feel the evidence of his lust prodding her hip.

He was close enough now. Mariel reached up with her bound hands and let her fingertips glide softly over the oiled skin of his chest. The Mohawk grunted in surprise, but he liked the sensation and moved closer, allowing more of his weight to rest on her. Her fingers slid all the way down his torso until they found what she was looking for. She had known she would find *something* down there.

Her fingers closed over the hilt of his knife. She plucked it free from his belt and drove the blade upward. The tip of the knife entered the Mohawk's throat just below the chin. It grated on bone, then sliced down through the soft flesh of his neck. He tried to scream, but nothing came out but a bubbling rattle and a gush of blood that soaked Mariel's dress. With both hands wrapped around the knife hilt, she ripped it to the side and out of the man's neck. He collapsed on top of her, and she had to use every ounce of self-control she possessed to keep from screaming out loud as she writhed frantically out from under the body.

Sitting up, Mariel fought the impulse to retch. She bent forward and carefully sawed through the cords that lashed her ankles together. The knife was sharp, and the task took only a moment. Her feet were numb, and she knew she could not walk, but she was able to get on her knees and quietly crawl toward Murdoch and Quincy.

Luck was with her, and she reached the two men without disturbing the Mohawks sleeping around the fire. Before she got there, however, Murdoch had raised his head, his woodsman's instincts rousing him as she approached.

"Mariel?" he whispered in surprise.

"I've got a knife," she whispered, her voice as agitated as his own. "Give me your hands."

Murdoch sat up and thrust out his arms. Mariel had to work by feel, but she found the length of rope that was wrapped around his wrists and began carefully cutting it. A time or two, she was sure she slipped and cut his flesh, but if that was the case, Murdoch did not flinch or make a sound when the blade cut him. "Good girl," he said so softly she barely heard him over the hammering pulse in her head. "Get these ropes off o' me, and we'll show these savages a thing or two!"

Finally the rope parted, and Murdoch tossed it aside,

then reached out to grasp her hands with his own. "Give me the knife," he whispered, and Mariel gladly relinquished the weapon. Working by feel, with an ease born of long familiarity with cold steel, he slipped the tip of the blade under her bonds and cut through them in less than a minute. Then he bent forward and slashed the ropes around his ankles.

He put a hand on her shoulder and leaned close to her ear. "I dinna ken how ye got free and got your hands on a knife, lass," he said, "but ye've saved all our lives. Good work!"

The words of praise from the big frontiersman made Mariel's heart swell with pride and went a long way toward easing the horror and revulsion she had felt after killing the Mohawk. Impulsively she threw her arms around Murdoch's neck and hugged him tightly, until he gently eased her arms down and went on, "Now we got t' get the others free and get out o' here!"

When alerted by his sixth sense that someone was coming toward him, Murdoch Buchanan had been as surprised as he had ever been to see Mariel. He had recognized the approaching person only by its size and the paleness of the girl's dress, which made her stand out a little in the darkness. Then, when she reached him and cut him free, his surprise deepened. *Where in the name of Bonnie Prince Charlie had she gotten hold of a knife?* He had never been one to turn his back on good fortune, however, and there would be time later for explanations—if they got out of here alive.

When Mariel and he were both free, Murdoch eased over beside Quincy. Hoping his aim was good in the shadows, he reached down and clamped his hand over Quincy's mouth. The youngster surged up, startled out of sleep, but Murdoch pushed him back down, careful not to cut him with the knife that he held in his hand.

"'Tis only me, lad," he whispered. "Lie still, and I'll cut ye free."

Quincy's head nodded in agreement beneath Murdoch's silencing palm. He took his hand away and used it to locate the bonds on Quincy's wrists and ankles, then sliced quickly through the cords. Quincy sat up, tried to get to his feet, and would have fallen heavily had Murdoch not grabbed him.

"Rub your legs and feet," Murdoch told him. "Ye got t' get the feeling back in them before ye can go running around."

Murdoch's own feet hurt abominably, a fiercer pain than the usual pins and needles of an extremity denied blood for a short time. He welcomed the pain, however, knowing that it meant no permanent damage had been done to his feet by their imprisonment. He was confident that in a few minutes he would be able to walk.

Working as quickly and quietly as possible, Murdoch woke and freed Cordelia and Howard, both of whom were as surprised as Quincy had been. He roused them in the same manner, keeping them quiet until they understood who was looming over them in the darkness with a knife. By the time he was finished, some of the feeling had returned to his feet, and he was able to stand up. Mariel was on her feet, too, although she was shaky.

The sky was turning gray in the east. The darkest part of the night was over, and dawn would soon be stealing up. Murdoch grasped Quincy's hand, hauled the young man to his feet, and gave him the knife. "As soon as Cordelia and her father can walk, get them into the woods and as far from here as ye can," Murdoch told Quincy, his mouth practically pressed against the youngster's ear. So far no one had stepped on a dry branch or a clump of leaves. But Murdoch knew that luck could not be counted on to last forever.

"What are you going to do?" Quincy asked.

"Try t' get us a wee bit better armed before we leave here," Murdoch replied, grinning. Between the grayness in the sky and the faint orange glow from the fire's embers, he could see muskets lying beside several of the slumbering Mohawks. Shot pouches and powder horns lay with the weapons.

Cordelia and Howard got to their feet and joined Quincy and Mariel at the rear of the second wagon. Murdoch was about to creep toward the sleeping Indians when Mariel stopped him by grasping his arm. "Dietrich!" she whispered urgently. "Where's Dietrich?"

Murdoch had already thought of the little boy, and his keen eyes had picked out Dietrich's form next to the Reverend Sabbath. Dietrich was curled up in the hollow of the preacher's arm and had instinctively moved against Sabbath for warmth during the night.

"We can't get him now," Murdoch told the girl, ready to grab her and put his hand over her mouth if she protested too loudly. "We'll rescue him later. Right now we got t' get away whilst we have the chance."

"No! I won't leave without—"

Cordelia acted before Murdoch was forced to. Coolly, she slipped an arm around Mariel and drew her toward the trees, putting a hand over her mouth as she did so. Mariel struggled but then realized the futility of fighting. If she caused a commotion, she would only wake up the Indians, and they would all be in worse trouble than before.

"Sabbath's got a soft spot for the boy," Murdoch said, following them. "He will'na allow Dietrich t' come t' any harm. And I give ye me word we'll get him back."

Then, as Quincy, Howard, and Cordelia, with an arm still around Mariel's shoulders, eased toward the woods, Murdoch moved along the fringes of the Mohawk camp. He bent over several times, noiselessly picking up muskets, powder horns, and shot pouches. He had to be careful to keep the weapons from clattering against each other. Using every bit of wilderness survival skill he had, in a few minutes he was in possession of three muskets and the ammunition to go with them. *'Tis time to get the devil out of here,* he thought.

Backing away carefully, he reached the woods and had gone only a few feet when he heard Quincy whisper his name. He handed the young man one of the muskets, gave another to Gresham Howard, and kept the third one for himself. Then, silently, he led his companions away from the place of their former captivity. As they put more and more distance between the Mohawks and them, Murdoch increased the pace, but they could only go so fast in the thick woods that were still cloaked in predawn shadows.

Finally he estimated they had come at least half a mile from the camp, called a halt, and said in a low voice, "We'll rest a few minutes and get our bearings. We dinna want t' go blundering right back into those red devils."

Mariel sank down on a large rock and dropped her face into her hands. Sobs shook her slender body. "Oh, God, what's going to happen to Dietrich?" she asked in a low, agonized voice.

Quincy put a hand on her shoulder. "I'm sure he'll be all right. The Mohawks wouldn't hurt a little boy like him, would they, Murdoch?"

"Not unless they were on a murder raid, which they aren't," replied Murdoch. "Like I told ye, lass, Sabbath'll see to it Dietrich isn't hurt. He may be the craziest madman me eyes have seen in a long spell, but for some reason these villainous Indians seem t' do what he tells them most o' the time. Dietrich'll be fine, and we'll get him out o' their clutches as soon as we can. Ye got me word on tha'."

Mariel looked up at him, her soft cheeks streaked with tears. "How?" she asked. "How will we save him?"

At this particular moment, Murdoch did not have a firm answer to that question, and he wished like blazes she had not asked it. But he murmured, "I got me an idea."

Chapter Twelve

Roxanne Darragh had witnessed violence: She had seen Quincy Reed, his trouser leg wet with blood, his face pale and drawn with pain, and she had helped some of the men who had been wounded in the battles of Lexington and Concord. But never had she beheld such horror as the scene before her now.

A middle-aged woman hurried past, her arms full of petticoats and sheets. She noticed Roxanne and stopped, then pressed one of the undergarments into the younger woman's hand. "Tear that into strips for bandages!" she commanded sternly, then hustled off to pass out the rest of the sheets and petticoats to other volunteers.

Roxanne took deep breaths to clear her head. She had to ignore the sickness in her stomach at the sight of so much torn flesh and shattered bone. If she was going to help these men, she had to be alert.

She ripped the petticoat into long strips as she had been instructed, then moved along the line of wounded men who lay in the street. Doctors went from man to man, kneeling beside the soldiers and doing what they could to ease their suffering. The air was filled with moans and cries, and Roxanne imagined this was what hell must sound like. There was even a stench of brimstone in the air—although it was actually powder smoke carried inland on the breeze, along with smoke from Charlestown, which was still burning.

There were not enough physicians to treat the wounded, and many of the men died before receiving medical attention. The women of Cambridge as well as Roxanne did what they could. The doctors would reach up as she passed and take some of the makeshift bandages from her, and when she had given out all she had, she joined a group of women who were tearing up more petticoats. When her arms were full once again of the strips of cloth, she returned to the gauntlet of wounded men.

She had taken only a few paces when a hand reached up and grasped her arm. "Help me, girl!" a voice ordered harshly. She gasped as she was pulled to her knees beside an injured militiaman. A silver-haired, coatless man knelt beside the soldier, and it was he who had grabbed Roxanne, pulling her down with surprising strength for one who appeared frail and elderly. The doctor thrust a pad of folded cloth into her hand and snapped, "Hold this on that wound! *Now,* girl!"

Roxanne felt faint as the doctor's hands urged hers down on the wounded man's bloody chest. His shirt had been torn open and revealed a hole from which blood pumped rapidly. Roxanne pressed hard against the wound, and the thick cloth was sodden within moments. She looked at the militiaman's colorless face. He was unconscious, but his lips moved slightly as he drew ragged breaths into his body. A thin whine of pain came from him when the doctor moved one of his legs. The thigh bone had been broken by a British musket ball.

The injured man was young, Roxanne realized, probably not much older than she. Looking around, she saw that
most of the men lying in the street were young, but there
were some middle-aged ones as well, thick in the middle,
hair turning gray, and some old-timers who should never
have been on Breed's Hill fighting the British.

It was dreadful to think of all the lives that had been lost
in the battle, but Roxanne knew the men had been there of
their own choosing. The soldiers had gone up on the hill to
fight for liberty for the colonies. It didn't matter to her how
the battle had turned out, she was proud of these men. They
had been willing to give their lives for the cause of freedom.

The pad was soaked with blood, and Roxanne threw it
aside as the doctor handed her another one. "Keep it up,"
he grunted. "Got to stop that bleeding. This leg wound's
about closed, so I can give you a hand in a minute."

"Do what you have to, Doctor," she said in a voice
that surprised her with its firmness. "I'm all right."

She had been holding the fresh pad on the soldier's
chest wound for a few minutes and was thinking that his
bleeding was slowing down when the doctor said, "You can
stop that now."

Roxanne looked up at him. "You mean the bleeding's
stopped?"

"I mean he's dead," the doctor said heavily. He stood
up and extended a crimson hand to Roxanne. "Come with
me. You kept your head well, and I can use someone to assist me. What's your name?"

Dead? Roxanne stared at the young man's face. It was
still, and his chest had stopped rising and falling. She
wanted to cry out that it was impossible, that he couldn't be
dead, but she knew he was. A shudder ran through her, and
she thought she was going to be sick. She swallowed hard,
forcing down the sensation, and then reached to take the
doctor's hand. "Roxanne Darragh, sir, and I'll do whatever
I can," she managed to say.

"Good. Come along. There's plenty to do."

For the next hour, she followed the doctor from place to place while he tended to as many of the wounded as he could. Her dress was spattered with blood, and her arms were deep purple to the elbow. But she did not pass out, although she felt nauseated and light-headed several times. And always, always lurking in the back of her mind was the fear that Daniel's might be the next face she would see when she knelt beside an injured man.

The only person she recognized, however, was Lemuel Parsons, and he spotted her first. "Roxanne!" he called out as he limped toward her, one of the bloody makeshift bandages tied around the calf of his right leg.

"Lemuel!" she cried, running to him and grasping his hands. "Are you all right?"

"Don't worry about me," Lemuel replied. He grinned. "I just got a little scratch on my leg from the ball of a Brown Bess. Give me a few days to rest up, and I won't even know it's there."

"Are you sure?"

"Certain sure," he told her. "Have you seen Daniel?"

Her hands tightened on his. "No. Have you?"

Lemuel shook his head and said, "No, dear. Not here in Cambridge and not out there during the fighting."

"Maybe he wasn't there," Roxanne said. "Maybe he's hundreds of miles away."

"Could be," said Lemuel, "but I wouldn't count on it. If he was anywhere around, he'd've wanted to be in on this one."

Roxanne knew he was right.

"Please, Miss Darragh, we've got work to do," the doctor called.

She squeezed Lemuel's hands one last time and said, "I have to get busy. If—if you see Daniel, will you stay with him for me?"

"Aye," agreed Lemuel. "You can count on it."

She turned to join the doctor once more, and a few moments later, they were laboring to save the life of a soldier who had been wounded in the side by a bayonet. There was no time to worry about Daniel, or anything else but the life that was in their hands.

Roxanne labored beside the elderly doctor until dusk settled over Cambridge. While she still didn't know his name, she knew that she would never forget him or this afternoon's grisly work. The things she had seen would stay in her nightmares forever.

Finally all the wounded had been attended to, and many had been moved indoors to beds given up by the citizens of the town. Most of the men still lying in the street were beyond help, and they waited in the silent stillness of death for the ones who had the most unpleasant duty of all. Wagons moved slowly through the streets, and the bodies were loaded on them.

Roxanne trudged into an empty cross street. She had no idea where she was going or what to do next. She had not eaten since early that morning, but her stomach rebelled at the thought of food. All she wanted was a long drink of cool, clear water.

Unexpectedly her eyes fell on a huddled shape in the doorway of one of the buildings she was passing. The way the shadows of twilight had gathered, it was difficult to be sure, but after a moment Roxanne was convinced that it was a man. But he was lying so still—

Had one of the wounded soldiers staggered into that doorway looking for help, only to collapse and die there all alone? Roxanne prayed that was not the case. Her heart pounding, she hurried toward the figure. If he was still alive, perhaps she could help him.

There was still a garish red glow on the western horizon, but the faint illumination barely penetrated the shadowy doorway. Roxanne knelt beside the man and looked closely at him. His face was turned away from her, but she could see his back moving as he breathed, and she sighed in relief to see that he was still alive. Gently, she put a hand on his shoulder and tugged on it to roll him toward her. "Sir?" she said tentatively. "Sir, can I help—"

Daniel heard a scream, far off and echoing through the caverns of his sleep-dulled mind. The cry was enough to wake him up, but what he heard then pulled him to full consciousness.

A voice that was achingly familiar was calling a name. *His* name.

Ignoring the shrieks of pain from his sore, stiff muscles, he bolted upright. His eyes snapped open, and despite the shadows that met his gaze, it seemed as though the brilliance of the rising sun burst upon his eyes. The last feeble rays of daylight struck a tumbled mass of red hair, and he plunged his fingers into it and held the young woman's head tightly as he stared into her green eyes.

"Roxanne?" he whispered.

"Oh, yes, Daniel," she answered hoarsely, her voice showing the emotions coursing through her.

He slid his hands down to her shoulders, then threw his arms around her, hardly able to trust his senses. Yet he could feel the warmth of her body pressed against him, smell the special fragrance of the red hair, and taste the sweetness of her lips as he brought his mouth down on hers.

He never wanted to let her go and would have been happy to remain here just like this forever. "Is—is it really you?" he asked.

A smile tugged at her mouth. "I could ask you the same thing. Oh, Daniel, it's been so long." She leaned back to look at him. "Are you all right? Were you wounded in the battle?"

"A couple of scratches," he said. "Nothing to be concerned about." Suddenly he frowned as he noticed the blood on her dress. "What about you?"

She looked down at the red splotches and said, "I've been helping tend the wounded. I'm fine, Daniel, really. Now that I've found you again."

She came into his arms and rested her head on his shoulder. Daniel stroked her hair and her back as he held her. Gradually he became aware that they were both on their knees in a filthy doorway, so he got to his feet, gently pulling her up with him.

"We've got to get out of here," he murmured. "Find someplace to be alone—"

She tipped her head back to look up at him. "What about your apartment?"

His apartment—of course! It was not far off. He and Thad and the other militiamen had spent time there while they were in Cambridge. If George and Ben and Fred had survived the battle, they might return there, and if they did, Daniel would have some bad news for them. The memory of Thad's death sobered him and took away some of the giddy happiness he felt.

He turned and slid his arm around her shoulders. "Come on," he said. "That's where we'll go."

When he stood and put his weight on his wounded leg, it threatened to buckle underneath him, but Roxanne caught hold of him around the waist and cried, "You *are* hurt!"

"Just a scratch," Daniel insisted. She did not know about the wound he had suffered when he had been ambushed on his way to Fort Ticonderoga by Perry Faulkner, Cordelia's bandit husband. Daniel knew Roxanne would fuss over that scar once she saw it.

It would be a good idea to get her to clean and bandage the two bayonet gashes, however, just to make sure they did not fester. With his arm around her shoulders and her arm around his waist, they made their way toward the apartment. The streets were almost deserted. After the fierce battle, everyone was staying indoors, fearful that the British would attack Cambridge itself now that they controlled the Charlestown peninsula. Daniel and Roxanne were slowed by Daniel's limping gait, and the night was dark by the time they reached the building where his rooms were located.

As he went up the familiar stairs with Roxanne, he remembered the peaceful time when Quincy and he had lived here. They attended classes in those days, Daniel at Harvard, Quincy at the Boston Latin School, and it had been a good time in Daniel's life. But even then the shadows of war loomed over the colonies. He recalled the night Quincy had participated in the Boston Tea Party and had come home filled with patriotic fervor.

Daniel had wanted nothing but to get on with his life. The talk of war had been a distraction he did not need—or so he had thought. But everything had changed since then.

His leg ached badly, and by the time they reached the door of the apartment, his face was ashen from the throbbing pain. Roxanne opened the door and led the way inside. It was dark in the apartment, and Daniel knew that none of the militiamen had come back here. That did not have to mean they were all dead, he told himself. Perhaps they were only wounded, or unharmed but staying elsewhere.

"I'll light a candle," Roxanne said as she slipped out from under Daniel's arm.

"Candles and tinderbox on the mantel," he told her.

"I remember," she said softly.

Within moments she had a small blaze burning in the fireplace. It cast a rosy glow over her face as she knelt beside it. Taking a burning sliver of wood, she lit one of the candles on the mantel, then turned to face Daniel. She gasped as she got her first good look at his haggard features.

"I don't imagine I'm very handsome at the moment," he said dryly. He smiled at her. "I could use some cleaning up."

"You look wonderful to me," she said as she placed

the candle on the table and then helped him into a chair. "Let me take a look at those wounds."

Moving in the same efficient manner she had adopted during the long afternoon of assisting the elderly doctor, she tore back his sleeve and cut the leg of his breeches so that she could get at the bayonet gashes. Both wounds were ugly and crusted with blood, but they did not appear too deep. Daniel leaned his head against the back of the chair and closed his eyes as she ministered to him, fetching water from the well in the back yard of the building, heating it in a pot over the fireplace, then using a cloth and hot water to clean away the dried blood. She was as gentle as possible, but several times his lips tightened to hold back an expression of pain.

"I wish there were a doctor here to look at these," she said, "but I think they'll be all right if I bind them up."

"Go ahead," Daniel told her. "I'd rather stay here with you than go out looking for a doctor."

Roxanne agreed and tore strips off her petticoat and wrapped them tightly around the wounds, which had started to bleed again. "There's still some warm water in the pot," she said. "I'll wash your face."

Before Daniel could tell her that was not necessary, she was crouched beside the chair with the warm, wet cloth, using it to swab away the dirt and grime from his colorless face. What she was doing felt so wonderful that he lay back and closed his eyes to enjoy the sensation. His mind drifted off, and he was barely aware of it when he felt her hands tugging at his shirt, working it up over his head and off him.

But then she gasped in surprise, and when he opened his eyes he saw she was looking down at the scar on his side where the ball from Faulkner's pistol had pierced his flesh. He took hold of her wrist and said softly, "It's nothing. It's all healed up, and I'm fine."

"But—but how?"

"It's a long story, and I don't really feel like telling it right now. But soon I will. I want you to know everything there is to know about me, Roxanne."

"Yes," she murmured, "I want that, too."

For an instant, he thought he saw a flicker of uneasiness cross her eyes, but then it was gone, and he told himself he had imagined it. He was not going to waste energy worrying when he could be luxuriating in the feeling of the warm cloth against his chest.

It moved in circles across the mat of fine brown hair on his torso, the movements taking it ever lower across his belly. And suddenly Daniel found himself forgetting about the aches and pains that only seconds earlier had seemed to extend from his toes to the top of his head. He looked at Roxanne, studying the way the warm yellow glow from the candle struck highlights in her red hair. There was a logical part of Daniel's brain—a small part, admittedly—that told him her hair was tangled and disheveled and her face was as gaunt and hollow-eyed as his own. But to him, she had never looked more beautiful than she did at this moment.

"Daniel," she whispered, leaning over him.

He slid his arms around her and pulled her into the chair with him, and the cloth fell to the floor unnoticed. Her mouth descended on his, her lips parting so that he could more fully taste her sweetness. The soft warm globes of her breasts flattened against his bare chest, and through the fabric of her dress he could feel the insistent prod of her erect nipples. The urgency of his response washed away any vestiges of the soreness and exhaustion that had gripped him earlier.

They kissed for long moments, but finally Roxanne slipped out of his embrace. She stood up, and when he followed her, she placed her fingertips on his chest and stopped him. "No," she said, her mouth curved in a faint, mysterious smile. "You stay right here."

She stepped away from the chair, and her fingers went

to the buttons of her dress. Quickly, she flicked them open, then shrugged the garment off her shoulders, withdrew her arms from the sleeves, and let the dress fall around her to the floor. She stepped out of it, still wearing a shift and the petticoat she had used for Daniel's bandages.

Daniel swallowed hard. He seemed to be having trouble breathing. The lump in his throat was probably his heart, he thought fleetingly, because it was pounding so hard it might jump out of his mouth. His eyes were fastened on Roxanne, and he could not have torn his gaze away even if a thousand redcoats had come storming into the room.

No one came in; no one was going to bother them. They were alone—the way it was meant to be, and all the horrors of the day were pushed aside by their growing passion.

Roxanne removed her petticoat, then grasped the hem of the shift and pulled it up over her head. Her hair caught in it for a second before she tugged it free and tossed it aside. A mass of red hair tumbled loosely around her shoulders, and she stood nude before Daniel.

He could sit in the chair no longer and came to his feet without realizing it. He was too busy drinking in her loveliness: His gaze followed the sleekness of her legs up to the gentle curve of her hips, the triangle of fine red hair at the juncture of her thighs, the softness of her belly, then the small but proud breasts riding high on her chest that was lightly dusted with freckles. Her skin was fair and creamy and beautiful, and as he stepped closer to her, he reached out to rest his palms on her forearms. He slid his hands up her arms, over the wispy hair and the tiny freckles to her shoulders, and then he pulled her toward him and sought her mouth again with his own. This time there was no barrier in the way as her breasts nudged against his chest.

"This is what you want?" he asked her.

"More than anything," she whispered in reply.

Her hands were working at the buttons of his breeches.

His hands slid down the smoothness of her back to caress her hips, and the touch made her moan and press her belly against his. His breeches came loose, and she pushed them down over his strong thighs. Now there was nothing between them, nothing to stop them from reveling in the heady sensation of their nude bodies coming together in a gathering storm of heat and passion.

Daniel was uncertain how they got to the bedroom. Surely he had not picked her up and carried her, not in his condition. But it did not matter; they were there, and he was gently placing her on the bed and moving over her, and she was reaching for him, and then they both gasped into each other's mouths as they joined together, and the heat that had enfolded them exploded into an all-consuming inferno.

But through it all, through the love and passion and need that swept them away, they both sensed the desperation at the core of their lovemaking. Daniel had come close to death more than once, and with the war going on, neither of them knew when the other might be ripped away. So they had to make the most of moments like this.

That feeling of despair was shoved to the back of their minds, however, as they became lost in each other, and for this night, at least, the war was far, far away.

They were together, and right now, that was all that mattered.

Chapter Thirteen

Mariel Jarrott was reluctant to leave the vicinity, but when the sun came up, Murdoch led the party west as fast as it could travel through the thick woods. The others agreed with Murdoch's reasoning: Even though they had escaped, with the exception of little Dietrich, the Mohawks would keep moving west, too, toward Lake Ontario and the village of Oswego, instead of searching for the prisoners. Murdoch recounted the conversation he had overheard between Sagodanega and Reverend Sabbath and how it appeared they were under some time pressure to reach their destination. Whatever was going to happen, it would take place at Oswego. And Murdoch wanted to be there when it did.

The small group of men and women was able to move faster than the larger band of Mohawks. Now that the captives had escaped, Murdoch thought, the Indians might abandon the wagons, or they might consider the mules and the wagons a better prize than nothing. At any rate, Murdoch and his companions pushed on, and by noon, the big frontiersman estimated they had put several miles between them and their former captors. He knocked down a squirrel with a shot from his musket, and they cooked the animal over a small fire and made a meager meal of it.

While they were eating, Gresham Howard played devil's advocate by asking, "Wouldn't it be easier to rescue the boy from those savages before they reach the lake? Once they get there, they'll have a great many more of their fellow tribesmen to pursue us."

"I dinna think they'll chase us," Murdoch replied. "Whatever is going t' happen at Oswego, 'tis more important than a handful o' captives who got away. Sabbath'll likely be upset if we snatch Dietrich back, but I have an idea that Sagodanega won't be in any mood t' listen t' him then."

"I hope you're right, Murdoch," sighed Quincy, with a pitying glance toward the still wan and distraught Mariel. "It seems to me we'll be walking right into a hornet's nest."

"Ye could be right, lad," Murdoch admitted. "We'll have t' wait and see."

Mariel had been silent most of the morning, caught up in her own thoughts, unable to speak of the hideous thing she had had to do in order to stay alive. She had nothing to say now, either, as they moved out again. Murdoch looked at her and was sorry they had been forced to leave Dietrich behind. The two survivors of the Jarrott family had endured more suffering and danger than anyone had a right to ask of them. But there was nothing Murdoch could do about it now, except hope that his plan succeeded.

Over the next three days, the travelers journeyed west, skirting the small body of water known as Oneida Lake to the south and then hitting the Onondaga River. They could have followed this stream to the great lake and Oswego, but the area was teeming with Mohawks going in the same direction. Murdoch, Quincy, and their companions were forced to leave the river and make their way across country.

But as they forged through the wilderness, Murdoch took advantage of the opportunity to refine his plan. By the time they reached Oswego, he would know what to do. Unless, of course, they got there and found that nothing was as he suspected it would be. In that case, there was no way of knowing what would happen—except that they would all die, and it would be his fault.

Murdoch shook off that thought whenever it intruded into his brain. A man did what he had to do, did the best he could, and fate took care of the rest.

Late in the afternoon, four days after escaping from the Mohawks, the group topped a ridge and saw the dark blue sheen of water in the distance. *One hell of a lot of water,* Murdoch thought, and he knew it had to be Lake Ontario. That meant they were close to Oswego.

Each of the five travelers wore gaunt, hunted expressions, and for the first time, Murdoch thought he understood how animals felt when men stalked them. He and his companions had spent four days and nights hiding from the Mohawks, traveling when they thought it was safe, ducking into the nearest hiding place several times a day when they came too close to one of the bands of warriors moving toward the lake.

Now they were close to their goal, but they had to get closer. Murdoch let everyone sit down on the ridge and rest for a few minutes. There were enough trees to keep them from being noticed from a distance, but after only a short time had passed, he said, "We best get moving again. We dinna want t' stay in one place too long."

Wearily they got to their feet.

"Do you know which way Oswego is from here?" asked Quincy.

"By my reckoning, we're a wee bit south o' the place. We will'na go all the way t' the lake and follow the shoreline; too exposed tha' way. We'll have t' stick t' the woods and hope we can find Oswego from this side."

Cradling his rifle in the crook of his left arm, Murdoch walked, and the others trailed along behind. He used game trails when he could find them, as long as the paths were not too open. When there was no other way through the underbrush, he hacked a path for them with the knife Mariel had taken from the Mohawk guard who had tried to molest her.

She had finally washed the dried blood from her dress in a small stream. When the stains had dried, she told her companions about the incident that had happened two nights earlier. She spoke in a halting voice as they huddled in yet another cold camp. Telling the story had lifted some of the burden from her, although she was still consumed with worry about Dietrich.

Murdoch did not call another halt when the light of evening faded and darkness closed in. Instead, they pushed on. A little later when full night had settled down on the landscape, the others understood why. Pointing with a blunt, knobby finger, Murdoch indicated a ruddy glow in the sky to the northwest, along the shore of the lake.

"Tha' be the glow from council fires in Oswego," he said. "We can use it t' steer by now."

He led the others toward the reddish light, and as it got brighter it became evident that Oswego was a sizable village with a great many fires burning. Whatever its purpose, this clearly was a major gathering of the Mohawk tribe.

They reached a road that led straight toward the village, and only after Murdoch had watched closely from the brush for several minutes did he allow the others to dart across the open area. The road was deserted, and no one saw them run into the brush on the other side. Not long after, they came up to a small stream that was shallow enough to be forded, although the water came up to Mariel's neck, and she had to be helped across by Quincy.

When they emerged from the river, their clothes were plastered to them, and given the warmth and humidity of the night, the sodden garments would not dry any time soon.

But Murdoch and Howard had held the guns and powder horns up out of the water as they crossed the stream, and that was what mattered the most right now. The weapons had survived the crossing high and dry.

The light from Oswego was on their left as they circled around the village, searching for some high ground that would give them a view of the settlement. Not long after they crossed the stream, they found a small, wooded hill that rose just enough to let them look down into the Mohawk encampment. Looking to the right, they had a good view of Lake Ontario, although at the moment the lake's surface was dark and forbidding under the cloudy night sky.

Silently, Murdoch touched each of his companions and motioned for them to get down. They lay on the ground at the top of the hill and studied the village two hundred yards below them.

The lodges of the Mohawks were grouped in a rough circle with several large fires burning in the open area in the center of the ring. There were other lodges, besides the ones that formed the circle, scattered irregularly around the periphery. Oswego was crowded with the visitors who had traveled from other Mohawk villages in Iroquois territory. Murdoch estimated he saw several hundred people sitting around the fires and milling about the village. Nor were all the inhabitants warriors; he saw many women and children. This was a major gathering of the tribe, and he wondered what it was that they had to discuss.

Murdoch had an idea what it was. He had said nothing to the others because he was not sure his hunch was correct. If he was right, though, what happened in this lakeshore village might have repercussions that would stretch all the way across the embattled colonies.

"Where's Dietrich?" Mariel asked into the silence atop the hill. "Do any of you see Dietrich?"

"They're not here yet, lass," Murdoch told her. "We moved faster than tha' bunch could. I reckon with all the hiding out we had t' do, though, they're not far behind. Ought t' be here tonight, or in the morning at the latest."

"I hope he's all right." Mariel's voice cracked from the strain she was enduring.

"He will be," Quincy told her gently. "You just wait and see. Dietrich will be fine."

After he had tried to reassure Mariel, Quincy edged closer to Murdoch and asked, "What do we do now?"

"We wait," Murdoch said, not liking the answer himself and knowing the others would not care for it, either. But it was all they could do until Sabbath and Sagodanega showed up.

The wait was not a long one, and Murdoch was grateful for that. Less than an hour after they had begun their watch, a commotion drew their attention. Striding along the road into the village was a party of warriors led by Sagodanega and Jason Sabbath, and Mariel let out a sob of relief when she saw that Sabbath was carrying Dietrich. It was difficult to be certain, but it appeared the little boy was in good health.

The arrival of Sagodanega's band created a stir. A tall, well-built Indian who walked with the firm step of a young man greeted the group. He wore buckskin trousers, a white man's silk shirt, and a bright red scarf tied around his neck. A plume of gaudy feathers decorated his scalp lock.

"Brant," muttered Murdoch as he watched. "Got t' be."

"What did you say, Murdoch?" whispered Gresham Howard.

"Tha' bright-colored gentleman talking to Sagodanega and Sabbath is Joseph Brant. He's the chief o' the whole bloody Mohawk Nation."

"With a name like Joseph Brant?" Cordelia asked.

"He's said t' be half white. Raised by an Englishman named Johnson, had his schooling in Connecticut and England. I never met the man, but I've heard plenty about him."

"If what you say is true, surely he's not a savage like the others of his tribe," Howard commented. "Perhaps we could talk to him—"

Murdoch's grim chuckle stopped Howard in midsentence. "Begging your pardon, Mr. Howard," the big frontiersman said, "but Joseph Brant's as much a Mohawk as any o' the rest o' them. He speaks our tongue a wee bit better and has traveled more, but he's still a Mohawk through and through, white blood or no."

"Then how are you going to get Dietrich away from them?" asked Mariel. Her voice crept up, bordering on hysteria, as she went on, "You promised you'd get him back!"

"And I will, lass," Murdoch replied. "But ye got t' wait—"

"I'm tired of waiting! I'm going down there!"

Cordelia reached out and grabbed Mariel's arm before the girl could get to her feet. "Wait!" Cordelia said urgently. "You'll ruin everything if you go running down there."

"Let me go," Mariel said, trying to pull her arm out of the older woman's grasp. "You've no right—"

Cordelia's hand cracked across Mariel's cheek in a sharp slap. "Hush! If you bring those Indians down on us, we'll never get Dietrich away from them." She grasped Mariel's shoulders tightly. "And I've every right to stop you from getting us all killed. Six weeks ago, I was nothing but a spoiled, willful child. I've learned a great deal since then about courage and endurance. I know you've gone through a lot, Mariel, but so have I. So have all the rest of us! Please just be quiet and pay attention to what Murdoch says, or so help me, I'll tear a strip off that petticoat of yours and gag you with it!"

The unexpected outburst was hissed in a low voice that penetrated the anxiety that had clouded Mariel's brain. She lay weeping on the ground, her head buried in her arms. "I— I'm sorry," she managed to say.

Cordelia patted the girl's back. "That's all right. We know you're afraid. We all are."

"Aye," said Murdoch. "Truer words were never spoke. But we'll come through this trouble, lass. Just ye wait and see."

It was all well and good to mouth reassuring words, Murdoch thought, but there was still the matter of rescuing Dietrich and getting away from the Mohawks. It was not going to be easy, but he knew the first step to take.

"Mr. Howard, I want ye t' wait here with Cordelia and Mariel. Me and Quincy'll get a mite closer to tha' encampment."

"What are you planning to do?" asked Howard.

"Leave tha' t' us. Just keep an eye on the girls and keep the three o' ye safe. When we come back, God willing, we'll have little Dietrich with us."

Mariel reached over in the darkness and put a hand on his arm. "I'm sorry I lost my head, Murdoch. Please be careful—both of you."

"Oh, aye, we will be. Won't we, lad?"

"Sure," Quincy said. "Come on, Murdoch." He sounded eager to get started.

Moving slowly and carefully to avoid making any unnecessary noises, they slipped down the hill toward the Mohawk village. When they had gone fifty yards and were out of earshot of Howard, Cordelia, and Mariel, Quincy put his mouth close to Murdoch's ear and asked, "Just what is it we're going to do, my friend?"

"We're going t' pay a little visit to Oswego as soon as I stop by this stream t' give meself a quick shave. You best use the knife on your tender face, too, me boy. Keep your eyes open, lad, and follow my lead."

Their skin stinging from the dull blade and the ice-cold stream water, the two men crawled on their hands and knees as well as their bellies, and covered the distance to the outskirts of the village. The brush grew right up to the rear wall of one of the lodges, and when Quincy and he came to a stop, they were right behind the dwelling and less than ten yards from where Mohawk warriors paced back and forth in front of it.

They could not even whisper now. Murdoch motioned for Quincy to remain quiet. Flat on his stomach, he edged forward toward the hut. With the coming of night, some of the Indian warriors had thrown hide cloaks over their bare torsos, and some also wore caps decorated with eagle feathers, complete with the heads of the dead birds sticking up like topknots. If Quincy and he could get their hands on two of those cloaks and a pair of caps, Murdoch thought, they could disguise themselves as Mohawks. The imposture would not hold up for long, but it might give them the chance they needed to grab Dietrich and get out.

When Murdoch reached the rear wall of the lodge, he listened intently for several long moments but heard no sound coming from inside. He slipped the knife from his belt and sawed on the thin branches that formed the wall. He had to proceed cautiously, without making too much noise, just in case it was occupied.

Luck was with him, and soon he had a large enough opening to wriggle through into the empty, darkened lodge. Finding what he was looking for piled in a corner, he grabbed the cloaks and the feathered caps and slipped out the rear of the hut.

It had been too easy thus far, and Murdoch worried that such good fortune would not last. Dropping to all fours again, he tugged Quincy deeper into the woods. When they had crawled far enough away from the lodges, Murdoch whispered to the young man, "Take your shirt off, and put this garb on."

Quincy let out a small, astonished gasp as Murdoch pressed the cloak and cap into his hands. "We're going into the village dressed as Mohawks?"

"Aye. What did ye think?"

"I don't know." Quincy hesitated, then asked, "Do you think it'll work?"

"We'll find out soon enough, won't we?" Murdoch took off his coonskin cap, pulled his own buckskin tunic over his big shoulders and his head, and reached for a cloak.

In a matter of minutes both men were attired as Mohawks, at least to a certain extent. Murdoch's buckskin trousers and high-topped moccasins would not look out of place. Quincy's homespun breeches and boots were unusual, but it was not unheard of for Indians to wear such items, looted from the cabins of white settlers. The same held true of the muskets Murdoch and Quincy carried. While Murdoch was taller and burlier than most of the Mohawks, Sagodanega himself was of roughly the same stature as the redheaded frontiersman.

Murdoch jammed the cap down as tightly as he could over his thatch of red hair. Its color would betray him if an alert Mohawk spotted it. He was counting on the fact that the night was dark and the flames of the council fires tended to throw a reddish tinge over everything. The cloaks would conceal their pale skin, at least for a while.

"Are ye ready?" Murdoch asked.

Quincy's expression was a mixture of nervousness and anticipation. He had always had a love of adventure, and this daring masquerade was thrilling enough to satisfy any headstrong young man. "Let's go," he said. "I haven't dressed up like an Indian since the Boston Tea Party."

"Ye're not on the city streets now, lad. Mind that."

"I will," Quincy promised. "What if somebody speaks to us?"

"I can talk a wee bit o' their heathen tongue. We'll just grunt if we can get away with it, though."

They waited until no one was passing by. Then, they sidled alongside the dwelling and joined the dozens of Mohawks who were milling around the village. Murdoch knew that the Indians were renewing old acquaintances from other gatherings of the tribe, but the activity made it easy for Quincy and him to blend in. Stooping a bit to disguise his

great height, Murdoch led the way toward the large fire at
the center of the camp.

As they drew closer, they could see Sagodanega and
Sabbath sitting cross-legged on the ground. They shared a
pipe with the man Murdoch had pegged as Joseph Brant.
Brant inhaled deeply, then passed it to the war chief. Sagodanega took the ritual puffs and offered it to Sabbath, who
refused. No doubt smoking tobacco was against the man's
religious beliefs. *Sabbath would hold to something like that,*
Murdoch thought grimly, *even while encouraging the Mohawks to raid and slaughter white settlers.*

"Where is the boy?" Sabbath suddenly asked Brant.
"What have you done with him? He's mine, you know."

"Do not fear, my friend," Brant replied in flawless
English. "He is with my wife and children in the lodge we
have been given for our stay here in Oswego. He will be
safe with them." Brant raised an eyebrow quizzically and
went on, "I was unaware that you had any other children,
Reverend Sabbath. I thought all of them had been killed in
the fight at Silver Creek."

Murdoch listened with great interest. He touched
Quincy on the arm to stop the young man, and they came to
a halt not far from the big fire. They could hear every word
as Sabbath said in a choked voice, "The heathens destroyed
my family, this is true, brother. But the boy is a gift from
great Jehovah, sent to replace the children murdered by the
Americans."

Now Murdoch understood. When he had passed
through Pittsburgh on his way east the year before, he had
heard talk about a battle between the colonists and a band of
Mohawks at a place in the southwestern territory of New
York called Silver Creek. Obviously, Sabbath had been living
among the Indians, perhaps with a Mohawk wife and children, and his family had been killed in the fighting. The
Church of England had sent numerous missionaries to the
new world to "convert the savages." Sabbath—if that was his

real name—must have been one of them. Maybe the Mohawks had converted him instead, taking him into the tribe. The theory was guesswork, but it made sense to Murdoch.

He leaned close to Quincy's ear and murmured, "We'll wait and find out where Brant goes. Then we'll have t' grab the lad from his lodge."

"Do you think we can?"

" 'Tis our only chance," he replied, then fell silent. Brant and Sagodanega were still talking, and he wanted to hear what they were saying.

"—men of the council have spoken for many hours on both sides," Brant stated. "But the decision is mine, and I have not yet reached it."

Sagodanega glowered at him. "And I say we fight for the English. The men in red coats are our friends, bring us guns and powder."

"Don't you mean firesticks?" asked Brant. A hint of contempt in his voice revealed the animosity between them.

Sagodanega thumped his chest. "I say what I mean, Thayendanegea," he said, using Brant's Mohawk name.

"Of course." Brant shrugged. "I know you're not a stupid man, Sagodanega. I just wish you understood that this conflict between the British and the Americans is complex. It's not a matter of supporting the British simply because they've provided us with arms."

"I say we fight for the English," Sagodanega insisted stubbornly. "Brant be sorry if he think different."

Brant leaned forward. "Are you threatening me, Sagodanega?" he asked in a deceptively soft voice.

Sabbath spoke up. "Sagodanega speaks with the voice of the Lord," he intoned solemnly. "It is God's will that all the American settlers be driven out of the Mohawk Valley. Either driven out—or killed!"

"I'm sure you mean well, Reverend," Brant snapped, "but this is a decision that must be made by me, not by a representative of the white man's God. Now, if you'll both excuse me?" He stood and walked away.

No one had paid any attention to Murdoch and Quincy as they eavesdropped on the conversation between the Mohawk chieftains and the preacher. Now they turned away casually so that Brant would not get a good look at their faces as he strode past them.

While it was Quincy's instinct to follow the man, Murdoch stopped him because he had just glanced over his shoulder toward the fire and seen something very interesting. Quincy and he exchanged a glance as they watched Sagodanega speak angrily to Sabbath in Mohawk, then call over several warriors. Murdoch recognized them as members of the party that had held them captive.

"Something's up," Murdoch said softly. "Sagodanega doesn't like Brant going against him like tha'."

"What do you think he's going to do?"

"Let's wait and see."

For several minutes, Sagodanega spoke in a low voice to his men. Murdoch could not make out the words, but from the expressions on the faces of the warriors, they were being given orders they did not like. Still, their fear of Sagodanega's wrath was enough to make them willing to carry out his commands. Murdoch watched the exchange but kept the corner of one eye on Brant, who bypassed the lodges forming the ring around the council fires and headed for a large structure outside the circle. The lodge sat off by itself and was a fitting home for Brant and his family while he attended the conference of chieftains.

Finally Sagodanega's warriors moved off, fading into the crowd in the village. Murdoch's grip tightened on Quincy's arm, and he muttered, "Come on."

"What is it?" Quincy asked in a whisper. "What's going on?"

"Unless I miss my guess, Sagodanega just sent those warriors t' make up Brant's mind for him—permanently.

Sagodanega's got a lot o' ambition, and he figures he's the best choice t' lead the Mohawks, not Brant." By now, Murdoch and Quincy were walking quickly toward the lodge where Brant had gone.

"You mean Sagodanega's men are going to *kill* Brant?"

"And everybody else in tha' lodge, including Dietrich."

"But Sabbath—"

"Sagodanega's been using Sabbath for his own gain because the Indians are afraid of a crazy man. He will'na let Sabbath get in the way o' what he really wants, though."

Murdoch stalked across the village, no longer worried about disguising his long stride. Quincy hurried to keep up with him. If Sagodanega's men stole into the chief's lodge and murdered everyone in there, Sagodanega could step forward to seize power and take control of the entire Mohawk tribe. No witnesses would mean there would be no one to lay the blame for the massacre at his feet, and even though many of the Mohawks would suspect he was responsible, they would be unwilling to oppose him.

Then the Mohawks would enter the war on the side of the British in full force, drawing other tribes into the clash with them, and the colonists would be caught between the Indians and the British, trapped in a gigantic cross fire that could crush the rebellion. Somehow, Murdoch thought, Quincy and he had to prevent that.

His keen gaze searched for the four warriors Sagodanega had spoken to following the confrontation with Brant. They were nowhere to be seen. Undoubtedly they had slipped out of the village and would be working their way around to approach Brant's lodge from the rear, but Murdoch did not know if they would strike now or wait until later, when the village had settled down for the night.

Quincy and he moved past the ring of lodges and made their way toward Brant's dwelling. As they did so, Murdoch spotted movement in the thick shadows under the trees behind the lodge. He stopped in his tracks and pulled Quincy next to him, close beside one of the other huts.

"Look back there," growled Murdoch. "Sagodanega's men are closing in."

"You think Brant's alone in there with his family—and Dietrich?"

"Aye. Brant's a fine warrior, from everything I've heard, but four against one isn't good odds." A fighting grin plucked at Murdoch's broad mouth. "Let's see if we can even 'em up a wee bit."

As they moved quietly toward Brant's lodge, the bearskin robe that covered the entrance was thrust aside and a tall, powerful-looking Mohawk emerged. The man was not Brant, but from the way he assumed a position in front of the door, arms crossed over his chest, Murdoch knew he was a guard who kept watch over the chief's family. Now the warrior had taken up his post at the entrance of the lodge.

Suddenly someone darted out of the shadows next to the lodge, and a faint glimmer of firelight shone on the blade of a knife as it was lifted high in the air. The attacker looped one arm around the guard's neck and jerked him backward, cutting off any cry he might have made. Then, slashing down over his shoulder, he buried the knife in the guard's chest. The killer yanked the blade free and dragged it across the guard's throat, silencing him forever. He flung the guard's body aside, and more shadowy figures joined him; the four knife-wielding men darted through the unprotected door of the lodge.

"Come on!" Murdoch barked to Quincy, abandoning all attempts at stealth.

They were still fifty yards from the isolated lodge, and Murdoch covered the distance with surprising speed for a big man. Quincy was right behind him. As Murdoch neared the lodge, he heard the sounds of a struggle inside, but no one had cried out.

Pushing aside the bearskin robe with the barrel of his musket, Murdoch leapt into the lodge, and by the light of the fire built in the center of the dwelling, he saw Brant struggling with two of Sagodanega's warriors. He was silent except for some strangled grunts because one of the men had an arm locked across his throat. The warrior was hanging on doggedly while his companion tried to plunge a knife into Brant's chest. The chief had caught the wrist of the knife-wielder, though, and was holding off the blade with both hands. Across the lodge floor, a third man had a hand clamped over the mouth of a young Indian woman who was writhing and struggling so that he had not yet been able to plant his knife in her slender body. The fourth man was menacing a pair of adolescent Indian children, a boy and a girl, and little Dietrich was cowering at their feet.

The instant Murdoch's eyes took in the situation, his canny mind reached a decision. Brant was holding his own for the moment; his wife was in more danger right now.

The would-be assassins had heard Murdoch and Quincy bound into the lodge, and the one holding Brant's wife turned to meet the new danger. He was too slow. Murdoch's musket roared, and the man pitched backward against the wall of the lodge.

Meanwhile Quincy turned toward the Mohawk who loomed over the children, and as the man's face contorted savagely and he drew back the tomahawk he held to hurl it at the newcomers, Quincy fired. These were close quarters to be using a musket, but the shot went true. Quincy had aimed high to avoid hitting the children, and the ball took the Mohawk in the forehead and killed him instantly. The man's head snapped back, and he fell at the feet of the youngsters, who overcame their fear enough to let out screams of terror.

Murdoch dropped the empty musket and threw himself across the fire, scattering ashes and embers as he crashed into the man who held Brant. Both men fell heavily, and

Murdoch grasped the man's wrist and hung on desperately as his blade darted toward him. He turned the thrust aside, and the knife bit into the ground, sticking there momentarily. Murdoch took advantage of the opportunity to slam a big, knobby fist against the Indian's jaw. The man yanked the knife free and again tried to stab Murdoch, but the Indian was weaker and slower now, half stunned by the punch. Murdoch caught his wrist, turned it, and shoved down. With a hideous gurgle, the Mohawk died with his own knife through his throat.

Murdoch rolled off the dead man, spotted the tomahawk that was dropped by the man Quincy had shot, and snatched up the weapon as he surged to his feet. His gaze darted around the lodge in search of another enemy, but he saw that the threat was over. Brant himself had disposed of the last man.

There was a shocked look on Brant's face as he regarded the two strangers, and Murdoch knew what the Indian leader was seeing. His cap had been knocked off in the struggle, and his red hair was in plain sight. A few feet away Quincy stood, breathing heavily, and even though his cap was still on his head, anyone who looked closely could see that he wasn't a Mohawk.

Shouts sounded outside, and running footsteps approached the lodge. The shots and the cries had drawn plenty of attention. No doubt Sagodanega and Sabbath would be among those hurrying toward the chief's lodge at this very moment.

Murdoch glanced at the door. If he had hoped to snatch up Dietrich and make a run for it, that hope was gone. So he looked at Brant, tossed the tomahawk casually onto the body of one of the dead warriors, and grinned. "Well, Chief," he said, "looks like we've saved your bacon."

Chapter Fourteen

Daniel Reed stirred sleepily, relishing the feel of the sheets against his nude body. A cool morning breeze swept through the bedroom, carrying away the heavy feeling of the hot, humid night, and birds sang in the trees that surrounded the small common across the street from the apartment. Even though he was awake, his eyes were still closed, and he did not want to open them, preferring to stay in bed for a while to enjoy a few quiet moments with Roxanne. Intending to draw her close, he turned onto his side and slid an arm across the bed, but his hand touched only cool, empty sheets.

He lifted his head from the pillow, opened his eyes, and looked around. Where was she? A faint drumbeat of panic thumped at the back of his mind, but he relaxed when he saw Roxanne standing at the open window, silhouetted against the morning sunlight. Her back was to him, and she was staring distractedly out the window. He called her name softly, and when she did not respond, he said it again, a little sharply. "Roxanne."

When she turned away from the window, he saw that she was wearing one of his linsey-woolsey shirts. It came halfway down her smooth thighs, and the sun shining behind her rendered the shirt translucent enough so that he could see the elegant curves of her body beneath it. She smiled and walked over to him as he sat up in bed.

"I thought you were gone," he said. "I reached out for you—" He broke off and shook his head. "I'm sorry. I've no right to worry so."

"I don't mind," she said as she settled down cross-legged at the foot of the bed. The shirt was just long enough to decently cover her as it draped across her thighs. "I'm glad you worry about me. But I woke up early, and you seemed to be sleeping so well I didn't have the heart to disturb you."

"You have leave to disturb me anytime you desire," he said with an intimate growl. The words as well as the tone of voice would have sounded faintly ludicrous under most circumstances, but here in this sunny bedroom, between lovers, they rang utterly true.

She leaned forward, slipped her arms around his neck, and kissed him. The gentle kiss soon turned urgent, and Daniel's hands crept under her shirt and cupped and caressed her breasts.

Five days had passed since the battle of Bunker Hill, as it was being called, though nearly all the fighting had taken place on Breed's Hill. Daniel and Roxanne had spent most of the time in the apartment, venturing out only to buy a loaf of bread and some fresh meat and vegetables. The talk in the market had been of how demoralized the British were by the battle; even though they had won, the cost of victory had been so high that patriot leader Nathanael Greene had been heard to say, "I wish we would sell them another hill at the same price!"

At the moment, Daniel cared little about military victories and defeats. He only wanted to rest, to let his wounds heal, to forget the horrors he had witnessed and participated in the previous Saturday. He wanted to spend time with Roxanne.

And so for the last five days they had been together, making love, talking, laughing, sleeping in each other's arms—keeping the world as far away as they possibly could. They knew this idyll had to come to an end sometime.

But not yet, Daniel prayed fervently. *Please, God, not yet.*

This morning they took each other with the same desperate urgency that had characterized their first lovemaking. In the past few days, there had been times that were slower and sweeter, but neither of them cared about that now. It was a fierce coupling, punctuated by gasps and moans and hissed words of passion. They were left spent and sweating on the tangled sheets.

Daniel rolled onto his back and looked up at the ceiling. His pulse was racing, and he was panting like a man who has just run a mile or more. Roxanne nestled against his side, draped an arm across his chest, and rested her head on his shoulder. He lightly stroked her flank with his hand.

The idea that had been forming in his head for the past few days suddenly burst from his mouth almost before he knew what he was saying. "Roxanne, I think we should get married."

She stiffened and turned her face away from him.

Alarmed, Daniel came up on an elbow and leaned over her. "What is it?" he asked. "Did I do something wrong?"

"No, Daniel," she said softly, her voice little more than a whisper. "You didn't do anything wrong. I love you, and I wish we *could* be married—but we can't."

"Why not?" he asked. "We love each other. There's no reason we shouldn't be married."

"No reason?" she echoed. She slid away from him, got out of bed, and stood up, then turned to look down at him. The shirt had been discarded in their lovemaking, so she stood there nude. "What about the war?" she asked.

"It's managed without us for the last five days," said Daniel, and no sooner were the words out of his mouth than he regretted the lightness of his tone.

She turned sharply and paced back and forth, crossing her arms over her breasts and hugging herself as if she were cold. "What kind of life could we have if we were married?" she demanded. "You have your duties, and I have mine. We couldn't even have a semblance of a normal life!"

Daniel's temper flared. "Duty be damned!" he said as he stood up. "We've both risked life and limb more than once for the cause. Isn't that enough?"

An ironic smile touched Roxanne's lips. "You sound like Lottie Parsons talking to Lemuel. Think about it, Daniel. Yes, we've both risked a great deal, but are the colonies any closer to freedom? Can we only think about ourselves now?"

He blinked but made no reply. He could not honestly say that liberty was any nearer. The American patriots had just suffered a defeat, and the British hold on the colonies was as unshakable as ever.

"It'll take time—" he began.

"Yes, time," agreed Roxanne, interrupting him. "Time and the efforts of people such as you and me. We can't give up, Daniel."

"But I'm not asking you to," he protested. "All I'm asking you to do is be my wife."

She shook her head, and although it pained her to do so, she said, "I can't. Not now. Perhaps someday, when the war is over and this land is free."

Daniel sighed heavily. He was not going to change her mind, and he knew it. Beyond that, he was not sure he had any right to try to persuade her otherwise. She was a grown woman with a mind of her own, as he was well aware.

"All right," he said. "I won't pretend to like your decision, but I'll abide by it. Where does that leave us?"

Roxanne shrugged her sleek shoulders. "Right here, just as before."

"Not exactly the same," said Daniel, slowly shaking his head. "You're right, we do have our duties, and I've been neglecting mine. I have to find someone from the Committee of Safety to report on the New York campaign."

Roxanne picked up the shirt from the floor and slipped it over her head. "I've heard that Samuel Adams and Mr. Hancock as well as most of the others are in Philadelphia for the Second Continental Congress."

Daniel found his breeches on the floor by the side of the bed and stepped into them. Now that they were talking business, he felt decidedly uncomfortable being nude. "I don't want to go all the way to Philadelphia if I can avoid it. Who's left in Boston?" he asked.

"Dr. Church is still there, as far as I know, and I'm sure some of the other committee members are, too."

Daniel frowned in thought. "Dr. Church, eh?"

He had never fully trusted Dr. Benjamin Church. True, the man had been of considerable assistance the night Roxanne and Murdoch had rescued Daniel and Quincy from the Brattle Street jail. However, there was still some question in Daniel's mind about why the physician had been in a British stronghold in the first place. Church's statement about accepting medical work from the British so that he could spy on them had not rung completely true to Daniel's ears.

"What about Elliot?" Daniel asked. He had thought about his cousin before now but had been too caught up in his passion for Roxanne to ask her about him.

She hesitated for a second, then replied, "Elliot is still in Boston, too, as far as I know. Where else would he be?"

"True. He has had to stay there to spy on the Tories, hasn't he?" Daniel made his decision. "We'll get a message to Elliot. Perhaps he can get here and then relay my report to the proper people in Boston. At any rate, it will be good to see him again!"

"Of course," Roxanne murmured.

"Do you still have some contacts who can get word into Boston, people from the old days, I mean?" A wry smile appeared on Daniel's mouth as he spoke. Those "old days," as he had just referred to them, covered only the last eighteen months, since he had been drawn into the espionage activities of the patriots.

"I think so," Roxanne answered, sounding slightly reluctant. "I can try, anyway."

"All right. I'll leave that to you, since you know more people than I do."

"I'll see about it today," promised Roxanne.

"Thanks." Daniel went over to her and rested his hands on her shoulders. "You've opened my eyes, Roxanne. Our personal lives have to come second, at least until we've shaken off the British yoke. But someday—"

"Someday may be a long time off," she cut in. She came up on her toes and kissed him. "For now—know that I love you, Daniel."

"And I love you," he said huskily, folding her into his embrace. That was enough for him—it would have to be.

Several days later, Roxanne waited nervously at the window of the apartment, watching the street outside. She had received word that Elliot would be arriving sometime that afternoon. The message had come to her from a greengrocer who smuggled produce into Boston. Technically, the city was under siege and cut off from the rest of Massachusetts, but one of the results of that was a lucrative business slipping food and other goods into the city. With the supply line between Boston and England already stretched as thin as it could be, the redcoats had a tendency to look the other way when Tory sympathizers from the surrounding countryside showed up at Boston Neck with fresh fruits and vegetables.

Of course, not all the smugglers were loyalists, although it paid them to pretend to be. Some, like Roxanne's friend, were ardent patriots who were not above making a few coins for themselves in addition to serving as couriers, passing information back and forth between the revolutionaries outside and those still inside the city of Boston.

Getting a message to Elliot had not been difficult, nor had Roxanne expected it to be. Still, she had almost refused Daniel's request, and even after she had promised him she would help, she had come close to changing her mind.

The past week and a half with Daniel had been wonderful, even though they had been reunited in the aftermath of a bloody battle. That respite was about to come to an end, however. She had a feeling that when Elliot showed up, they would be plunged back into the whirlpool of espionage and counterespionage.

And she was decidedly uncomfortable about the prospect of having Elliot—the man who had taken her virginity—in the same room as Daniel, the man she loved with all her heart.

Would he be able to read the truth on her face? Surely not. And yet she was as nervous as a cat this afternoon as she waited for Elliot to arrive.

She heard the front door open, and Daniel walked through the sitting room and into the bedroom. He had been downstairs talking to Gidden, the landlord. The man was a strict Puritan and none too happy about Daniel and Roxanne sharing the rooms without the benefit of marriage. It was quite scandalous, of course, but then she had already been branded a scarlet woman in Boston for her alleged affair with Elliot Markham.

Roxanne was uncertain whether to laugh or cry. Growing up, she had always paid little attention to young men. Her intelligence, curiosity, and stubborn nature, as well as her father's profession, had led her to be much more interested in books and abstract ideas than in what went on between men and women. That attitude must have been apparent to would-be suitors because in spite of her looks, she had not been pursued to any great degree by the young men of Boston.

And now she found herself regarded as a trollop. Perhaps there was something to it, a side of her that had been slumbering until now. She had certainly been making love to Daniel with joyous abandon.

Now she turned from the window and said, "How did it go? Does Mr. Gidden still want us to leave?"

"I'm afraid so," sighed Daniel. "However, he said he wouldn't force us to move out, not with things in such an unsettled state in the area. I have a feeling we're going to have to put up with a great many frowns of disapproval if we stay."

"Why don't we go back to the farm?" Roxanne suggested. "I'm sure Lemuel and Lottie wouldn't mind us staying there."

A grin lit up Daniel's face. "You're right. That's an excellent idea. And I'd certainly like to see the two of them again. We'll get ready to leave as soon as we've talked to Elliot."

It was exciting to think about going back to the Parsons farm. The place was a haven to her; she had been safe there, and that was where the love Daniel and she felt for each other had blossomed and grown. Yes, it would be good to return to the farm.

As soon as they had seen Elliot.

As he reined his horse to a stop, Elliot Markham gazed up at the familiar building. He had visited Daniel here in Cambridge several times and had no trouble finding the place, just as he'd had no trouble getting past the British guards on Boston Neck. Even if he had lost his job at Markham & Cummings, he was still Benjamin Markham's son, and that carried some weight with the British.

He hesitated before dismounting. *What the hell is*

going to happen in there? he wondered. *Just how much has Roxanne told Daniel about what went on between us?*

Elliot knew his cousin very well, knew that while Daniel was slow to anger, the young man from Virginia *did* have a temper. They had always gotten along well as boys and young men, but Elliot had never deflowered a woman Daniel loved before. Was he about to walk into a beating—or worse?

Elliot sighed and swung down from the saddle. As he did so, he spied a flash of red hair in an upstairs window and knew Roxanne was watching for him. His heart beat heavily in his chest.

This would be the first time he had seen her since the day off the New Hampshire coast when they had helped a small fleet of patriot fishing boats hijack a cargo of British munitions from the Markham & Cummings ship the *Carolingian.* More nervous than he had ever felt, Elliot strode up the short walk to the building and went inside.

He was wearing a rather threadbare, undistinguished suit, as he always did whenever he left Boston. His powdered wig was in his bedroom at his father's house, and he wore his sandy hair loose, rather than clubbed at the back of his neck. His tricorn was pulled low over his eyes, and he was sure he looked disreputable—which was exactly the way he wanted to look.

Daniel was waiting for him at the top of the stairs, and from the broad grin on his cousin's face, Elliot did not think this was a trap. He was relieved when Daniel grabbed his hand, pumped it up and down enthusiastically, then threw his arms around Elliot in a bear hug.

"God, it's good to see you again!" exclaimed Daniel. "How have you been? Are you all right?"

"I will be if I can extricate myself before you crush my ribs," Elliot replied dryly. "It's good to see you, too, Daniel."

Daniel steered him into the apartment. "Come on. I'm sure Roxanne's eager to see you."

Elliot was not so certain of that, but he allowed Daniel to lead him through the door. Roxanne waited inside, as lovely as ever, wearing a dark green dress. Her hair was loose and tumbled around her shoulders, and Elliot felt a sharp pang of desire. He tried to stifle it as he said softly, "Hello, Roxanne."

She stepped forward, surprising him by coming into his arms and kissing him briefly on his cheek. Well, it hardly qualified as a kiss, he thought. More of a sisterly peck. Not at all like the kisses they had shared before leaving on their mission six weeks earlier. He forced that thought out of his head.

"I'm glad you're here, Elliot," she said. "Please, sit down."

The three friends took seats around the table in the front room, and as Elliot looked from Daniel to Roxanne and back again, he came to the conclusion that Daniel knew absolutely nothing about his affair with Roxanne. A feeling of relief surged through him. If Roxanne had not said anything about it, then he certainly was not going to! This was a chance to put it all behind them, to go back to the friendship that, as far as Daniel was concerned, still existed.

"How are things in Boston?" asked Daniel.

"The food supply is running low, the British have clamped down on everyone they consider connected to the insurrectionists, and the general feeling is that the American army is going to attack any day now, especially since Washington was elected commander in chief."

"Washington?" Daniel exclaimed. "You mean Colonel George Washington from Virginia?"

"He's General Washington now," Elliot replied with a smile. "The Continental Congress picked him to lead the army two weeks ago, even before Bunker Hill. I hear that he's on his way to Cambridge even now."

"That's amazing," Daniel exclaimed. "You know

more about what's going on than we do, and you've been stuck in Boston!"

Elliot leaned back in his chair. "The rumors fly fast and furious across the harbor, I'll admit that. But I assume you've been busy, or you'd have heard the same things here in Cambridge."

Roxanne blushed, and suddenly Elliot felt like an utter fool. *Of course they had been busy; they were lovers, weren't they?* he thought.

There was no mistaking the way they sat near each other or the flashes of emotion in their eyes. It was clear to him that their love had progressed to the next logical step.

Daniel looked at Roxanne and smiled, then said to Elliot, "Have you talked to any of the committee recently?"

"From time to time," Elliot replied. "In fact, I spoke to Samuel Adams not long ago."

"Sam Adams? But I thought he was in Philadelphia."

"He was. He came back briefly to talk to me." Elliot chuckled. "That makes me sound more important than I really am, I assure you. Adams merely sought me out to give me a new job." Elliot hesitated, but only for an instant. There was no one in the world he trusted more than these two people. "He wants me to discover the identity of the traitor within the committee who's working with the British."

That revelation brought exclamations of surprise from both Daniel and Roxanne. "I've long thought that there might be a turncoat inside the committee," Daniel said. "So Adams is sure of it now, is he?"

"Sure enough to ask for my help. So far, though, I've had little success. There aren't too many of the inner circle left in Boston; Samuel and John Adams are in Philadelphia along with John Hancock. I've heard that Dr. Warren was killed on Breed's Hill—"

"He was," Daniel said. "I was there."

"It must have been horrible," Elliot sympathized. "Mr.

Revere and William Dawes are still in the city, as are James Otis and Francis Rotch. And Dr. Church, of course."

"Of course," repeated Daniel. "There's a man I've never fully trusted."

"Perhaps not, but there's no proof he's our double agent. In fact, there's no proof pointing to anyone. That's one of the reasons I'm here. You see, I've got a plan to catch the traitor."

Daniel and Roxanne looked at each other for a moment, and then Daniel said, "I speak for both of us, Elliot, when I say we'll do anything we can to help you with this mission."

"Good! Now, along with your information about what happened at Ticonderoga, what I need to know is the troop strength and the amount of munitions and supplies on hand for the Provincial Army."

"We can get those numbers for you," agreed Daniel. "I know several of the officers, and I'm sure I can find out anything you need to know. That's vital information, though. What do you intend to do with it?"

"I'm going to give it to all the committee members who are still in Boston."

Roxanne shook her head and said anxiously, "I don't understand. If one of them is a traitor—"

Elliot waved off the objection. "The exact numbers aren't that important. I'm sure the British commanders already have a fairly good idea how strong the patriot forces are. The only reason I need to know the information is so I can pass along reasonable estimates to the committee members." He leaned forward and smiled. "But here's where my plan is inspired. I'm going to give each man a slightly different set of numbers."

Daniel frowned. "I'm afraid I still don't understand."

Warming to his subject, Elliot went on, "You see, there's a girl in Boston—a doxy, really—whom I suspect of carrying messages for our spy, whoever he is. Old Pheeters at the Salutation Tavern put me on to her. He hears a great deal, and it seems that she's been traveling in and out of the city with more impunity than someone such as she should be able to. She's made several trips to Rhode Island lately and has more money than she should."

"Rhode Island?" repeated Roxanne. "What does Rhode Island have to do with anything?"

"I'm not sure," Elliot admitted. "My best guess is that the lines of communication between the traitor and the British are purposely complex. The information being sent by the turncoat might well take a roundabout journey and end up right back in Boston."

"That makes sense," mused Daniel. "And I think I'm beginning to see what your plan is. You're going to provide different information to each of the committee members— information that you can identify with its possessor—then try to intercept the spy's report to the British containing that information." Daniel grinned as if he were a little boy who has just mastered a difficult trick. "Am I right?"

"As right as you can be, cousin," Elliot said. "If I can get my hands on the message that wench is carrying, I can compare the numbers with what I reported to the committee members, and the finger of guilt will point straight to the treasonous party." He leaned back again and spread his hands. "Well, what do you think? Does this stratagem have a chance of success?"

"It has a chance," Daniel agreed. "How much of one, I couldn't say."

"It's complicated," Roxanne put in. "And rather risky. There are no guarantees everything will turn out just as you need it to in order to unmask the traitor."

"Life is complicated," Elliot responded, adding silently, *as you and I should know better than most, dear Roxanne*. Aloud, he continued, "And there are no guarantees of anything. All we can do is try."

"Very well," Daniel agreed. "I'll get those facts for

you, then Roxanne can pass them along through her contacts. You should have it in a few days."

"The sooner the better. I want to ferret out this turncoat and be done with it." Elliot grimaced. "It's an unpleasant chore."

"I can imagine. Knowing that someone you trusted is unworthy of that trust—" Daniel shook his head. "That's difficult indeed."

Only with great effort did Elliot keep his composure. Daniel might as well have been talking about *him*. He had betrayed Daniel's trust with Roxanne.

Daniel slipped an arm around Roxanne's shoulders and said, "The next time you come to see us, we'll be at Lemuel Parsons's farm."

Forcing himself to smile, Elliot said, "That sounds like a good idea."

"We've had enough of Cambridge, I think. Now, there's something you can do for me, Elliot. I'm going to tell you what happened in New York, and I want you to pass it on to whomever you deem proper in Boston. I've already told General Ward and General Putnam here in Cambridge, and they can get word to the Continental Congress if Colonel Arnold and Colonel Allen haven't already done so."

"Wait a moment," Elliot said. "Why don't you start at the beginning?"

Daniel did just that, telling Elliot of his adventures in New York as well as passing along the details of the capture of Fort Ticonderoga that he had gotten from Quincy and Murdoch. This was the first time Roxanne had heard the tale all the way through, and both Elliot and she sat listening raptly.

When Daniel was finished, Elliot let out a low whistle. "You do tend to get mixed up in some interesting things, cousin," he said.

"No more than you, I'd wager. What have you been up

to since I saw you last, other than this affair of the turncoat?"

Elliot glanced at Roxanne. Daniel was not looking at her at the moment, so she was able to give a minuscule shake of her head. Clearly she had told Daniel nothing about the *Carolingian* and the theft of the British munitions, and certainly she had not mentioned what had gone on between them. If that was what she wanted, Elliot was more than willing to go along with her wishes.

Sooner or later, though, Daniel was bound to find out. When he did—Elliot told himself sternly not to worry about the future. With the way things were in the world, the three of them might not have a future.

With those bleak thoughts playing in his head, he spun a few moments of fluff about his activities over the past two months, utilizing just enough truth to make the story sound good. He could tell by the look in Roxanne's eyes that she approved.

When they were all caught up on everything and had their plans straight, Elliot stood up and said, "I'd better be going. It'll be easier getting back into Boston if I arrive before dark. The guards tend to check everyone more closely once night falls."

"I'm still surprised you're able to get in and out of the city so easily," Daniel commented.

Elliot grinned. "Well, a siege is only as good as the people in charge."

"I suppose so." Daniel held out his hand. "Good luck with your plan."

"Thanks. I have a feeling I'll need it."

Roxanne leaned toward him and kissed him again, another meaningless brush of the lips. "Take care of yourself, Elliot."

"Oh, I always do, you know that," he replied lightly. Settling his battered old tricorn on his head, he tipped its brim with a finger in a casual salute, then left the apartment.

As he rode away, he glanced back and saw them standing at the window, watching him leave. Daniel's arm was around Roxanne, and Elliot had never seen two people who looked more at ease with each other. They were meant to be together, he realized, and the one night of passion Roxanne and he had spent together had been a mistake. He hoped that one transgression would never cause trouble between Daniel and Roxanne.

Surely one mistake could be forgiven.

As he approached Boston Neck, Elliot slowed his horse in order to get a better look at the commotion on the narrow strip of land that led to the Shawmut Peninsula and the city of Boston. The area was bristling with red-coated British infantrymen.

Most of the guards who were stationed at the barricades knew Elliot and were well aware of his status as the son of Benjamin Markham. They also knew that he sometimes slipped them a few coins to look the other way as he passed back and forth over the Neck. Like the tradesmen who ran illegal goods into the city, Elliot was a source of extra income for the underpaid troops, many of whom had been unwillingly conscripted, ferried across the Atlantic to the colonies, and dumped here in the midst of brewing trouble that was not of their making.

He had not anticipated trouble getting into Boston following his visit to Daniel and Roxanne in Cambridge, but from the looks of the hubbub on the Neck, entering the city might not be easy.

He heeled his horse into motion and trotted up to the guard post at the end of the land bridge. "What's going on?" he asked one of the soldiers. The best course, he had decided, was to brazen his way through.

The redcoat looked up at Elliot from under his tall black hat and recognized him. "Oh, hit's you, Master Markham. You'd best get back 'crosst the Neck, guv'nor. The bleedin' rebels are about to attack."

Elliot stiffened. He had not heard anything about a patriot assault on the city being imminent. "Are you sure?" he asked in surprise.

"That's wot the rumor says. Oi'd like to see 'em try hit. We'll pin their ears back good an' proper if they does."

So it was just rumor, Elliot thought. Rumors had been flying fast and furious since the battle of Bunker Hill. This alarm would probably come to nothing.

On the other hand, it was possible the patriots *were* about to attack. Boston Neck was not a very strategic place to do so, but there was no telling what some of the hotheads on both sides might do. Elliot smiled his thanks at the guard, touched a finger to the brim of his tricorn, and put the horse into a gallop as the gates in the makeshift barricades were swung open for him. He breathed a sigh of relief when he was back on the cobblestone streets of Boston proper.

He was eager to put his plan into operation. It felt good to be doing something again. Benjamin Tallmadge and Robert Townsend, who had helped plan the theft of the munitions from the *Carolingian,* had not been in touch with Elliot since, and he was anxious to get back to work on behalf of the patriot cause.

If he could discover the identity of the turncoat, he would strike a blow against British espionage efforts. And the Americans were going to need all the help they could get, Elliot sensed. It was going to be a long, difficult struggle. But it would all be worthwhile; the colonies would be free to chart their own destiny.

At least he hoped it would be so. Otherwise his own sacrifices and the sacrifices of countless others would have been for nothing.

Chapter Fifteen

"**W**ho in the name of all the spirits are you?"
Joseph Brant asked slowly, staring at the two
white men who had appeared so mysteriously in
his lodge and saved the lives of his family and him.

"Name's Murdoch Buchanan," replied the frontiersman as he shed the cloak that had become tangled around
his shoulders during the fight. "The lad is Quincy Reed.
Glad we got here in time t' give ye a hand."

Dietrich scrambled to his feet, ran over to Murdoch,
and threw his arms around the big redhead's leg. "Murdoch!" he said as he sobbed. "Bad men try to hurt me!"

"No one will hurt you, child," Brant promised in a
gentle voice and touched Dietrich's shoulder. The boy
flinched away from him and held tighter to Murdoch. Brant
glanced up at him and said, "It appears the boy knows you,
Buchanan."

"Quincy and I been traveling with him and his sister
and some other folks. At least we were until a big bruiser
name o' Sagodanega got hold of us. Speaking o' which, 'tis
his men getting blood all over the floor o' your lodge."

Grimly, Brant looked down at the bodies. "I thought I recognized them," he muttered.

Several warriors burst into the lodge, tomahawks held at the ready. "Thayendanegea!" one of them said excitedly. "We heard shots and cries!" The man's eyes widened as he saw the two white men. Quincy was still holding his musket, and the Mohawks had no way of knowing it was empty. All they saw were white men and the bodies of four of their fellow warriors lying bloody on the ground. The four Mohawks surged toward Murdoch and Quincy, tomahawks uplifted to strike.

"Hold!" cried Brant. "These men are friends!"

Murdoch tried not to let the chief see how relieved those words made him. Brant could have ordered the warriors to kill them, but Brant's curiosity had prompted him to spare Quincy and him. The leader had to be wondering what had just happened. They had managed to kill three of the four would-be assassins due to the element of surprise, but that advantage was gone, and Murdoch was glad they did not have to fight their way out now.

Brant turned to his men and barked, "Go out and guard the door. Let no one else enter." Then he took his wife in his arms and spoke rapidly to her in Mohawk. She nodded shakily, and Murdoch gathered that Brant was asking her if she was all right. When Brant was satisfied that she was, he went to his children and calmed the youngsters.

Dietrich was still clinging to Murdoch's leg. Murdoch bent down, swept the boy up, and cradled him in the crook of his arm. "Are ye hurt, Dietrich?" he asked.

The toddler was sniffling, but he smiled at Murdoch. "Me all right," he managed to say.

"Good! Ye're a brave wee bairn."

"Now," Brant said, "I want to know how you came to be here at just the right moment to save my life and the lives of my family."

"Tha' part was just luck," Murdoch answered honestly. "We came t' get Dietrich out o' here and take him back t' his sister. Tha' be why we had these disguises on. But whilst we were sneaking into the village, we overheard the argument you were having with Sagodanega and Sabbath."

"You know the good reverend?" Brant asked dryly.

"Aye, all too well. He was with Sagodanega when they grabbed us, and he laid claim t' wee Dietrich here as his own."

"Yes, I thought there was something strange about that," Brant murmured. "I had just about come to the conclusion that the child had been kidnapped by Sabbath."

"Ye got the straight o' tha'. Anyway, after ye left the fire, we saw Sagodanega send some o' his men skulking after ye, and I supposed he was tired o' waiting for ye t' make up your mind. He wants t' be the only leader of your tribe."

"Yes, I know," Brant affirmed. "Everything you say has the ring of truth. But will you be so forthright when you have to confront Sagodanega himself with these accusations?"

Murdoch had been hoping for just that chance. He glanced at Quincy, grinned, and then said to Brant, "Bring him on. Ye'll see I be telling the truth."

From the sound of the din outside the lodge, a crowd had gathered. Brant motioned for Murdoch and Quincy to go to the door. "Leave the child with my wife," the chief said. "She will see that he comes to no harm."

Dietrich desperately grabbed hold of Murdoch's neck when he tried to put him down. "I ken ye're scared, Dietrich," he said as gently as he could while prying the boy's grip loose. "But ye'll be all right, and I'll be back for ye. Ye got me word on tha'."

But Dietrich was too young to understand the concept of a man's word, and in the end Murdoch had to have the assistance of Quincy and Brant's wife to get Dietrich to release him. The Indian woman cuddled the little boy against her breast and spoke softly to him until his wails of fear died away to a series of quiet sobs and hiccups. Then Brant led the way out of the lodge, and Murdoch and Quincy followed him as the crowd of Mohawks closed in behind them.

There had been little response from the throng when Brant appeared, but the reaction was different when Murdoch and Quincy stepped into the light cast by torches carried by several of the warriors. At the sight of the white men, shouts of anger and hoots of derision came from the assembled Indians.

No one was more surprised to see them than Sabbath and Sagodanega, Murdoch realized, and he chuckled at the expressions of shock on their faces. The war chief and the preacher stood in the front ranks of the Indians.

Brant raised his hands for quiet and spoke for several minutes in Mohawk. Murdoch understood enough of what he was saying to know that Brant was explaining, with typical long-winded eloquence, what had happened inside the lodge. Brant concluded by saying that the craven snakes who had crept into his lodge to strike him down had been sent by the most craven snake of all, a traitor within the tribe who sought to enhance his own stature by murdering women and children. Only the courageous intervention by the pair of white men had saved the lives of Brant and his family. More cries of rage sounded from the crowd as they realized what Brant was saying.

"You want to know who among you would sink so low as to do such a thing," Brant went on in Mohawk, with Murdoch translating as best he could in a low voice to Quincy. "These men will tell you the name of the dog who sought by murder to replace Thayendanegea." Brant turned to Murdoch and said in English, "Point out the man."

Murdoch raised his hand and leveled an accusing finger straight at Sagodanega.

The burly Mohawk looked shocked and insulted. He wrapped his fingers around the shaft of his tomahawk, yanked it from his belt, and growled, "White man lie!"

"I know this man," added Sabbath, pointing a quivering finger right back at Murdoch. "He's a sinner, an unbeliever! He speaks with the tongue of Satan! Cast him out like the demon he is, Lord, cast him out!"

"Ye might be interested t' ken, Sabbath, tha' Sagodanega's men were going t' kill little Dietrich, too, as well as the chief and his family."

Sabbath blinked and stared at Murdoch.

"Murdoch's right, Sabbath," Quincy added. "We stopped them just in time to keep them from killing the boy."

Murdoch glanced at Quincy, proud of the way the youngster was keeping his wits about him. He had to be scared—there were a few butterflies in Murdoch's belly—but Quincy was as cool as could be.

Sabbath turned, grabbed Sagodanega's arm, and looked directly into the war chief's cruel face. "Is this true, Sagodanega?" he demanded. "Is it true?"

Sagodanega brushed him off, sending Sabbath staggering away from him with a shove. "Lies, all lies!" Sagodanega rasped. "Is Brant fit to be chief when he believes a white man over a Mohawk?"

It was a cunning question, and it brought mutters of agreement from some of the warriors gathered behind Sagodanega. He was a big, crude brute, but he had a compelling air about him, a sense of leadership that could reach out and find support, no matter what lies he told.

Brant looked from Murdoch to Sagodanega and back. The big frontiersman and the equally brawny warrior were glaring at each other in a contest of wills that neither man was willing to concede. Brant's own position as leader of the Mohawk Nation was fairly secure, Murdoch thought, but it was clear that Sagodanega had made inroads into

Brant's popularity. Brant might be better off to accept Sagodanega's word even though it was patently false, have the two white men killed, and deal with the threat from Sagodanega at a later time. Gratitude would carry only so much weight with a pragmatist like Brant, and Murdoch realized he had to do something in a hurry to keep Brant from deciding that option was the most attractive one open to him.

"I challenge Sagodanega," Murdoch said abruptly. "Trial by combat, and the winner is the one who be telling the truth."

That surprised everyone, including Quincy, who gasped, "Murdoch, you can't—"

"We dinna have a choice, lad. We got t' show these men the truth."

There was a glint of admiration in Brant's hard eyes when he looked at Murdoch. Then the chief swung his gaze around to Sagodanega and asked, "Do you accept the challenge? Or do you agree that the white man is telling the truth?"

There was only the slightest hesitation on Sagodanega's part before he thumped himself on the chest with his habitual, bombastic gesture. "I will kill white man!" he declared. "Sagodanega—the Fist of the Spirit World—will follow destiny!" He glared defiantly at Brant.

The chief was a smooth one, Murdoch had to give him that. Brant knew good and well that Sagodanega was behind the murder attempt, but now he had someone else to do his dirty work for him, and all Murdoch had to do was kill Sagodanega in the trial by combat.

Aye, Murdoch thought grimly. That was *all* he had to do.

The preparations did not take long. Murdoch and Quincy were marched to the center of the village, where a large circle was drawn on the ground near the biggest of the fires. Murdoch felt the heat from the flames on his bare chest as he stepped into the circle, his hands empty. As the one challenged, it was Sagodanega's right to decide in which manner this combat would be conducted.

Sabbath was still plucking at Sagodanega's arm. Angrily Sagodanega thrust him aside. "Leave me!" he snapped at Sabbath.

"I am the voice of the Lord—" shouted Sabbath.

Sagodanega whipped his cloak off and tossed it aside, then reached out and clamped his hand around Sabbath's throat. "Be quiet or die, little man," he warned coldly.

Sabbath's protests subsided as Sagodanega shoved him away. The Indian then turned slowly toward the circle, rolling his shoulders as he did so, relishing the power he felt in his strong, muscular body. With his back to Sabbath, he could not see the crazed look on the preacher's face.

But Murdoch could, and he knew that even if Sagodanega survived the fight, the big Mohawk would die in the night with his throat cut—a victim of what Sabbath would regard as divine vengeance.

Sagodanega handed his tomahawk to one of his warriors, then wrapped his fingers around the hilt of his knife and slid it from its sheath. Murdoch had been unarmed, but Brant stepped forward and extended a knife to him. "Sagodanega has made his choice," Brant said. "Let the combat begin."

Murdoch glanced at Quincy and saw the lad's tight, colorless face. If Murdoch lost the fight—if he were killed by Sagodanega—then Quincy would no doubt die moments later. Murdoch spared a second glance for the hill where they had left Gresham Howard, Cordelia, and Mariel in hiding. If they were left on their own in this wilderness, it would be only a matter of time until something or someone killed them, either beasts or Indians or the elements. He was well aware that six lives, including Dietrich's, were riding on his broad shoulders.

Sagodanega lunged at him, his knife sweeping toward him with astonishing speed.

Murdoch darted aside and whipped a blow at the Indian. The crowd erupted, their traditional stoicism forgotten in the excitement of this highly personal combat. Sagodanega dodged Murdoch's thrust and quickly stepped back, and the first exchange was over, with both men still untouched. Sagodanega retreated almost to the edge of the circle, and Murdoch did likewise on the opposite side of the ring.

They had taken each other's measure and confirmed what they had suspected: Considering their size, both were fast on their feet.

Sagodanega sneered and gestured for Murdoch to come to him. Murdoch just grinned and shook his head. Neither man wanted to waste his breath on verbal taunts. This fight would be long and brutal, and they would need every reserve of strength they had.

Murdoch wondered fleetingly if Howard, Cordelia, and Mariel could see what was going on. They must have heard the shots earlier, and now the shouts of the Mohawks would be plainly audible up on the hill. He hoped they had the good sense to stay put; they would only be in the way if they tried to slip into the village.

While Murdoch was woolgathering about the others, Sagodanega launched another attack, but he was able to leap aside as Sagodanega's blade sliced through the air where his shoulder had been a fraction of a second earlier. The big Mohawk was too close and in a bad position for Murdoch to strike back with his own knife, so he kicked out instead, slamming the heel of his foot into the Indian's right shin. Sagodanega stumbled, and Murdoch struck like lightning, bringing his knife around in a blow that, if it connected, would remove Sagodanega's head from his shoulders.

Sagodanega threw himself forward, going down and

away from Murdoch's knife. As he landed, he rolled into a somersault and stood up, spinning around in a surprising display of agility. Steel rang against steel as Sagodanega blocked another of Murdoch's blows.

The warrior snapped a punch into Murdoch's midsection, and the blow rocked the frontiersman back on his heels. This time he was the one who had to fling up his blade in desperation as Sagodanega's knife flashed toward his face. The Mohawk sensed his advantage and pressed it, making Murdoch retreat from a vicious flurry of jabs. From the corner of his eye, Murdoch saw the edge of the circle behind him. He dropped beneath Sagodanega's sweeping strike and kicked out, aiming for his opponent's groin.

Sagodanega took the kick on his thigh, but the impact knocked him back a few steps, giving Murdoch a chance to roll over and spring to his feet. Murdoch had known French fur traders who fought with their feet, but he was sure he could not match their prowess. He was good with a knife, too, but Sagodanega was his equal or better.

It was about time to admit that the odds were against him in this fight, Murdoch told himself grimly. But he could win despite them. His Highlander blood was calling out to him, and somewhere in the back of his mind he could hear the skirling of the bagpipes. If he'd just had his hands wrapped around the hilt of a broadsword, rather than a hunting knife, he'd have shown Sagodanega some fancy carving.

The warrior let out a screech of hate and charged him, and Murdoch met him with a ringing cry of "For the honor o' the Clan Buchanan!"

Grunting with effort, knives clashing, bodies colliding, the men came together in the center of the circle. Sagodanega's torso was slippery with sweat, and although Murdoch got a grip on him for an instant, the Mohawk twisted free. Murdoch tried to dart back, but as he did so, he felt a finger of fire rake across his chest.

He looked down and saw blood well from the shallow cut Sagodanega's knife had sliced in his flesh. The crimson fluid leaked out into the thick mat of rusty hair on the Scotsman's broad chest. Sagodanega had drawn first blood. But what mattered was who drew *last* blood.

The surroundings grew vague for Murdoch as he fought on. The hundreds of Mohawks who had gathered around the circle to cheer for Sagodanega became a noisy, faceless blur. Murdoch could not even pick out Quincy's face, although he knew the youngster was there. The glow cast by the fires and the torches became a hellish glare. *Surely this is what the pits of Hades are like,* Murdoch thought as he blocked blow after blow from Sagodanega and tried to respond with thrusts of his own. And, he thought, Sagodanega had to be Satan's own twin, dancing and capering and laughing as he tormented his victim. The Mohawk's blade bit into Murdoch's flesh again and yet again, but Murdoch's knife answered, and both men's torsos gleamed with blood and sweat. Murdoch's legs were as heavy and stiff as tree trunks, and the breath burned in his throat as he gulped down air. His pulse hammered in his head as if it were all the great thunderstorms rolled into one.

He was going to lose. He knew that now. Sagodanega was going to kill him, and everything would have been for naught.

Murdoch tripped, and it saved his life. He fell backward just as Sagodanega thrust past his guard, aiming straight at his throat. The point of Sagodanega's knife missed by inches as Murdoch stumbled backward. Sagodanega staggered toward him, unable to halt his momentum.

The back of Murdoch's head banged sharply against the ground, and as though the blow had jarred loose a curtain over his eyes, his vision cleared. He saw Sagodanega looming above him, lashed upward with his foot, and the kick hit its target. Sagodanega was unable to keep from screaming when Murdoch's foot smashed into his groin. Sagodanega doubled over against the pain.

With his other foot, Murdoch hooked Sagodanega's right ankle and pulled it out from under him. Already off balance, Sagodanega toppled like a tree, and as he did, Murdoch rose to meet him. With a force that shivered all the way up Murdoch's arm, he felt the knife in his hand enter Sagodanega's chest. The point glanced off the Mohawk's sternum, and its hilt was almost ripped out of Murdoch's fingers. He hung on as the long, heavy blade slid through Sagodanega's lung and then penetrated his heart. At that instant, Murdoch's face was only inches from Sagodanega's, and he saw his enemy's mouth open in shock and agony and fear. The realization that he had just been killed bloomed in Sagodanega's eyes and burned fiercely for a second, then died out along with his life. His knife buried in the ground only inches from Murdoch's left ear, Sagodanega collapsed on top of him.

A stunned silence settled over the village of Oswego. The warrior Sagodanega had been known and feared throughout the Mohawk Nation. Now he was dead, killed by a white man in fair combat.

Groaning with the effort, Murdoch rolled Sagodanega's dead weight off, then turned onto his belly and pushed himself up to his hands and knees. He stayed in that position for a long moment, his head hanging from his shoulders as he gasped for air. Blood dripped from his cuts onto the dirt under him.

Finally Murdoch raised his head. He got one foot under himself, lurched forward, and struggled to his feet. Then he stood in the center of the circle of Indians, bloodied, swaying from exhaustion, the knife he had pulled from Sagodanega's chest still gripped tightly in his right hand.

Triumphant.

Joseph Brant stepped forward and faced him. "You

were telling the truth," Brant said. "Sagodanega is dead, and you and your friend shall live."

Quincy ran to Murdoch's side and threw an arm around him to help him stand up. Murdoch tried to blink the sweat and blood out of his eyes so that he could meet Brant's level gaze, but he had to lift his hand to wipe away the gory mixture. He looked directly at the Mohawk chieftain and asked, "What about the boy?"

"He will go with you and be returned to his proper place, wherever it may be."

"No!" cried Sabbath in a ragged voice. "The child is mine!"

Brant turned his head and coldly regarded Sabbath. "You are here, Reverend, because my people do not believe in harming one who has been touched by the spirits. I warn you, do not test that belief."

Sabbath opened his mouth to say something but fell silent when several of the Mohawk warriors crowded closer to him. The reverend was insane, not stupid, Murdoch knew. He watched, his sight getting blurry again, as Sabbath turned and stalked away, the crowd parting to let him pass.

Despite this setback, Murdoch had a feeling they had not seen the last of Reverend Jason Sabbath.

"Come to my lodge," Brant went on, ignoring Sagodanega's body on the ground at his feet. "Our women will cleanse your wounds and bring food and drink." The chief's voice became sterner as he continued, "Do not mistake this for friendship, Buchanan. I owe you a debt of honor, and it must be paid in full."

"Aye," said Murdoch, nodding wearily. "I understand."

With Quincy beside him, Murdoch walked slowly to Brant's lodge. He looked at the faces of the Mohawks they passed and saw dislike but grudging acceptance. As long as he and the others were under Brant's protection, they would be safe here. He did not see any more of Sagodanega's men. With their leader dead, it was likely they had left the encampment.

"We have friends waiting nearby," Murdoch told Brant as they entered the lodge. "I'd like t' have Quincy go get them."

"It shall be as you wish," Brant assured him. "You and all your friends are welcome. Sit by my fire, Buchanan. I will send for the women to care for you."

Murdoch sent Quincy to fetch Howard, Cordelia, and Mariel, then sank down cross-legged beside the fire. It was going to feel good, he told himself, mighty good indeed to have women clean up his wounds and bring him something to eat. Now, he thought, with a wry chuckle that drew a puzzled look from Brant, all he had to do was stay awake.

They stayed in the village of Oswego for the summer of 1775 while Murdoch recovered. Initially Howard and the two young women, especially Mariel, were reluctant to come out of hiding, but after Quincy had assured them it was all right, they accompanied him to Brant's tent. There, in a flurry of hugs, kisses, and happy tears, Mariel was reunited with Dietrich.

Brant was as good as his word. Several young Mohawk women cleansed Murdoch's wounds with warm water, then smeared them with an herbal poultice that stung like the very devil but took away most of the pain. There was a brief moment of embarrassment when Brant indicated in no uncertain terms that these same young women would be glad to share the blankets of Murdoch, Quincy, and Howard for the duration of their stay, but Brant quickly sensed their discomfort and graciously let the offer pass without a response.

When Brant learned that their destination was the Allegheny River, he was quick to promise them safe passage to that point. "Never again return to the land of the Mohawk after that," he warned, "or you will be killed on sight, like any other American interloper."

"Fair enough," Murdoch told him.

As his health improved Murdoch took walks to test his recuperation from his wounds, and Brant often went with him. One day when the leisurely summer was coming to an end, the men stood on a hill overlooking Oswego and Lake Ontario. "What about the British?" Murdoch asked, bringing up their favorite topic of conversation.

Brant smiled. "You mean, will we fight for the British in this war your people have with them? You must remember, Buchanan, I was raised by Sir William to be loyal to the Crown. Not only that, but some of my education took place in London. My detractors among the tribe have been known to say that I'm more English than Mohawk. That is not true, of course, but I will not deny that I support the British." Brant gazed out over the flat blue surface of the lake and went on, "However, that does not mean I will fight for them. Not now. You did me a great service by killing Sagodanega. I tell you this only when we are alone. And since I have come to know you, I feel a new respect for the Americans." He nodded decisively. "For the time being—and I cannot promise for how long—the Mohawks will remain neutral. This will be my last payment on the debt I owe you."

Brant extended his hand in the fashion of the white man, and Murdoch shook it. "Ye're a good man, Brant," said Murdoch. "I hate t' think we may wind up looking at each other over the barrels o' guns one o' these days."

"Then don't think about it, my friend," Brant advised. "Think instead of the journey still in front of you."

"We'll be leaving first thing in the morning. I know Mariel and Dietrich aren't comfortable staying here, and now that I've rested, I'm ready t' go meself. Besides, tha' fellow Sabbath is still skulking around."

"Leave Sabbath to me." Brant smiled. "I shall miss you, Murdoch Buchanan—but not too much."

"Aye, likewise." Murdoch grinned.

It would be good to be on the move again, he thought as he looked out over the lake with Brant. Both men stood silent for a while. After the trouble they had been through, Murdoch was looking forward to making some real progress.

But he had a hunch their problems were not over; they were heading into wild territory, and trouble might just follow them all the way to the Ohio River valley.

Chapter Sixteen

On July 3, 1775, a party of blue-coated officers rode into Cambridge and paused at the outskirts of the camp that had grown up around the Massachusetts Provincial Army. It was a sorry sight, a mixture of huts, lean-tos, and tents that served as sleeping quarters for the more than fourteen thousand men who had come to Cambridge to fight the British. A fetid breeze blew from the sea several miles away and carried the stench of latrines, cook fires, and unwashed bodies. The tall, slender man leading the group of riders regarded the unimpressive scene spread out before him and shook his head.

"Gentlemen," said General George Washington as he turned to speak to his hastily assembled staff, "I give you the Continental Army." He sighed. "I realize I've not taken a good tone, and I promise you the men shall not hear such from me—or any one of you. If we are to win this war, we must *believe* we can win it. Now—let's set about restoring a little order around here, shall we?"

* * *

Elliot Markham urged his horse into the thick shadows under a spreading elm tree beside the road south of Roxbury. Two hundred yards away sat a small tavern with a thatched roof. A buggy driven by a young woman had just pulled up in front of the building and stopped, and Elliot watched with intense interest as she got down from the carriage and, with a sweep of her skirts, entered the tavern.

Elliot grimaced and wished he had made his move earlier. It was possible that inside the tavern, the woman had already carried out the task that led Elliot to follow her. Or perhaps she had just stopped for a drink; she was known to have a sailor's fondness for rum.

And just as well, since she has a fondness for sailors, too. Elliot grinned as that thought crossed his mind. In truth, he knew little about the woman. She called herself Maureen, although that was likely not her true name. She had red hair, but he was sure she had the leaves of the henna plant to thank for her russet curls. And she was a whore, that was undeniable, but what he really needed to know was if she was a courier for the British spy whose identity he sought.

Even though he had been unable to discover where she lived, he had been keeping an eye on her ever since Pheeters at the Salutation had tipped him off about her mysterious trips out of Boston. Tonight was the first time she had left the city, and Elliot was convinced she was carrying a message for the turncoat. That was not the only reason a woman in her profession might make a nocturnal journey, of course; she might be on her way to an assignation with a wealthy squire. Somehow, Elliot had to find out.

Maureen had been inside the tavern for several minutes when Elliot heeled his horse into a walk and rode up to the establishment. There were quite a few horses, wagons, and carriages tied up at the hitching rail, and Elliot swung down from the saddle and added his mount to their number.

When he went inside, the first thing he spotted was ~~~en's garish hair. She had thrown back her bonnet and was leaning over the bar, letting the proprietor of the place have a good look down the valley between her ample breasts. She laughed in response to something that was said by one of the men who crowded around her, and while she was receiving a good deal of attention from them, she was also the recipient of some jealous looks from the serving girls.

Elliot sat at an empty table in a corner, and after several minutes, one of the wenches came over to him. "What can I bring you?" she asked.

"Just a tankard of ale," replied Elliot, adding, "and perhaps a little information?"

"The ale first," the girl said.

When she brought the drink on a pewter tray, he had several coins in his hand, more than enough to cover the cost of the ale. She put the tray down, and Elliot placed the coins on it next to the tankard. She looked at the money, then at him, and murmured, "You must think this information you seek is worth something."

"It is, but only to me." Elliot nodded toward Maureen. "What can you tell me about her?"

The girl looked over her shoulder at the bar, where Maureen was laughing and swilling rum. "Her? She's a trollop, and a drunken one at that." A smile played around her mouth. "What's the likes of you interested in a slut like her for? You can do much better, I promise you that."

Elliot smiled at her. He guessed the girl was about eighteen, with blond hair and a dusting of freckles across her pretty features. Her body was slender, her breasts high and firm, although Elliot was only speculating on that last point. He was tempted to ask her to join him, but he reminded himself he was here on business.

"Maybe some other time," he murmured to himself.

"What was that, sir?"

He shook his head. "Nothing, nothing." Lifting the tankard of ale, he went on, "Thank you—for the drink and for the information."

"You're welcome, I suppose." Reluctantly, she picked up the tray and walked away.

He sipped the ale while keeping an eye on Maureen, and as he watched her, he drew some conclusions: If she were carrying a message for the turncoat, she had probably not passed it on in here. The tavern was too crowded, and she was the object of too much attention. Also, she was not drinking nearly as much as she seemed to be. She was putting on an act, Elliot realized, and he was more convinced than ever that she was the courier he sought.

After another quarter hour, Maureen got ready to leave the tavern. Elliot slipped out first, and when the woman emerged from the building and went to her carriage, he was sitting on his horse, in the shadows across the road. He watched as she left, let her gain a slight lead, then set out after her.

He had already risked allowing her to pass along the message she carried, and her act in the tavern made him certain that she was bent on espionage activities. Unless she was on an errand of great consequence, she would have drunk herself into a stupor, picked out a man—or men—to bed her, and carried on in a disreputable manner. It would be too big a gamble to wait any longer, Elliot decided; he had to strike now.

He urged the horse into a faster gait, and as he drew nearer to the carriage, he saw Maureen lean to the side and look behind her. He knew she must have heard the hoofbeats as he approached, and the bright moon would allow her to see him without any trouble.

The cry she let out as she whipped her horse to a greater speed floated back to his ears. She was fleeing from him, and Elliot, holding his tricorn on with one hand as the wind tugged at it, leaned forward and pressed his horse to go faster.

The road curved up and down and around the wooded, rolling hills. Elliot stayed behind the carriage and gradually closed the distance between the vehicle and him. When only a few yards separated them, he called on the horse for still more speed, then drew alongside. He prepared to reach out and grab the harness of the carriage horse and pull it to a halt.

But as he passed the seat he glanced over and saw Maureen delving into her bag with her free hand, and when it emerged, she clutched a small pistol in her fingers. She swung the gun toward him.

Elliot let out a yelp of surprise and bent forward. The pistol cracked, spitting orange flame into the night, and the shot, fired from an unsteady platform, went wild. But being shot at made Elliot's pulse race; he wanted to get to her before she had a chance to reload.

His mount pulled up beside the carriage horse, running neck and neck, and Elliot leaned over and grabbed the harness. However, his horse stumbled slightly, and Elliot was almost jerked out of the saddle. If he had fallen, he would have landed under the carriage wheels, and he was sure that Maureen would have taken great pleasure in running over him. He clamped his legs tighter around his horse's belly and hauled back hard on the harness of the animal pulling the carriage.

The beasts came to a skidding, sliding halt, and Elliot dropped out of his saddle and ran toward the seat. He was afraid Maureen might try to run away into the fields bordering the road, but instead, the woman let out a screech of anger, flung herself off the seat, and dove straight at Elliot. He staggered as she crashed into him and clawed at his eyes with her long fingernails. Unexpectedly he found himself with an armful of spitting, cursing hellcat.

He cried out in pain and surprise when her fingers raked at his face, narrowly missing his eyes. In all probability she had a knife concealed somewhere in her flashy clothes, and he knew he had to put a stop to this, so he balled his right hand into a loose fist and swung it at her jaw.

The blow clipped her perfectly, and she sagged forward into his arms. Elliot caught her to keep her from falling, then dragged her to the side of the road and gently lowered her to the grass. His hand hurt. It had been a while since he had punched anyone, and now that he thought about it, he had never hit a woman before. Maureen's jaw had been just about as hard as a man's.

As he fetched her bag from the seat of the carriage and pawed through it, Elliot hoped no one else would come along while he was thus engaged. With Maureen sprawled out on the ground and him looking through her bag, he supposed he did look like a highwayman.

The situation worsened when he realized there was no message, secret or otherwise, in the bag. A quick look through the carriage told him nothing was concealed there, either. That left Maureen herself.

"This isn't the first time you've checked to see what some doxy has under her clothes, old boy," he muttered to himself as he knelt beside her and ran his hands over her body. She was stirring, moving her head from side to side, and letting out a faint moan. She was only stunned; he had to hurry.

The crinkle of paper from underneath her dress was his reward. The sound came from her midsection, and Elliot knew there were only two ways of getting there. He chose the quicker route and shoved Maureen's dress and petticoat up around her waist. She muttered a curse and shook her head harder as he slid his hand up to her soft, rounded belly.

His fingers touched a folded piece of paper, stitched to the inside of her petticoat. Elliot grasped it tightly and pulled it free, and as he did so, Maureen cried out in shock. She must have realized that she was sprawled on her back beside the road, her garments up around her waist, with a man's hand shoved up under them.

Elliot stepped back quickly, the paper in his hand.

Maureen sat up and glared at him, and a stream of profanity came from her lips as she got to her feet.

Reaching under his coat and slipping out a small pistol, he pointed it at her and said, "Be still." He would never have used the gun on her, but she did not have to know that.

"What'd you want wi' me?"

"That'll be quite enough," he told her sharply. "You're coming with me."

"The hell I am!" she snorted. She peered at him more closely in the moonlight. "Say! Don't I know you? I seen you in the tavern. It's a sad day when even a highwayman sinks so low as to rob a poor, defenseless woman—"

"Defenseless?" Elliot said. "You took a shot at me and then tried to rip my eyes out!"

"And you deserved it, too, you bastard!"

Wearily, Elliot stepped forward and raised the pistol as if he were going to lash out at her with it. She flinched and raised her arms to cover her head. "Stand up and turn around," he told her.

This time she did as he ordered, and he quickly grabbed her arms, jerked them behind her back, and lashed her wrists together with cord he had in his pocket for just such a purpose. Then he shoved her toward the carriage and lifted her into it, depositing her none too gently behind the seat. With another length of cord, he bound her ankles so that she could not do anything but squirm around and curse him. He was willing to put up with that for a while, and if it became too much, he could stop and gag her.

As soon as his horse was tied to the back of the buggy, Elliot climbed to the seat and took up the reins. Swinging the vehicle around, he headed toward Boston, but instead of trying to enter the city when he reached it, he guided the carriage onto the Cambridge road and drove on toward Concord and Lexington. He was going to need help to complete this mission, and as far as he was concerned, there was only one person who fit the requirements of the task.

Lemuel Parsons shook him awake and said, "Wake up and come downstairs, Daniel. You've got company."

The farmer sounded excited, and Daniel wondered what was going on. Lemuel was not frightened or upset, so clearly they were not in any danger, but Daniel hurriedly pulled on a pair of pants and followed him downstairs.

In the light from a lamp on the kitchen table, Daniel saw his cousin, Elliot Markham, sitting at the table, and huddled miserably on one of the other chairs was a woman he had never seen before. She was glaring at Elliot and rubbing wrists that were chafed raw by a rope.

"Elliot!" exclaimed Daniel. "What is this?"

Holding up a piece of paper he had been studying in the lamplight, Elliot grinned and said, "Success—I hope."

Excitement gripped Daniel as well. "You've found the turncoat?"

"Perhaps. Take a look at this."

Daniel pulled out a chair and sat down, then took the paper from Elliot. It was covered with carefully inked letters—and it made no sense whatsoever. "I don't understand," he said.

"You're not meant to. That letter is in code. I took it from this *lady* here. I suspect she was supposed to deliver it to a British officer somewhere outside of Boston."

"That's a damned lie," the woman spat. "I don't know what you're talkin' about!"

"Keep your voice down," Elliot warned her. "I don't want you rousing the whole house." He glanced at Daniel. "Is Roxanne asleep upstairs?"

"Yes," Daniel said. "We've been here just a month. Lemuel and Lottie were kind enough to take us in."

And a wonderful month it's been, Daniel thought. Although they slept in separate bedrooms for the sake of propriety and the Parsons children, they had been able to steal several opportunities to make love. Even when they were not doing that, the time spent with Roxanne was still joyous for Daniel. He enjoyed walking through the woods with her, holding her hand, even doing chores around the farm with her. He was in love. What more was there to say?

Daniel tapped the coded letter. "If this is from the spy, the information in it will point to his true identity once it's deciphered."

"That's right. I think the plan worked perfectly." Elliot looked at the woman. "But you could save us a great deal of trouble, my dear, if you'd just go ahead and tell us who gave you that letter to deliver."

"Get stuffed," she said, sneering.

"Very well," Elliot said. "If that's the way you want it, fine. But I warn you, this letter *will* be deciphered and its message read!" He hesitated and glanced at Daniel, then added sharply, "And Dr. Benjamin Church will be exposed for the traitor he is!"

The woman's head snapped up in surprise, and both Daniel and Elliot knew that their suspicions of Church were correct. However, all the woman did was glare at them and say, "You'll not get anything from me."

"So be it." Elliot turned to Daniel. "I brought this doxy here tonight—her name's Maureen, by the way—so that I could ask a favor of you, Daniel."

"Of course. But what can I do?"

"I want you to take her and this letter to General Washington for me."

"But you caught her, Elliot," Daniel said. "You should be the one to bring her in."

"I don't want any glory," Elliot responded. "Nor do I want it widely known I'm working for the patriot cause. I have to get back into Boston and resume my life there." He slipped another piece of paper from his coat and handed it to his cousin. "Give that to the general as well. It's a list of the information I gave to the members of the committee. One set of numbers in it should match the numbers in this coded message."

"You're sure this is the way you want it?"

"I'm certain."

"All right, then. I'll get dressed and head for Cambridge right now."

Elliot stood up and extended his hand. "Godspeed, Daniel. And say hello to Roxanne for me."

Daniel got to his feet and took his cousin's hand. "I'll do that. Thank you, Elliot. With any luck, you've performed a great service for the colonies tonight."

Elliot grinned, waved to Lemuel Parsons, who had listened to the discussion in silent awe, and left. A moment later, the sound of his horse's hooves drumming on the road could be heard through the night air.

"They arrived in a buggy," Lemuel said to Daniel. "I suppose you'll be taking it to Cambridge."

"That's right. Keep an eye on this lady for me while I get dressed, would you, Lemuel?"

"Glad to. Just keep it quiet. I don't want Lottie to come downstairs and find me sitting at the table with the likes of this one!"

Daniel grinned and clapped his friend on the shoulder, then turned and hurried up the stairs to dress.

General Washington had done a remarkable job in the short time since he had taken over as commander in chief of the Continental Army. More tents had been secured to house the men, and the squalid, makeshift huts had been razed. Latrines had been covered and fresh ones dug. Intensive drilling had instilled a sense of discipline in the men, and as Daniel drove the carriage into the encampment, he had to admit the place had a sharp military air to it.

A sentry directed Daniel to Washington's headquarters, an impressive-looking structure known as the Vassall House, which had been commandeered for the army's use during this emergency. The guard had looked curiously at the woman on the seat next to Daniel, but he had not asked any questions.

As for Maureen, much of the defiance had slowly leaked out of her following Elliot's mention of Dr. Church. She was sullen, but she had stopped cursing and threatening. As Daniel brought the carriage to a stop in front of Vassall House, Maureen stepped down from the vehicle and allowed him to take her arm and lead her into the building.

A sentry stopped them and demanded to know their business.

"We must see General Washington," Daniel said. "It's a matter of the utmost importance."

"The general's in a meeting with some of his staff and the Committee of Safety," the guard replied. "He's not to be disturbed."

"The Committee of Safety," repeated Daniel. "That's

perfect. I assure you, they'll want to hear what I have to say. Will you take my name in?"

The guard considered it for a moment, then finally said, "I can do that much."

"Thank you. Tell them it's Daniel Reed, and I have news of the turncoat."

"Daniel Reed, news of the turncoat. Sure, mister. Wait right here."

The sentry was back in less than a minute and looked at Daniel with new regard as he said, "Follow me. They are right anxious to talk with you."

Daniel was ushered into a meeting room with a long hardwood table in its center. General Washington, tall and impressive in his blue jacket with buff trimmings, stood at the head of the table. Several officers were in the room, as well as a few men in civilian clothes.

"You're Daniel Reed?" Washington asked in clipped tones.

"Yes, sir." Daniel tugged Maureen up alongside him.

"Mr. Elbridge Garry here speaks highly of you, Mr. Reed. What can I do for you?"

Daniel recognized Elbridge Garry, whom he knew from his days in Boston as an agent of the committee. Garry smiled at him and said, "You can speak freely, Daniel. You're among friends."

Daniel slid two pieces of paper from beneath his coat. "This is a coded message from a highly placed British agent who is a member of the Committee of Safety. The other is information that will enable us to discern the traitor's identity."

A stunned silence greeted his announcement. Finally Washington said, "This is a serious matter, Mr. Reed. Are you certain you know whereof you speak?"

"Absolutely certain, sir." Daniel inclined his head toward Maureen. "This woman has been acting as the spy's courier, delivering his dispatches to the British. She was caught tonight by a patriot agent who wishes to remain anonymous."

Elbridge Garry strode toward Daniel. "I have some knowledge of ciphers," he said, holding out his hand. "Let me see that message, if you will."

Without hesitation, Daniel passed it over, and Garry studied it for several moments. When he looked up he said, "I'm certain I can decode this message, especially if you'll be so kind as to lend me the services of Captain Elisha Porter, General. Captain Porter is a friend of mine, and familiar with ciphers as well."

"Of course," agreed Washington. "Have to, Mr. Garry."

"Wait!" Maureen cried suddenly. "You don't have to decipher it. I'll tell you who gave it to me." She cast a surly glance at Daniel. "This man already knows, anyway."

"Let us hear it from your own mouth," Washington told her. "It will go easier for you that way."

In a harsh voice that was little more than a whisper, she said, "It was Church, Dr. Benjamin Church."

Immediately there were exclamations of protest from some of the men in the room. Church was widely known and admired, and he had been one of the most ardent supporters of the patriot cause in the days before the war. No one wanted to believe he was capable of such treachery.

Washington looked solemnly at Daniel. "Is this accusation true, Mr. Reed?"

"I believe it to be," Daniel answered.

With the decisiveness of a true leader, Washington said quickly, "Very well. Mr. Garry, find Captain Porter and get to work on that message. Mr. Reed, I'm going to assign a detail of soldiers to you. Bring Dr. Church to me."

"Do you know where I can find him, sir?" Daniel's heart was thudding heavily in response to the trust Washington was placing in him.

"Indeed I do," he replied. "Dr. Church is now my chief surgical officer. You should be able to find him making his rounds in our hospital."

Five minutes later, Daniel walked at the head of a small group composed of a sergeant and four troopers.

They entered the large building near Vassall House that had been converted to a hospital. An orderly directed them to the second floor, and when they reached the ward, Daniel spotted Dr. Church at the far end of the big room. The light was faint, coming from several candles and lamps scattered around the ward, but the illumination was enough for Church to see them coming. The tramp of the soldiers' feet must have alerted him.

Church stiffened as Daniel walked toward him. A mixture of apprehension and confusion crossed his handsome, distinguished face. "Daniel Reed!" he exclaimed heartily. "I've not seen you in months. How are you, my boy?"

"I'm fine, Doctor," Daniel said, coming to a stop in front of Church. Nervously he went on, "You're to come with us. We're taking you to General Washington's headquarters."

For an instant, panic flared in Church's eyes, but it just as quickly vanished. He looked baffled and said, "I don't understand. Why does General Washington want to see me?"

"Because you're under arrest, Doctor," Daniel said bluntly. "Your days as a turncoat and British spy are over."

Church drew back, and Daniel thought he might try to make a break for freedom. The physician was intelligent enough to know he could not escape, however, and after a moment he relaxed. He gave Daniel a sardonic smile and said, "I helped you get out of that jail in Boston, you know. And I treated your brother when he was wounded. I daresay I may have saved his leg."

"You may be right, Doctor, but that doesn't change anything. Come along."

"Of course," Church said smoothly. "But you're wrong, Reed. I'm no traitor. You'll see. This is all insane."

"Doctor, I almost wish I could believe you."

Then Daniel and the soldiers with him led Dr. Church out of the hospital to the headquarters of General George Washington. Fate had caught up at last with Benjamin Church, noted physician, patriot—and spy.

* * *

With the help of a chaplain from Dartmouth, Massachusetts, the Reverend Samuel West, Elbridge Garry and Captain Porter made short work of deciphering the letter taken from Maureen. Reverend West supplied his own translation, and it matched letter for letter with the job of deciphering done by Garry and Porter. The information contained in the message also matched perfectly with the figures Elliot had given Dr. Church. Along with Maureen's testimony, it was abundant proof of Church's guilt, even though he continued to insist that he was innocent, that this was all some sort of dreadful misunderstanding.

But it was not a misunderstanding. Daniel knew that.

Now, several days later, he was in the conference room of Vassall House, facing the stern countenance of General Washington. They were alone, and Washington had just finished telling Daniel the results of the investigation into Dr. Church's espionage activities.

"We can only hope he did not do irreparable damage to our cause," Washington concluded. He sighed. "What leads a man to betray his fellows like that?"

"I don't know, sir," Daniel replied honestly. "What's going to happen to him now?"

Washington chuckled humorlessly. "That's a good question, lad. Some of my men favor hanging him, others would prefer a firing squad. As for me, I don't want to see him executed, and so far I've resisted that pressure. I've a feeling Dr. Church could come in handy for our side sometime in the future. A bargaining chip, as it were." Washington had been lounging in his chair, but now he sat up and went on briskly, "So for the time being, Church is in custody, under heavy guard, as is that doxy of his. But I have a more important matter to discuss with you today, Mr. Reed. That's why I summoned you."

"Yes, sir?" Daniel said, trying to conceal his surprise. "Whatever you want of me, I'd be honored to give it my best effort."

"I'm glad to hear that. I want you to join my staff, Mr. Reed."

Daniel blinked at the unexpected offer. "But I'm not officially a member of the army, sir," he finally said.

"We can quickly take care of that. I've been discussing your contributions to our cause with some of the committee members, as well as with General Ward and General Putnam. You fought bravely at Breed's Hill, and before that at Concord. In addition, you were responsible for capturing a supply train filled with British munitions in New York. And, young man, you've performed admirably as an espionage agent—the capacity in which I want you to join my staff." Washington laced his fingers together on the table and leaned forward. "If we're going to win this war, Mr. Reed, we're going to need all the information we can possibly get our hands on concerning the British and their activities. To that end, I'm going to form an intelligence network, making it as far-flung as possible. I've already recruited a friend of yours, a gentleman named Nathan Hale, as well as two of his friends, Benjamin Tallmadge and Robert Townsend. I believe you're acquainted with them as well?"

"Yes, sir," Daniel said, his mind numb from the implications of the conversation.

"What I need now is a man to function as a liaison between this network of secret agents and me, a man who can also serve as my personal intermediary on matters requiring special attention. *You* are that man, Daniel Reed." Washington settled back in his chair and smiled. "What say you?"

There was only one thing Daniel could say. He held out his hand to Washington. "I'm honored, sir, and I accept."

"Good man!" Washington gripped his hand firmly. "We'll soon have those British on the run, won't we, lad?"

"As a member of your staff, General, I assume you want me to speak frankly?"

"Of course."

"Then I think we have a long, hard fight in front of us, but sooner or later, we will win. The colonies will be free."

"Yes," agreed Washington solemnly. "I pray that it's so." He got to his feet, and Daniel stood as well. "For now, you're dismissed, Mr. Reed. I'll be in touch with you when I have need of your services. Where can I find you?"

"At the Parsons farm outside Concord, sir. I'm free to return there?"

"Yes, of course. Good day, Mr. Reed."

"Good day, sir."

Still dazed by the developments, Daniel left the head-quarters building, swung up on his horse, and headed toward Lexington and Concord.

He had been on this road many times before, but never as a member of George Washington's staff. There was no way of knowing what this might bring, but he felt sure the days to come would be hard, bloody, and dangerous, just as the past had been.

For now, though, he had time, time to be with Roxanne, to savor the love he had found with her, and when the call to duty came, he would answer it, even though leaving her behind would sadden both of them. But until then he had the long, warm summer days and Roxanne, and for now, that was enough.

ABOUT THE AUTHOR

"ADAM RUTLEDGE" is one of the pseudonyms of veteran author James M. Reasoner, who has written over sixty books ranging from historical sagas and Westerns to mysteries and adventure novels. Reasoner considers himself first and foremost a storyteller and enjoys spinning yarns based on the history of the United States, from colonial days to the passing of the era known as the Old West. He lives in Azle, Texas, with his wife, Livia, and daughters Shayna and Joanna.

PATRIOTS—*Volume IV*

LIFE
AND
LIBERTY

by Adam Rutledge

Reunited after the bloody battle of Bunker Hill, Daniel Reed and Roxanne Darragh spend an idyllic summer on a farm just outside the British stronghold of Boston, until redcoat raiders leave Daniel for dead and take Roxanne— and her secret—prisoner.

On the frontier, Quincy Reed falls in love and plans to marry—much to the concern of his friend and guardian Murdoch Buchanan. But the wedding feast ends tragically with the arrival of unexpected and unwelcome guests: the mad Reverend Jason Sabbath, three vengeful British deserters, and a band of angry renegade Indians.

In Boston, Elliot Markham and his father, a loyal Tory, are badly beaten by a gang called the Liberty Legion. But is its leader, Lazarus, an American patriot or merely an extortionist taking advantage of the personal and political passions of the times?

Look for LIFE AND LIBERTY, Volume IV in the PATRIOT series, on sale April 1993, wherever Bantam paperbacks are sold.